A Bargain Sealed

"Is that what you want, Audrey?" he asked in a husky voice.

She felt the pressure of his thigh, no longer just next to her skirts, but against her own.

"To have people think you a scandalous widow?"

"I want to be respected, to become part of the village society, not the fast London Society."

He eased his thigh away. "That's what I want for you, too, Audrey. So we will remain engaged for a while longer. Shall we continue our walk about the grounds?"

He took both her hands and pulled her to her feet, and for just a moment, she stood before him, skirts tangled with his legs, their hands joined.

Suddenly, she felt him looming over her, bending near.

"But if we're engaged," he whispered, "cannot a fiancé steal a kiss?"

By Gayle Callen

GAYLE CALLEN

PAPL
DISCARDED

SURRENDER
TO THE
EARL

AVON

An Imprint of HarperCollinsPublishers

This is a work of fiction. Names, characters, places, and incidents are products of the author's imagination or are used fictitiously and are not to be construed as real. Any resemblance to actual events, locales, organizations, or persons, living or dead, is entirely coincidental.

AVON BOOKS
An Imprint of HarperCollins*Publishers*
10 East 53rd Street
New York, New York 10022-5299

Copyright © 2013 by Gayle Kloecker Callen
ISBN 978-0-06-207607-6
www.avonromance.com

First Avon Books mass market printing: June 2013

Avon Trademark Reg. U.S. Pat. Off. and in Other Countries, Marca Registrada, Hecho en U.S.A.
HarperCollins® is a registered trademark of HarperCollins Publishers.

Printed in the U.S.A.

10 9 8 7 6 5 4 3 2 1

*To Molly Herwood, fellow Purple, dear friend.
I can't think of this book without remembering
the laughter and ah-ha moments of our
brainstorming sessions. Thanks so much for
your time, your creative brain, and for showing
me that perseverance and love of the craft
are crucial to a writer's happiness.*

Chapter 1

Oxfordshire, England
1843

Robert Henslow, Earl of Knightsbridge, late of the Queen's army, paced the drawing room in Lord Collins's modest country mansion and debated how best to see to the welfare of the baron's daughter—considering he'd never met her before. Robert had spent the six-week journey home from India pondering this dilemma, but he was no closer to an answer. He hoped he wouldn't have to tell her the real reason: a military decision he'd help make had cost the life of her husband, Martin Blake. The guilt would never leave him, but at least the nightmares had ceased in the last year.

Blake hadn't been the only man to die. Two others in their regiment had met a bloody end, including their commander, leaving Robert and two of his good friends to feel the need to make amends. He had made Mrs. Blake a widow, and he didn't know how to make that right.

Robert was staring broodingly at the rolling grass fields of the park and the gold- and red-tipped trees when he heard the first chords from a piano in a nearby room. The sound grew into a merry melody, reminding him of a springtime awakening during this blustery autumn day.

And still Lord Collins did not come.

Robert decided to investigate the next room. It only briefly occurred to him that it might be impolite, but he was an earl, and his father had bred into him the loftiness of his title. It hadn't taken the army long to beat the worst arrogance out of him, but he still had his moments. So he went back out to the entrance hall and peered through the next doorway into a small parlor. A young woman sat alone at the piano, her eyes closed, her face luminous as she enjoyed her music. Her light brown hair was caught simply at the back of her head, and it gave a faint sheen in the shaft of sunlight streaming through the window. She looked neither tall nor short, a perfectly average figure clothed in a dark blue day dress with a bit of lace above the bodice. Her face held him, with its pixieish pointed chin, slanting eyebrows, and the hollows beneath her cheekbones that made her striking rather than truly beautiful.

And then she started to sing, her voice angelic, her expression distant, as if her music took her away from her life, from the pain of loss.

He took a step into the room, and she suddenly stopped, although not even a floorboard had creaked.

She tilted her head at an angle, her face turning toward the doorway, her gaze off to the side. "Is someone there?"

She was blind. This couldn't be Mrs. Blake. Surely her husband would have said something during the six months they'd served together. It must be a sister, he told himself. But his stomach was clenched tight, and he had an instinct for the truth, after all his years with the army.

"Forgive me for intruding," he said, then cleared the roughness from his throat. "I am Knightsbridge, come to visit Lord Collins and Mrs. Blake."

Her face smoothed into a polite expression. "The Earl of Knightsbridge? Mr. Blake's fellow officer?"

"He wrote of me?"

"My husband was not given much to letter writing," she said candidly, "but I heard your name more than once."

Heard. Of course, the letters would have been read to her. Mrs. Blake was blind, and from the perfection of her features, it was not a recent injury. Had she been born that way? He found himself powerfully curious to know everything about her. She was a blinded invalid, who'd never have a normal life. And it certainly made him think differently of Blake, who'd seemed a shallow, though good-natured, man. To marry a blind woman, he must have had depths of compassion Robert had never seen.

Before they could exchange another word, an older man came up behind Robert and made a polite coughing sound. Robert stepped out of the doorway.

"Good afternoon, Father," Mrs. Blake said, her tone impassive rather than loving.

Lord Collins was a portly man, with long, gray, muttonchop sideburns and a red face. Without responding to his daughter, he eyed Robert with interest and said, "Knightsbridge?"

Robert gave a brief bow. "We have not met, sir, but it is a pleasure."

"Come in, sit down," the man said heartily.

Robert had heard this unctuous tone of voice before. Mrs. Blake smoothly slid off the piano bench and crossed the room. She didn't use a cane, only allowed her hand to gently slide along the back of a chair as if to navigate. She pulled the bell cord hung in the corner, then glided with unerring accuracy back to a small sofa across from him. He almost warned her about the low table between them, but she obviously knew it was there. Her father didn't seem to notice her movements at all.

"Audrey, your brother and sister aren't here?" Lord Collins asked, faint disappointment in his voice.

Mrs. Blake shook her head. "Edwin is shooting this afternoon, and Blythe is visiting a friend in the village."

Lord Collins grimaced. He probably wanted both of his daughters to meet an earl—or maybe just the sighted one, Robert speculated.

A young footman dressed in dark livery entered the room and bowed.

"Please have Cook prepare us a tea tray, Richard," Mrs. Blake asked.

It was obvious she knew the workings of the household, and controlled the servants as the mistress of the home. Robert was impressed.

Lord Collins turned a speculative glance on him. "To what do we owe this visit, Knightsbridge?"

"As I mentioned to your daughter, I served in India with Mr. Blake. I know two years have passed since his death, but I've only just returned to England permanently, and I thought I would pay my respects and condolences."

"You sold your commission?" Lord Collins asked, without acknowledging his daughter's loss.

"Yes. I'm home for good." Home. And he'd never felt so useless, for the entire estate ran smoothly without him. He'd wanted a steward to make that happen all those years ago when he'd left—and the man had succeeded. But now . . . Robert was at loose ends, as if he were unnecessary. And since it was autumn, even Parliament was not in session for him to take his place in the House of Lords.

He was used to being in charge and living an exciting, dangerous life. Oh, he'd been invited to country house parties and shooting parties from the moment of his return, but he'd only been able to focus on meeting Mrs. Blake. He snuck a glance at her, as if she'd even notice. Though her eyes appeared normal, they were strangely blank, and she wasn't quite looking at him. They were an unusual color, a light amber that seemed to shine from within dark lashes. One wanted to focus on their beauty, which only made it even more apparent that they were so very different in *every* way.

"Thank you for your kind condolences, my lord," she said with quiet dignity. "You were in the same regiment as my husband?"

"He joined us because so many from our parish were in the Eighth Dragoon Guards."

"Cavalrymen," Lord Collins said approvingly.

Robert nodded, then added, "Yes," because Mrs. Blake couldn't see his response.

A maid pushed a teacart through the open door, and Mrs. Blake rose. Robert watched, astonished, as she poured the cup herself, noticing that she left one finger just inside the rim. She didn't need to actually touch the tea, since she must have felt the rising heat.

"How do you take your tea, Lord Knightsbridge?" she asked.

"Black is fine," he said.

She held the cup and saucer toward him and he took it. She poured more for herself and her father, adding milk and sugar in the appropriate amounts. Her father took his almost without looking at her. She placed a little plate of iced cakes on the table, then sat down with her own tea.

Robert had thought such a woman would be an invalid, but he'd heard her play the piano, watched her move gracefully about the room and serve refreshments like any competent hostess. He admired her, yet he felt pity that she could never live a normal life.

"This may be an awkward question, my lord," she began slowly, "but were you with my husband at the end?"

Memories swamped him of the dark jungle

night, and the swarm of unexpected attackers. "Yes, ma'am, I was."

"Did he . . . suffer?"

"I do not believe so. The head wound was swiftly mortal." Blake had died in his arms, and Robert had found the last letter from his wife that Blake hadn't even had time to read. Robert had kept that letter for the next two years, reading several times the innocent, cheerful details of home and hearth.

She stared down into her tea—no, she didn't stare, he amended to himself. But her head was bent, and he wondered at her emotions, though he could guess: grief and perhaps despair.

"I am glad he did not suffer," she said at last.

Her father glanced at her almost impatiently. "Such sorrow is in the past," he intoned. "No need to dwell, now that we are out of mourning."

Mrs. Blake's mouth tightened briefly, and Robert guessed she and her father had not reacted the same way to Blake's death.

Lord Collins glanced out the window at the faint sound of harness jingling and the clop of horse hooves on the drive. A curricle, driven by a groom with a lady at his side, moved past the house and took the corner. "Ah, there is my youngest daughter," he said with satisfaction. "She will be so pleased to meet you, Knightsbridge. I will hurry her along." He rose and waddled from the room.

Mrs. Blake took another sip of her tea before giving Robert a fixed smile. "My sister came out several years ago, my lord."

"And it must not be as successful as your father wished, considering the speed with which he departed."

Her expression lightened, and her smile, though faint, eased his tongue.

"While we have a moment alone, Mrs. Blake, I would like you to know that, as your husband's friend, I wish to be of service to you in some way. He saved my life once, and I was not able to save his. I owe a debt in his memory, and it would ease me to assist you."

He expected her to downplay such an offer. After all, she was a blind widow who had a comfortable life with her family.

She slowly set down her cup, and for the first time he felt the intense focus of her interest, even though she was not looking directly at him. But those eyes were mesmerizing, and the line of her body grew slowly tense.

In a lower voice, she said, "Do you mean that, my lord? I could ask a boon of you?"

He set down his own cup and leaned toward her. "If I can grant it, I will."

"I am trapped here," she said, her voice impassive even though her words were startling. "I inherited my husband's manor, but my father refuses to allow me to live there, though I am twenty-five years of age and have managed this household for many years. No one will go against him. But you can, my lord. Will you help me?"

Chapter 2

$\sim\!\!\infty\!\!\sim$

Audrey Blake knew her request was too forward, too impolite—but she no longer cared. She was desperate, and Lord Knightsbridge's arrival might be her only chance. He sounded pleasant, his voice deep, manly, and obviously he had compassion and a sense of justice to come all this way to offer his assistance.

"I am not an invalid, my lord," she continued, knowing she rushed her words. She couldn't hear anyone in the foyer, but they'd be interrupted soon. "And I'm not a fool. I would have servants to assist me, and my lady's maid, who acts as my eyes when necessary. And I remember what things look like—I went blind from scarlet fever at seven years of age, and I've done my best to remind myself every night of the images of my relatives' faces, the grounds of my home."

"But you would be going to a place with none of those things, Mrs. Blake," he said in a gentle voice.

"You are a soldier, sir—did you not wish to explore places you'd never been before? Why would I be different? And the house is *mine*," she added with emphasis, "although my father tried to weave an elaborate deception to convince me the house went to a distant male relative of my husband. I wrote to a lawyer and discovered the truth. I do not want to spend my days as my sister's companion, to intrude on her marriage as a poor relation. That is what they plan for me, all of my family, when they aren't trying to keep me hidden."

She heard the inhalation of his breath, forced herself to remain calm, though she could barely control the trembling of her hands. This was her chance—would the earl deny her, when he obviously felt he owed her?

She knew he heard the footsteps in the hall when he lowered his voice and spoke quickly.

"You make a good argument, Mrs. Blake, and I do understand your frustration. But I don't know you or your situation, and could be doing more harm than good."

He must have leaned closer, for she could smell the clean, outdoor scent of him.

"Then stay," she said. "My brother is having a shooting party with his friends for the next few days. My family would be honored at your presence—especially my sister Blythe," she added with just a touch of sarcasm. "I will invite you if my father or sister doesn't. And then you will see the family I have, who believe they know best for me, when I'm a grown, competent woman, and not a drooling invalid."

"Very well, I will stay," he said.

"Thank you, my lord."

The surge of relief Audrey felt was enough to make her teacup rattle in the saucer as she picked it up. She was sipping slowly, casually, when she heard the rush of swirling garments, the prancing steps of Blythe entering the parlor, the heavy footfalls of her father.

With the creak of the padded chair, she knew Lord Knightsbridge had risen to his feet.

"Knightsbridge," her father said with his overly cheerful tone, "may I present my daughter, Miss Blythe Collins."

"Miss Collins, it is a pleasure to meet you."

The earl's voice was full of the warm admiration men always showed a lovely woman. Even though Audrey had last seen Blythe as a two-year-old, she well remembered her pretty brunette curls and the dimples whenever she smiled. She'd been Audrey's little doll baby from the moment of her birth and she'd enjoyed caring for her and dressing her under their mother's loving supervision.

Both children had contracted scarlet fever, but only Audrey's fever had raged so high as to take her sight. And it had altered their relationship ever since. Her father and siblings were ashamed of her infirmity, of her very differentness, as if it were a mark on their family that might be carried to future generations.

While their mother had been alive, she made certain Audrey was treated as any normal child, and the seasons had passed with some moments of harmony. But her mother had died seven years ago. Gradually, Audrey's visits to the outside world had been restricted, as if she were a ghost who shouldn't be seen. Blythe had more and more mimicked their father, who tolerated Audrey's blindness, especially since he could use the few skills he thought she had. But treat her like a normal daughter? No. Only Blythe could regularly visit neighbors or go to London. Audrey's control of the household freed Blythe to concentrate on finding a husband.

Audrey had never been beyond their village. She had no women friends of her own except dear Molly, her nanny's daughter. They'd been raised together since infancy, and Molly was now her lady's maid and secretary all rolled into one cheerful package.

Would things be better if she lived alone in her

own home? Would strangers give her the benefit of the doubt, unlike her own family? Audrey didn't know, but at least she'd be free to do as she wished, go where she wished. That had seemed just a distant, unattainable dream this morning—until the arrival of the Earl of Knightsbridge.

She knew Blythe would have swept into a deep curtsy at meeting a peer of the realm. And by her breathless, "How do you do, my lord?" Audrey assumed his lordship must be an attractive man, and not too old for Blythe's consideration.

Their father didn't even bother to tell Blythe the real reason Lord Knightsbridge had visited them, only said, "Knightsbridge is newly returned from India, lately a cavalryman for the Queen."

"Oh, what an exciting and dangerous life," Blythe said, her voice full of awe and eagerness.

Didn't she hear her own desperation? Audrey wondered. She'd once tried to point it out, but Blythe had dismissed her concerns, saying Audrey knew nothing of the flirtation between men and women. But Audrey could hear when someone made a fool of themselves.

"I consider myself honored to serve my country," Lord Knightsbridge said in a somber voice. "But it is not a life for the faint of heart." He hesitated. "I inherited the earldom at twenty, but did not have the maturity for the title. The army seemed like the only way to achieve that. And I had an excellent staff who kept the estates running smoothly in my absence."

Oh, there was a deeper story there, but she would not be so impolite as to ask about it.

"We don't need to talk about the army," Blythe said in a too cheerful voice. "I imagine you simply want to forget it."

"Sometimes, I would like to," he said quietly.

Audrey felt a chill at the emptiness in his voice.

"But I must honor the memory of the friends I lost," he continued. "That is why I'm here, to pay my respects to the widow of my fellow soldier, Mr. Blake."

"Oh, I didn't realize," Blythe said faintly.

Audrey could already feel her sister's mind working, as she imagined that yet another man was connected to Audrey, besides her late husband. And Audrey wanted this new connection. She didn't want to hurt Blythe, but for once, she had to put herself first.

"Surely you weren't planning to share tea and then leave," Lord Collins blustered. "We have several young men arriving for my son's shooting party. Do stay, Knightsbridge. We have plenty of room."

On cue, Lord Knightsbridge said, "That is a gracious invitation, sir. I accept. I've been away nine years, so it will do me good to reacquaint myself with other young men."

"Oh, I am so glad, my lord," Blythe gushed.

"Perhaps you wish to retire and rest before dinner?" Audrey asked.

Sometimes it was good not to be able to see, if her sister was angry to have the earl snatched away from her so soon.

"I imagine I look dusty from the road," the earl said lightly, then his voice sobered. "Forgive me, Mrs. Blake, of course you cannot see that—"

She put up a hand and interrupted. "My lord, figures of speech are not offensive to me, so do not be concerned. I understand you are probably not used to dealing with the blind." But she felt rather relieved that he was considerate. After all, she'd just recklessly asked him, a stranger, to take her away from home. Perhaps it was good that they *both* learned about each other.

But he wasn't a stranger—he'd been a friend of Martin's. That didn't exactly recommend him in her eyes.

"You are very understanding, ma'am."

"I'll have a footman escort you to your room." Audrey rose to her feet. She was always very careful to sit at the end of furniture groups, so she wouldn't have to stumble over people. At the door, she leaned out to give instructions to the footman.

She could hear the party rise behind her as Lord Knightsbridge thanked her father once again before following her to the entrance hall.

"Rest well, my lord," Blythe called.

They were all briefly silent as the earl's footsteps faded away up the stairs. Then Audrey heard her sister excitedly whisper, "Oh, Father! An earl—"

Audrey heard her father rubbing his hands together.

"I know something of Knightsbridge," he said. "Though he has not taken his place in the House of Lords for these nine years, there is gossip to be had."

Blythe asked, "What kind of gossip?"

Audrey did not want to be a part of passing along rumors, but she could not pretend disinterest.

"I believe when he became the earl at twenty, he was considered by some to be too arrogant for his own good."

"And it seems the army cured him of that," Blythe countered.

"Maturity and experience help, too," Audrey added.

"There was something about a business investment that failed, and a man involved took his own life. That was when the young earl bought his commission."

Audrey frowned. "His lordship could be innocent or guilty of . . . anything."

"No one believes the earl had a hand in this man's death," Lord Collins assured them, his voice full of blustery conviction.

"Then it was the investment that people questioned?" Audrey asked warily. Had she just beseeched an unscrupulous man to take her away from her home?

"This doesn't concern you, Audrey," her father said.

She'd heard that her whole life.

"But, no, nothing underhanded was discovered, only bad judgment."

"And he was only twenty," Blythe said. "Anyone can make foolish mistakes at twenty."

"You're twenty," Audrey couldn't help pointing out.

"Oooh!" Blythe said with a groan. "You are impossible to speak with!" And she marched out, her slippers making scuffing sounds on the stairs.

Audrey sighed and was about to follow her.

"Audrey, I would like a word."

She remained still as her father brushed past her to close the door.

"I could confine you to your room," he said in his *I know best* voice.

She clenched her teeth together so hard she felt

a spasm in her jaw. Then she calmed herself. She had intrigued Lord Knightsbridge, she knew, and he felt obligated to do something for her. If she were confined to her room, it might make him even more determined to help. *I can't lose here,* she told herself firmly. But she didn't want to be confined, to hear other people having fun, to be unable to even sit among them.

"But confining you would cause talk during a shooting party, since Knightsbridge has already met you," he continued, heaving a sigh. "So I must trust you to be circumspect in your dealings with him. Your sister deserves her chance to shine."

"Father, the man is an earl," she insisted. "He will not be interested in a blind woman, except for compassion's sake. I am no threat to Blythe."

"See that you remember that," he warned her. "You didn't before."

She could feel him take a step toward her, and much as he'd never physically harmed her, his complete control of her was threatening enough. It was as if the air around her shrank, and she could smell the cologne he used to mask his body odor.

"I warned you about Blake," he reminded her for the thousandth time.

"And you were right," she said, trying to sound humble instead of furious. "Believe me, it is a lesson I have not forgotten."

"Good." He stepped away. "What do you have planned for dinner tonight, once all the young men have arrived?"

She briefly, impassively sketched out the menu for him, while her mind churned at her helplessness. He would confine his own daughter, but for talk and her usefulness to his guests. It had happened before, when she'd been cloistered alone and miserable but for Molly. Every time she thought herself immune to her family's subtle humiliations, another rose to wound her again.

"You look tired, too," he suddenly said. "You should rest before dinner. I don't want Blythe to have to take over coordinating the meal. She needs to be free to converse and make our guests feel at ease."

Audrey sighed. "I do feel tired, Father. I'll spend a quiet hour in my room."

But once there, she couldn't truly rest. She let Molly help her out of her gown into a dressing gown over her chemise and petticoats, the better to lie down. Throughout, the maid chatted about the other young men who had arrived, four more of them. Molly was her own age of twenty-five, and Audrey remembered she had dark blond hair and freckles across her nose. Once Audrey had sheepishly asked if Molly still had them, and Molly had only laughed and said they'd since spread across her face. Audrey had then explained that the people she'd last seen as a seven-year-old must now look different, but she had no way to tell. Molly had told her to touch her face and feel the difference. To Audrey's amazement, she really could "feel" the contours of Molly's pert nose and apple cheeks and imagine what she must look like. Though grateful for Molly's thoughtfulness, she knew she could ask no one else, especially her family, for such a personal favor. So she just had to go by what she remembered of them.

Molly's conversation came to the forefront when the maid said, "I caught a glimpse of his lordship in the hall."

"What does he look like?" Audrey asked with a bit too much eagerness. Now she was sounding like Blythe.

"Don't go moving your head while I'm trying to brush your hair, Miss Audrey."

Audrey had tried for years to have the maid call her by her Christian name, but she refused— although she did agree that "Mrs. Blake" was too formal for their relationship. And it was a true relationship, not mistress and servant. Molly was her dearest friend in the world, closer than her own sister. With no one else could Audrey be herself, ask silly questions, make mistakes. In front of her family, she had to always be at her best, for fear they'd start to treat her as an invalid again. Her mother had put a stop to that, but Audrey never felt safe now that she was gone. She kept waiting for someone to suggest there were hospitals for people like her.

"Hold on, miss, I'm looking for a pin."

Audrey gritted her teeth until she felt Molly pluck the offending pin from her hair. "Well?"

"You're mighty interested in the earl," Molly pointed out. "I wonder why that is."

Audrey couldn't tell her the truth—not yet. Even Molly might think she risked too much, going off with a stranger. "I hear Blythe's interest, and so I'm curious on her behalf."

"So are you wondering if this earl will finally take your sister off your hands?"

Audrey grinned. "You know me too well, Molly. Now what does he look like, so I can decide if he meets Blythe's standards."

"Oh, he does," Molly said with easy humor. "He's an earl, and he's young and handsome."

"I could tell all of that just by listening to her breathless chatter."

Molly laughed. "But as for what he *really* looks like . . . he's got the blackest hair, like a shadow in the night."

"I think your Irish stories are coming out."

The maid snorted. "That's a compliment, Miss Audrey, and you know it. As for the earl, his eyes are this intense green, very vivid. Think of clovers, and you'll know the color. He has laugh lines at his eyes and mouth, which I always consider a good sign in a man."

Laugh lines *were* a good thing. He must have gotten beyond the tragedy that had caused his business partner to lose hope. She admitted her own curiosity, but it was hardly something on which she would ever intrude.

"You and all your experience with men," Audrey said with mock seriousness.

Molly giggled. "Don't you remember my ma saying that?"

"Not exactly, but it sounds like her." Audrey sighed at the warm memories of her nanny, who, like her own mother, had treated Audrey as if she were a normal child, insisting she use her utensils correctly and even that she walk like a lady, though her hand might be following along a wall.

"Did I hear right, that his lordship knew your husband?" Molly asked.

"They were in the same regiment in India. You know Martin didn't write much," she said dryly, "but he did mention the earl. They're from the same parish. The earl's country seat is only a few miles from Martin's house."

"You mean your house," Molly said, her voice quiet and serious.

"Yes, my house," Audrey echoed. "He only wrote of his lordship in passing, his excellent skills on a horse. He might even have said he was brave—I think. If you can even count Martin's opinion for anything."

"Hmm," Molly said, still slowly drawing the brush through Audrey's long hair. "Now I think you need to do as you told your father, and rest. Just try to close your eyes."

"I won't be able to. All of the guests are arriving."

"And at last you're going to be a part of it." She squeezed Audrey's shoulder. "You know Mrs. Gibbs is taking good care of them. You work too hard, Miss Audrey. You should insist Miss Blythe help you."

But they both knew Audrey wouldn't. And it wasn't just that Blythe didn't care enough to do a good job—Audrey was simply afraid that if she didn't prove herself indispensable, they'd put a blanket on her lap like an old woman and never let her do anything again.

When Molly had gone, Audrey sat in the window seat, the window partially open to the cool autumn air. She could remember the view, had forced herself to think about it often so the memory wouldn't blur. The park surrounding the house had always been lush and green, but on this side was a lovely garden with winding pathways Audrey knew by heart. Off in the distance would be the rolling fields separated by hedgerows, the summer grain already harvested, fields being plowed for the winter wheat crop.

But although she tried to distract herself by remembering the grounds, she kept going back to Martin. Her father *had* warned her, she mused, but she hadn't wanted to believe him, had thought he only had selfish motives to keep her at home—but she should have seen beyond that. Martin had been visiting a school friend in their village when Blythe had had her first coming-out party. Blythe had thought every man should focus on her, but it was Audrey whom Martin focused on. In some ways, Audrey didn't think Blythe would ever forgive her for "luring" a husband so quickly. Audrey understood now that she'd been susceptible to Mr. Blake because she felt unloved after her mother's death, so grateful to be admired for her courage. And she'd really had no illusions—they'd never professed love to each other, and she knew he was a younger son. But she'd never imagined that the moment he had his hands on her dowry, he would purchase a commission in the army and leave her with her family so he could "see the excitement of the world." She'd had her first hope of freedom, until he'd cruelly denied her.

Of course her father wouldn't allow her to go to Martin's home, then or now. But she'd spent the weeks leading up to her wedding dreaming of being mistress of her own household, with the authority to do what she wished, *go* where she wished. And instead, her life changed barely at all—until she'd realized she was with child.

She'd been gloriously happy that their rather inadequate wedding night had still given her such a wondrous gift. Her father had been disappointed, her sister almost fearful, but not Audrey. She had been confident she'd meet the challenge, knew that having her own child to love would change her life forever. The baby grew inside her, and its first movements were like the touch of butterfly wings. Soon, it seemed to want to escape, and she loved the feel of its little feet pushing on her.

Then came the news of Martin's death. She didn't suffer terribly with grief, for they hadn't loved each other. But her child wouldn't have a father, and she might never have been allowed to raise it as she wanted. Her father could even have had the baby taken away from her. She'd lived in fear of this—until the worst happened. She'd gone into labor too early, and the baby died.

For several months, she'd existed in despair,

especially when her brother expressed relief that
at least she wouldn't have a blind baby. Did everyone wish she hadn't been born? Realizing how
dangerous her thoughts were, she'd focused on
the manor she'd inherited, a place of her own,
where she would have independence and never
risk losing herself again.

But she wouldn't tell any of this to the earl,
for fear he'd pity her. She didn't want his pity;
she wanted his help—as long as he seemed
trustworthy.

But how was she going to convince him to take
a blind woman away from her home against her
father's wishes?

Chapter 3

Robert came down to the drawing room before dinner and found Blythe Collins holding court like a princess, and Mrs. Blake nowhere to be seen. Were they keeping her out of the way? he wondered uneasily. Five young men were in attendance besides himself, and all turned to stare at him with curiosity. Several even looked familiar. But Lord Collins approached him first, leading a young man who resembled him in nose and in slightly expanding girth.

"Knightsbridge, this is my son, Edwin Collins."

Robert bowed to the other man, who looked near his own age, his expression pleasant and curious—not like a man who'd gone along with keeping his sister trapped against her will. Robert had to remind himself to be objective, to consider both sides.

"Good evening, my lord," Collins said. "It was kind of you to visit my sister. She is doing well, eh?"

Robert cocked his head. "You would know better than I."

He blinked. "Yes, you're right, of course. Come, let me reacquaint you with the men you might know, and those you don't."

Robert allowed himself to be drawn away and introduced to the group surrounding Miss Collins. He had been at Cambridge University at the same time with several of the men, but others had only come to London after his departure. Though he made the first overtures of conversation, it was hard to concentrate after he saw Mrs. Blake enter the room.

She walked without the aid of a cane, just occasionally ran her hand along the wall or across a piece of furniture. He noticed she stayed along the walls, and wondered if that was so she wouldn't accidentally bump into a guest. She inspired head turnings, and more than one of the men asked who she was. He felt bothered on her behalf that even her brother's friends didn't know her identity. She found the chair she was looking for and sat down.

"She's my blind sister," Edwin Collins said. "She insists on doing everything on her own, so you don't need to worry about her."

She didn't rate an introduction? Robert thought in astonishment. He was about to excuse himself and join her, when Miss Collins called his name.

As if Mrs. Blake had realized his intent, he saw her don the faintest smile—or did she simply understand that her sister would want his attention?

Miss Collins offered her hand, and he bent over it. She wore her hair in the most elaborate dark brown curls, shiny and smooth. She had her sister's pixie chin, but was of a more delicate frame. Instead of her sister's golden eyes, hers were light brown, but they sparkled with pleasure on being the center of male attention. She was young yet, he knew, so he could not fault her for enjoying herself.

"Good evening," he said smoothly.

"I am so glad you agreed to stay, my lord. Did my brother introduce you to everyone?"

"He did indeed. I look forward to the challenge of testing their marksmanship against my own."

"Those poor birds," she said, almost giggling. "But I must confess—they do taste delicious."

He smiled. "Then I shall do my best to make sure your dinner table is full of good things to eat."

"I imagine you are quite the marksman after serving in the army. My brother can use a good challenge, since he always bests his friends."

"Ah, but he's my host. I'll try to be fair."

He glanced once again toward Mrs. Blake, who sat very still, a serene expression on her face, her head cocked forward as if she were listening to everything going on around her. Still, no one had approached her.

"Miss Collins, shall I bring your sister to you? I'm not certain you can see her from here."

Something dark flashed in her eyes. "Audrey doesn't enjoy crowds the same way we do, my lord, so please forgive her shyness."

"There's nothing to forgive. I can imagine how difficult it is to see only blackness, to be at a disadvantage to everyone else. Yet she moves about so easily."

"She knows every space in this house," Miss Collins said. "Heaven forbid we move a piece of furniture."

"That is a sensible precaution, of course, and good of you to consider her situation."

He almost missed the brief wince, but it was there. Miss Collins was obviously not ignorant of the situation. But growing up with a blind sister, it was probably easy to imitate the way one's father treated her. Easy, yes, but disappointing, especially when age, maturity, and sympathy should have made her behave otherwise.

"Still, I cannot enjoy myself knowing she is alone," he said. "Excuse me, please."

He bowed, and this time she wasn't so careful about hiding her anger, as if she were jealous of her own sister. But then he did the math in his head. Blake had been recently married when he'd arrived in India, so that had probably put Miss Collins on the cusp of coming out. Had she been newly on display, only to find her blind sister snaring a wedding proposal instead of her?

Robert moved through the small crowd and reached Mrs. Blake. She was obviously aware of his arrival, for she lifted her head expectantly.

"Good evening, Mrs. Blake," he said.

"Good evening, Lord Knightsbridge."

"My voice gives me away?"

"And your courtesy," she reminded him, lowering her voice. "I trust you see that I was not exaggerating my dilemma."

She needed help—he could see that. But how to know what was best for her? Robert disliked feeling indecisive.

Before he could speak further, the butler announced that dinner was served. Mrs. Blake rose smoothly to her feet.

"Shall I escort you, ma'am? I believe the order of precedence will be satisfied that way."

"And so my sister can't be too angry?" she asked wryly.

He smiled. "You know her very well, of course."

"Of course. You'll enjoy her company at dinner, since she made certain she was seated at your side."

"I was once rather used to scheming females, Mrs. Blake, although I may be out of practice."

She stilled, and her smile died. "And I don't mean to be another one, my lord."

"Forgive me—I was not classifying you as such. I was merely making light of a peer's attractiveness to unmarried ladies."

"Oh, of course, I'm sorry. I am being too sensitive."

Robert guided her into the dining room until she touched the back of her chair, then after she sat, pushed the chair in for her. She smiled up at him.

With his inclusion, the numbers were uneven. He sat at one end, near the host and his younger daughter. Mrs. Blake sat at the other end, at her brother's right. Her brother started talking to the person on his left, and Mrs. Blake's other dinner partner turned to the person on his right. It was as if she weren't even there between them. More than once, he wanted to call across the centerpiece to her, but knew she wouldn't appreciate the attention.

As it was, many people glanced at her surreptitiously to watch her eat, and he found himself clenching his jaw, even as he realized he was doing the same. When the footman came around with each course, he would whisper something to

Mrs. Blake as he set whatever was being served on her plate, placing each selection carefully. Mrs. Blake ate quite normally, and the glances at last died away.

Dinner grew more and more awkward, because even as Miss Collins spoke to him about the countryside or London or the friends they might have in common, he kept glancing at Mrs. Blake and wishing this dinner over. And that probably didn't help Miss Collins's disposition, but he wasn't exactly feeling charitable toward her. At last the ladies retired to the parlor, and the men remained behind to drink and smoke and plan the schedule for their shooting party. Robert had little to add, except to quietly agree he might give them some competition if they challenged his shooting. They all seemed so . . . young, even though several were near his own age. Perhaps "young" was an incorrect word; "naïve" was probably better. Except for a jaunt to France or Italy, none of these men had traveled the world or risked their lives. All took their families and way of life for granted. Robert couldn't blame them, since he'd once felt the same way.

But now he'd experienced the wait before battle, when one looked to each side and wondered which fellow soldier—friend—would survive. He'd experienced the joys of triumph, and

the terrible, hollow sadness of death, and knowing one bore responsibility. He'd been hungry
and freezing—he'd almost lost several toes in the
Afghan mountains when they'd first taken over
Kabul. But that had been the worst of his injuries.
He'd felt almost miraculously incapable of being
harmed. And perhaps that had saved him, but not
some of his friends.

Audrey heard Blythe enter the parlor rather
than the drawing room to await the men, and she
knew that meant a musical evening at the piano.
Audrey didn't blame her for wanting to display
her talents; it was expected of a young lady.

But soon Audrey wished she'd fabricated an
excuse to check on something in the kitchen.
Blythe was full of icy silence. Audrey couldn't
guess what she was doing until she heard Blythe
curse under her breath. Needlework—she always
pricked her finger when she was upset.

She didn't know why her sister was so agitated
after her voice and laughter had filled the dining
room. After hearing Lord Knightsbridge's occasional chuckles, she'd felt a momentary worry that
her family would coerce the earl to *their* side. But
then she remembered his sincere wish to help her,
the widow of his fellow soldier. Could she trust
in that?

Audrey retrieved one of her embossed books from a shelf and began to read. The letters were large and raised, but she still had to move her fingers across slowly. Though she'd read this one many times, embossed books were expensive, and she didn't have easy access to her money. Usually Molly read aloud to her from the library, and the two of them had enjoyed exploring the world of books together.

Blythe's unending silence saddened as well as frustrated her, and at last she had to speak. "You sound like you're enjoying yourself with Edwin's shooting party, Blythe."

"I am."

At least she'd answered, even if her voice was clipped and angry.

"I thought the guests seemed to take pleasure in the meal."

"Trying to earn a compliment, Audrey?"

Audrey sighed. "I was making polite conversation, which might be all I ever have with you. It makes me sad."

Blythe made no response, and for the millionth time, Audrey wished she could see her expression. They suddenly heard a door being thrown open, and a genial burst of laughter from the men as they crossed the entrance hall.

The men swept into the room in a rush of exuberance, their very presence a powerful wave of maleness Audrey had never experienced. She was usually asked to retire to her room when her brother had company. But not this time. She had Lord Knightsbridge to thank for that. She was able to experience all their deep voices, the many scents of cologne and perspiration, the movement of air as if the young men couldn't stand still in anticipation of their hunt.

Someone bumped her leg, and she heard a young man say, "Forgive me, Mrs. Blake," in a voice so loud Audrey almost reared her head back.

Mildly, she answered, "Apology accepted, sir, although next you might try apologizing for the assault on my ears."

When chuckles swept around her, it was a little dizzying to imagine so many people in places she couldn't predict, couldn't see.

Someone sat beside her, and the cushions angled down from the weight. She balanced herself carefully.

"Interesting book, Mrs. Blake."

Lord Knightsbridge, she thought, relaxing. "It is, my lord, one made especially for the blind. You can feel the letters, if you'd like."

He did so, his fingers light across the page, but beneath the book, she could feel the faint pressure of them trailing across her thighs. It made her shiver, and she pressed her lips together. What was this? Such a strange sensation. The others continued to converse; it was reassuring to think no one watched them.

"It is good to know you have access to the world of books," he said.

"I am fortunate to have a lady's maid who will read for hours on end in the evening. Right now, we are studying the countries of Africa."

"Ah, you are a scholar."

Her cheeks felt hot—was he actually making her blush? "No, I am not so talented."

"What else do you do to pass the time?" he asked, then added, "If you do not mind telling me."

"I don't mind honest curiosity, sir," she answered. She wet her lips, knowing that how she portrayed herself would influence his decision. Conversely, his behavior would influence her as well. "I love to walk. I'm out every day with my maid, to strengthen my health and enjoy the air. I ride as well, although I sometimes need to be guided."

"Sometimes?" he echoed.

The surprised amusement in his voice wasn't condescending.

"My gelding, Erebus, knows his way about the estate, as do I."

"Erebus," he echoed. "Greek god?"

"Excellent memory, my lord. The god of darkness."

"Aah," he said, and the amusement was back. "Shaped like mist, not a man. Appropriate. Please continue with your pastimes."

He was well read. She liked that. "As for indoor amusements, besides reading, I can crochet and knit. We all know how important needlework is to a lady," she added dryly.

He laughed, and more than one conversation died.

Suddenly, Blythe spoke up in the silence. "So what are you two discussing that is so amusing? Do share!"

Audrey was surprised to feel a gentle understanding for her sister. Blythe also knew what it was like to worry about the future. She had been out for three years now, and though she'd turned down several inappropriate proposals, a good match had not presented itself. Blythe no more wanted to grow old in this house than Audrey did. Whenever Audrey grew angry with her sister's impatience and temper, she tried to remind herself of this.

"We are discussing needlework, Miss Collins," Lord Knightsbridge said.

Someone guffawed.

"I myself used to have terrible hobbies for a young future earl," he continued.

"Oh do enlighten us, my lord," Blythe urged.

"I thought myself quite the scholar and intellect."

"But you became a soldier," Blythe countered. "Would that not make you an outdoorsman in your youth?"

"My father would order my brother to drag me from my books to the archery field or fencing match."

"Surely your brother had your best interests at heart," Edwin said with hearty good cheer.

Audrey could imagine him giving Blythe a playful elbow to the side, but not her, as if it would be cruel to have fun with an invalid.

"Oh, my brother had more than my best interests—he was very competitive, being older than I."

"But you are the earl," Blythe said, confusion in her voice.

"My brother died at fourteen. Now, Miss Collins, do not look so sad. It was a long time ago, and I've since thought my brother has enjoyed watching me from above as I stumble from mistake to mistake."

So he has had other grief in his life, Audrey thought. Perhaps that was where his compassion began.

"Maybe your brother has guided you as well," Blythe said. "You were a captain in the army, yes? And you have the look of a man at ease in physical pursuits."

Audrey found herself trying to imagine what Blythe saw. Audrey knew something of men after all, even though she'd only had a wedding night before her husband had abandoned her. At first she'd thought herself lacking when he'd so quickly fled, but after a time, she'd realized he'd been a selfish man who cared little for her or making her feel at ease on their wedding night. She'd been a virgin, after all.

But she remembered what he'd felt like through his nightshirt, thin and bony, awkward with his hands on her body. He could not be a representation of all men. Lord Knightsbridge must look quite the dashing figure in comparison, if Blythe's reaction was any indication.

Not that she cared. The earl could be a hunched troll and it wouldn't matter, as long as he helped her. And then he could go away, because she was done with men, done with being under their control.

"I do enjoy outdoor pursuits now," Lord Knightsbridge admitted. "And I've been known to be an accurate shot. I imagine some of you here should fear my abilities."

There was laughter and answering challenges, so . . . manly to Audrey, thrilling in a new way. It was wonderful to participate like this, all because of his lordship.

As conversations began again, Lord Collins asked Blythe to play the piano, and soon her cheerful melody provided background.

Lord Knightsbridge murmured, "I do believe I must speak to others now, Mrs. Blake, or be accused of monopolizing you."

"I understand, my lord, but you are patronizing me. We both know all believe *I'm* monopolizing *you*."

"And we know it untrue," he murmured.

To her surprise, he lifted her gloved hand and brought it briefly to his mouth, so briefly she might have imagined it. Her fingers started to tremble, and she berated herself for a silly fool.

"You are a flatterer, my lord," she said, shaking her head. "I give you permission to go flatter someone else."

She heard his chuckle, felt the rush of warm air as he rose, and then she was alone at her end of the sofa. Listening to Blythe play, she heard the occasional wrong note that came from not enough practice, but overall, she thought her sister had improved. Blythe joined her voice to the music, and it was sweet and pretty. Audrey hoped many of the men looked upon her sister with interest.

Soon Audrey deemed it time for refreshments, so she walked to the bell pull and rang it, waiting patiently for the footman to appear. She ordered coffee and tea for her brother's guests.

"No, no, I can play no more," she heard Blythe say in a teasing voice. "My fingers will need time to recover."

"Then let us hear your sister play," Lord Knightsbridge said, his deep voice once again bringing all conversation to a standstill.

Audrey was caught standing alone, feeling almost adrift in surprise. She could sense their eyes on her, and her imagination made them all look wide-eyed with shock or revulsion or morbid curiosity.

"I don't think . . ." her father began in his big blustery voice.

"But I heard her this afternoon when I arrived," Lord Knightsbridge smoothly interrupted. "Mrs. Blake plays as beautifully as her sister. You have very talented daughters, Collins."

Audrey couldn't refuse the earl, for it would be poor manners, but she wasn't so certain this was a good idea. When she hesitated, not knowing who was between her and the piano, someone took her arm. She stiffened.

"It is only your proud brother," Edwin said, speaking tightly as if between gritted teeth.

Did he think she was ruining his shooting party? Or distracting attention from Blythe? Audrey straightened in anger, allowing him to lead her to the piano. Sitting down on the bench, she tried to clear her mind, the better to choose a selection. She panicked for a moment, never having been asked to perform for guests. At last one of Chopin's romantic piano ballades came to mind. As she hesitated, she remembered how long it had taken her to memorize it, note by note, with help from her mother. Those were such good memories.

She began to play, and let the pleasure of the music soothe her nerves and quench her unease. Only when she was done did she realize that everyone had remained silent throughout. A burst of warm applause made her bow her head with happiness.

She almost felt like a normal woman. But she wasn't—not yet.

Chapter 4

∽⟋⟍⟋⟍∽

The next morning, Robert walked the fields with the other men toward the marsh at the far end of the park, where they were supposed to find plenty of birds to shoot. The grass crunched beneath their feet from the frozen damp overnight. The sun was just rising, casting its rays through the brilliant foliage of a copse of trees ahead. A half dozen beaters had already gone in front, waiting for a signal to drive the birds toward them.

Robert couldn't keep his mind on what he was about to do, though he held his gun with well-trained caution. He was remembering Mrs. Blake's performance last night, and he still could not forget how impressed and awed he'd been. His bookish youth had made him familiar with the works of Chopin, and he knew the ballade she'd chosen to play was considered one of the most technically difficult. And yet she'd memorized it without ever reading the sheet music.

Seeing her with her eyes closed and her expression suffused with peaceful joy, one could almost forget she was blind. He'd looked around and seen the other men's faces show surprise and reluctant delight. Lord Collins's expression was far more inscrutable, and his son's simply impassive. But Miss Collins? She did not like to be upstaged, and surely knew she had been. Perhaps that was why Mrs. Blake chose not to sing. It would have only pointed out even more strongly who was the more talented of the sisters.

Robert hoped his request for Mrs. Blake to play hadn't further distanced her from her family. It was simply that he'd been annoyed at seeing her relegated to a corner alone, like a dotty old lady.

If she had wanted to show him her family situation, it was working. In less than twenty-four hours, he was already defensive on her behalf.

And he was also full of regret that he'd brought up the subject of his brother, Neil. They were only two years apart, and they should have been close, but their father had been a firm believer in raising up his sons to be competitive. Their tutor had taken that one step further and set them against one another to "spark their competitiveness." All it did was ruin their relationship, and made Robert retreat into his books. When Neil had died, Robert became the focus of their father's fanatic need to control everything around him.

And so he had to follow him around day after day whenever he was home for holidays, learning the man's obsessive methods for controlling his estates, watching other men cower to his father's bullying. Only one man could not be cowed, and that was a retired military officer who lived in their village. Robert would often seek him out to hear his adventures—which was probably why he bought a commission himself, when he felt himself turning into his father.

Robert was glad when they arrived at the pond and the beaters had begun their work. Birds took flight, and he aimed and shot. Some men had a servant reload one gun while they shot another, but Robert reloaded quickly by himself. Birds plummeted from the sky, and dogs brought them back without taking a single bite.

Several hours later, as they walked back toward the manor carrying bags of birds for the evening meal, Robert happened to glance down another path, and to his surprise, he saw Mrs. Blake walking with a plainly garbed woman. The sainted lady's maid?

Since he was already at the back of the small group of men, he simply turned down the path toward Mrs. Blake. She was far enough away that he had time to watch her move, still without the aid of a cane. She kept her head high, as if smelling crisp air redolent with recently picked apples and hearth fires.

"I'm quite sorry my sister distracted you, Knightsbridge."

Robert turned his head to find Edwin Collins catching up with him. "Not a bit. I thought I'd say good morning."

"It was foolish for her to be out when we're shooting," Collins said, his breath huffing. "She could have been hurt."

Robert almost pointed out that she wasn't anywhere near the pond, but he let Collins pull ahead of him and draw Mrs. Blake aside. The man spoke intently for several minutes, while Mrs. Blake's expression remained impassive. The other woman, red-faced, looked off as if she wasn't listening.

At last Collins strode back toward his friends, pausing to give Robert a look. Obviously realizing he had no say in what Robert did, he only gave an impatient nod and strode away.

The servant said something to Mrs. Blake, and her head came up quickly as he approached.

"Forgive me, Lord Knightsbridge," she said coolly. "I'm sorry you had to see that."

"I heard nothing, Mrs. Blake. It simply looked like a brother and sister conversing." But he knew he'd seen a warning. Apparently only Miss Collins was allowed to consort with their guests.

She gave a grim smile. "That is kind of you." Her expression eased and she turned her head slightly toward her servant. "This is my lady's maid, Molly. Molly, the Earl of Knightsbridge."

It wasn't often a woman introduced a peer to her servant; he admired that about her.

Molly sank into a deep curtsy and her blush emphasized her freckles. "Good morning, milord."

He smiled at her. "The two of you make quite a sight on an early morning."

Molly bit her lip, even as Mrs. Blake asked dryly, "You mean like Punch and Judy?"

He laughed. "Not at all. It is inspiring to see you out and about, without even a cane. I hope my admiration isn't offensive."

"It is not, my lord," she said at last, a faint smile curving her lips.

"May I walk with you?"

"You may."

He took her arm and placed it on his, and she seemed surprised.

"I know you can walk unassisted, but there is something about an autumn morn with a lovely woman on your arm that a man can't resist."

"You are a charmer, my lord," she said, shaking her head.

Molly fell behind them as they began to walk

toward the garden, giving them enough room to speak privately.

"You don't need to treat me like this," Mrs. Blake said at last.

He glanced down at her in surprise. "Like what?"

"Like you're flirting with me. We both know you're playing a part."

"I am so glad you see through to what you think I'm doing."

She gave a soft laugh.

"This isn't a part I'm playing, Mrs. Blake," he said, his voice a bit more serious. "I wanted to get to know you and your family. I'm doing so, am I not?"

"You are," she admitted with obvious reluctance.

"Do I make you uncomfortable—or cause you problems with your family?" he added, more to the point.

"I am not uncomfortable—simply unused to being brought to people's attention. There are some benefits to being invisible."

"Invisible," he mused, keeping his voice light although he felt a stir of anger on her behalf. "I often wished to be so when I served in the army. It makes one not a target."

"Exactly. And now you're home, taking up the responsibilities of the earldom, and I imagine you're far more visible than you're used to."

"Perceptive, Mrs. Blake. Then we have something in common." They strolled in silence for a moment as they entered one of the garden's gravel paths. The last daisies were dying, and other shrubbery had already been cut back. "Mrs. Blake, I mean no offense, but your husband never once mentioned you were blind. And I can see now he must have thought you quite the normal woman, regardless of your—"

"He was ashamed," she interrupted, her voice matter-of-fact.

Not surprised, Robert said nothing, only gave her gloved hand a squeeze where it rested on his arm.

"You don't need to show me sympathy, sir. I knew he did not love me. He only wanted my dowry."

And he suspected she was eager enough to be away that she wasn't too choosy.

"I'm sorry," he said.

She tilted her head as if she were looking up at him. "I hope I am not disillusioning you about your friend."

"I left England at a young age, and he was several years my junior. We only became more acquainted in the Eighth Dragoons."

"And that was only possible because of my dowry. It is how he purchased his commission. I didn't know his plans until he left England the day after our wedding."

Robert frowned. "That is a tragedy. I regret you had to suffer it."

"I would not normally confide such private sorrow in a stranger, my lord, but you need to understand my dilemma."

"I am understanding more and more each hour."

"Good. Then I will ask you not to repeat my past marital difficulties."

"Of course not."

"Even with my family. My father warned me about Mr. Blake's intentions from the beginning, and I didn't want to listen. Reminding him of it only makes him repeat his warnings all over again."

"About men in general?"

"About my suitability to marry. And though my father doesn't believe me, I have taken my hard-earned lessons to heart. I don't plan to marry again, ever."

She spoke so firmly, flatly, that he knew she believed it. And Robert couldn't blame her. It must be difficult to make oneself vulnerable, and then be so cruelly rejected.

"We all must react to our own lessons, Mrs. Blake," he finally said.

"Even an earl? I imagine that you're permitted—anything."

She sounded a bit intrigued, but he wasn't going to satisfy her curiosity.

"Even an earl."

They walked on in silence, taking the winding trails ever closer to the house, passing a fountain that sprayed a cold mist in the air.

"My lord, do you still have dead birds on your person?"

He shot her a glance. "I had forgotten."

"I had, too, until I smelled them."

He chuckled. "I'll guide you up to the house, and then head for the kitchens."

"Do not bother yourself on my behalf, my lord. I'll finish my walk with Molly, and see you at luncheon."

Robert watched in amazement as she turned back the way they'd just come and approached Molly. The servant murmured something, and they both took a right hand turn down another path that disappeared behind a vine-covered arbor.

Robert stood still, considering his dilemma. There was no doubt that he had to help Mrs. Blake, but after the close way her family watched her, he was beginning to think her suggestion that he simply escort her away wasn't going to work.

After luncheon, Robert accompanied the rest of the gentlemen for target shooting out on the lawn, which he won. Dinner ended up being a more elaborate affair, with neighbors as guests, followed by card games in the drawing room. He rather suspected he was being put on display by Miss Collins, who'd thrown the event together and sent footmen scurrying all over the countryside with invitations that morning. Robert was no longer surprised when only a few of the guests knew Mrs. Blake personally, although most had heard of her.

Since card games could not appeal to Mrs. Blake, she sat in a corner with an elderly woman, who kept up so much chatter that every time Robert looked their way, Mrs. Blake, though nodding politely, was never given the chance to speak.

Robert didn't need any more convincing. It was time to talk to Lord Collins. Would the baron allow him to simply whisk away his daughter? No. But Robert had another idea . . .

When the last guest from the village had gone, Miss Collins retired and Mr. Collins led his friends upstairs. Robert stopped their father in the entrance hall.

"Lord Collins, might we speak privately?" he asked.

Mrs. Blake was just entering the hall from the

back corridor. Her eyes narrowed as he spoke. There was no way to send her a reassuring smile. Realizing he was staring a bit too long, he turned and found Lord Collins frowning at him.

"We can speak in my study," Collins said, leading him across the hall to another door.

His study was lined with books and deep leather chairs, and the occasional masculine knickknacks of rocks, animal skulls, and a mounted deer. Collins indicated a chair for Robert, then went around and sat behind the desk, as if he needed a barrier against whatever Robert had to say.

But his expression was neutral enough as he asked, "Is something amiss, Knightsbridge?"

Robert was so used to making a decision and then the necessary physical preparations, it had never occurred to him to prepare a speech. He would definitely need to brush up on that before Parliament opened after Christmas.

"Collins, I came here with the intention of offering my sympathy to your daughter. I had heard a bit about her from Blake—"

"You can't trust a word that scoundrel ever said," Collins said, frowning. "He abandoned my daughter."

"He did, though I didn't know it. He spoke of her letters as giving him comfort, and in some ways, I think he was surprised by that."

The other man said nothing, only steepled his fingers together beneath his chin.

"I've spent two days in Mrs. Blake's company, and I've seen her courage, wit, and intelligence. I cannot express enough my admiration."

"What are you saying?" Collins demanded.

"I wanted to inform you that I will be asking for Mrs. Blake's hand in marriage tomorrow."

To his surprise, Collins began to chuckle, but it slowly died away as Robert didn't smile in return.

"You are serious," Collins said in a flat voice.

"I am."

"You have an earldom to lure any young woman. You've only just returned to England. And you want to choose the first woman you've spent time with—a *blind* woman?"

"I returned two weeks ago," Robert amended. "I met several debutantes in London, but most are in the country, I know. Your daughter is the first woman to fascinate me, and frankly, after nine years in the army, I've learned to trust my instincts."

"Her dowry went to Blake," Collins said smugly, crossing his arms over his chest. "But Blythe has a fine dowry."

Robert ignored the mention of the other daughter. "Mrs. Blake told me how her husband took her money and betrayed her. I would never do that. I've resigned my commission. I have no need of her dowry. Surely you know that the Knightsbridge estates have been well cared for. But, sir, it is your daughter's kindness and patience I value, not money. Her acceptance of her limitations, and the courage she shows every single day. The London debutantes want me for all the wrong reasons, my title and wealth. A mature woman like Mrs. Blake would best understand the moods of an ex-soldier."

Collins never took his eyes off Robert. At last he said, "I can't allow this."

Robert arched a brow. "She is an adult, sir, a widow. You have no say."

"She is an invalid. Any court will agree she's not capable of making her own decisions."

"She would testify on her own behalf and talk circles around any lawyer. You know that. And what will I be doing? I will be explaining to everyone in London about your resistance, and the way you treat her as your servant rather than your daughter."

Collins slammed his hands onto the desk, scattering papers. "I will not listen to such words in my own home!"

"You won't listen to the truth, you mean? I saw the local gentry tonight—most of them had heard of Mrs. Blake, but never met her. What kind of father keeps his daughter out of sight, simply because she's blind? Is it catching? We both know it is not. Is there a stigma attached? She has been convenient for you to take advantage of, but that is over now. You have another daughter. I suggest she learn to manage a household, so that she is not a disappointment to her future husband."

Collins jumped to his feet, and Robert followed, unstretching leisurely, until he was a head taller than the other man. Collins looked up, hesitated, then pressed his lips together in a narrow line.

"Have you already compromised my daughter?" he demanded. "Is that what this is all about?"

"I have not, sir. I have done all that is proper. But even I did not expect to feel such a connection after only two days. Now on to the practical matters. My country seat is only a few miles away from the house she inherited from Blake, which is why we were in the same regiment. The Eighth Dragoons are a tradition in our parish. I will escort her and her lady's maid there, so that we can live in proximity while the wedding is planned."

"That damned house—how did you learn of it?"

"She told me, of course. We are able to speak freely with one another. I had not imagined a woman could understand me so well."

Robert realized that for the first time in a long while, he was using the weight of the earldom to have his way, and there was satisfaction in that—too much like the old, immature days of his youth. But he wouldn't go back to being that spoiled young man who didn't know how to treat people with respect. This supposed marriage was for Mrs. Blake's benefit, not his own, he reminded himself.

"Do we understand each other, Collins?" Robert asked. "I wish to have a cordial relationship with you, but not if you can't respect your daughter."

Collins shook his head. "I have no choice, do I? But Knightsbridge, you are too full of yourself. She will refuse your proposal. She's been badly hurt before, and that was by a man who took the time to court her. You? She's too levelheaded to risk her future on a stranger."

"Then that will be her choice," Robert agreed amiably. He bowed to the baron and opened the door.

A footman waited with several candleholders, offering one for Robert's use.

"Not just yet," Robert said. "Please ask Mrs. Blake if she would speak with me. I'll be waiting in the parlor." He didn't want her father getting to her first.

Chapter 5

Audrey hadn't let Molly help her undress for bed. When she'd heard Lord Knightsbridge ask to speak to her father, her stomach immediately clenched and had been fluttering ever since. What was the earl saying? He hadn't even answered her request for help yet.

And then came a soft rap on the door, and she flung it wide.

"It is Richard, Mrs. Blake," said the well-trained footman. "Lord Knightsbridge requests your presence in the parlor."

"Now?" she asked in disbelief.

"Yes, ma'am."

"Very well, I'll be down in a moment."

When she shut the door, she could hear Molly's rushed footsteps, felt the maid clasp her arm.

"Miss Audrey, what is this about?"

"I'm not sure." *And that wasn't quite a lie.* Audrey hated to mislead her dearest friend, but her request of the earl was too important to speak of.

No candles were necessary for her as she moved through the manor in the dark of night—although more than once in the past, she'd startled a sighted person. She hurried down the stairs, crossed the entrance hall, and entered the parlor.

"Lord Knightsbridge?" she called.

"I am here, Mrs. Blake. Please close the door behind you."

That was nothing an unmarried woman normally heard from a man. Forcing down a shiver of nerves, she did as he asked.

"I'm seated on the sofa, Mrs. Blake. Come join me."

She moved forward cautiously, in case furniture had been moved as the servants cleaned. But they had all been well trained, and everything was where it should be. Lord Knightsbridge took her arm and guided her to a place beside him. It felt strange to sit so close when they were all alone. It had been almost three years since a man had showed any interest in her at all. She'd begged this one to help her—why could she not just hear his decision without feeling anxious?

"Why did you speak with my father?" she asked.

"Right to the point—I like that about you, Mrs. Blake."

"I had assumed you would discuss your decision with me first."

"I had to follow the rules of courtship. Which meant I had to inform your father I was marrying you."

Her breath caught in shock, and then fury and disbelief filled her up like a pitcher about to overflow. "I will not marry you!"

"Keep your voice down," he murmured. "I'm not truly planning to marry you—you've told me you'll never marry again."

She swallowed heavily, forced herself to breathe again. "Then why did you tell him that?"

"How else did you think I could get you away from here? I was not about to flee dishonestly in the night, as if I'd compromised you and we had something to hide."

"Now we just have a false engagement to hide."

"You are not thinking clearly. Since we're newly engaged, and you're widowed, I can escort you and your lady's maid to your new home—conveniently close to mine—to ease the wedding preparations. Once you're settled, you can break off the engagement, as is every woman's right. Who would blame you? We barely know each other, and thank God we took the time to discover our differences before we married, yes?"

She was still breathing deeply, realizing how frightened the thought of being married again made her. It was such a visceral, sickening feeling, that sense of helplessness she'd experienced being passed back from her husband to her father, as if she were but a possession, not a person with feelings to be hurt.

But his words calmed her, and at last she began to make sense of his plan. "Yes, I see what you're saying. You're an earl who wants to marry me, taking an invalid off her father's hands. People should think my father the luckiest man in existence. Or that I must have an incredible treasure in jewels."

"Now you're sounding sarcastic," he pointed out.

She was surprised to feel the beginnings of a smile. "I am sorry I reacted in quick anger when you're only trying to help me."

He put his gloved hand on hers. "Believe me, I understand your disillusionment with marriage. My parents' marriage was even colder than a mountain battlefield. They cared nothing for each other, and knew that from the beginning. It was a match to satisfy their families and their social status, that was all."

"I'm sorry. That sounds terrible for you."

"They didn't beat me, and they provided for me. There are many who have it worse."

She felt the cushions shift as he stood, bringing her hand up with him until she was forced to rise.

"Off to bed with you," he said. "You must fortify yourself before we break the news to the rest of your family. I'll let the hunting party go off without me in the morning and try to convince your brother to join his friends late."

She winced. "You had the worst of it, dealing with my father. I will find the words to explain to Blythe and Edwin," she insisted, smiling up at him. "I will take it from here. Thank you for your assistance."

It had been difficult for Audrey to fall asleep. For one thing, she kept secret from Molly her "engagement," deciding that her sister and brother should hear news of it before a servant—even though Molly was far closer to her than any of the others.

But she'd felt so fragile after Lord Knightsbridge's "proposal," she was worried she wouldn't be able to keep the truth from Molly—that it wasn't a real engagement. And that was something she had to hug to her heart as she played the part of a delighted bride. She couldn't risk anyone finding out the truth.

She'd waited to descend to the ground floor until Molly told her the shooting party had gone to the stables. Now, every step toward the dining room made her feel more and more apprehensive. *Why do you care what your family thinks?* They didn't care about how their feelings of shame hurt her; they didn't care if they kept her locked away forever, as long as she was useful to them.

But they were her siblings, and she didn't want to treat them as they'd treated her. It was her dearest wish—after her own independence—that she could heal her relationships with Blythe and Edwin.

She entered the dining room and came to a stop.

"Good mornin', Mrs. Blake," said the footman. "Yer chair is all ready for you."

"Good morning, Richard, and thank you. Is anyone else here?"

There was an awkward silence. And then Richard said hesitantly, "Lord Collins is readin' his newspaper, ma'am."

And he was so focused on his reading that he couldn't hear a greeting? Not from her, anyway.

"Good morning, Father," she said, moving past his chair and into the one she usually used near Edwin's end of the table.

"Did you say yes to the earl?" he suddenly barked.

Startled, she dropped her napkin. "I did."

At first, he didn't answer. Her throat tightened, her eyes stung, and she felt like a fool. She hadn't cried in so long; she wasn't about to give her father the satisfaction.

"I thought you'd learned your lesson," he ground out. "This man has the power to treat you far worse than the first."

"I'll be careful. Thank you for your concern."

He grunted his response.

Well, what had she expected? She managed his entire household, and now she was leaving him. He had a housekeeper, of course, but he never wanted to deal with her. Now he'd have to—or Blythe would. That was the only reason he was angry.

She was going to have her freedom at last, like any daughter would expect. That was what she'd wanted for so many years, even if it hurt others in her family.

"Yer usual breakfast, Mrs. Blake?" Richard asked.

"Yes, please."

He filled her plate from the buffet, then set it before her. She knew he'd placed everything where it belonged: eggs toward the north of the plate, toast to the east, the meat to the south—

"Do we have bacon this morning, Richard?"

"Pheasant, ma'am, from yer brother's shootin' party."

"Good, thank you."

"Don't sound too pleased with yourself," her father said. "You're making a foolish mistake."

She cocked her head, and said dryly, "The pheasant is too gamy?" Had she thought herself past the worst of her father's resistance?

"That will be all, Richard," Lord Collins barked.

She heard the servant leave, closing the far door behind him. More footsteps approached from the front hall, mixed with Blythe's chirping laughter and the deep voices of Edwin and Lord Knightsbridge. She couldn't decide if she was relieved or frustrated at the interruption.

"Good morning, Mrs. Blake, Lord Collins," said Lord Knightsbridge, sounding excessively cheerful.

"Good morning, my lord," she said softly.

Just hearing his voice made her think: *Will we leave today? Will I finally start my own journey, my own life?*

Something slammed on to the table, and she jerked.

"You are doing a terrible thing, Knightsbridge," said her father.

She closed her eyes and took a deep breath. This wasn't the way to explain the news to her brother and sister.

"Father, what are you talking about?" Blythe asked, sounding both nervous and good-natured, an interesting balancing act. "Lord Knightsbridge is our guest."

"A guest who takes advantage of innocent women—"

"Father!" Audrey interrupted. "Nothing underhanded has happened. Lord Knightsbridge and I—"

"—are engaged to be married." This time it was the earl's turn to interrupt.

She could imagine their shocked expressions. Blythe's gasp was piercing in the sudden silence. Audrey would have revealed their news another way, explained they'd come to an understanding . . . oh, what would have been the point?

But it bothered her that she'd told Lord Knightsbridge she wanted to handle the announcement, and he'd either forgotten—or ignored her.

"I—I—" Blythe stuttered.

Audrey could hear the shrillness in her tone, knew she was so angry as to be near tears. Blythe would think that once again, blind Audrey had captured a husband—her second—and Blythe had none.

"Sit down before you fall over, Blythe," their father said with exasperation.

"C-congratulations, my lord," Blythe stuttered.

"Thank you, Miss Collins."

"No congratulations are necessary," Lord Collins said. "I don't approve of this engagement."

"Audrey is an adult, Father," Edwin said impassively. "She doesn't need your permission."

Audrey's mouth almost dropped open. Was her brother actually on her side? Did he at last understand she'd been trapped like a wounded bird all these years—or did he just want to be rid of the embarrassment of her?

"But . . . you barely know each other," Blythe said in a soft voice.

Audrey was impressed by how hard her sister was working to control herself. She truly hadn't wanted Blythe to be hurt.

"It feels as if we've known each other much longer," Lord Knightsbridge said.

He took her hand, and she had to struggle not to show her surprise. She hadn't realized he'd come close, so lost in her thoughts she wasn't listening well.

And his hand was bare, and so was hers, his skin warm, calloused across the palm. It felt so different from her own, so . . . male. She was putting herself in those hands, trusting them. And Blythe was right—she barely knew Lord Knightsbridge.

"I have never conversed so easily with a woman," the earl continued.

His voice was low and smooth as a caress. Audrey could only imagine how it would feel if he were really using the power of that voice to woo her.

"I felt Mrs. Blake understood me, and I understood her. I don't see her blindness, I see everything she's accomplished."

Lord Collins snorted. "I've told him she has no dowry but that little house, and he doesn't care. That seems suspicious to me."

"How much more money does a person need?" Lord Knightsbridge asked.

"Audrey, how do you feel about this?" Edwin said. "You've only known him two days." He hesitated. "And as for your first marriage—"

"Do you not think I've learned from that?" Audrey asked. "I know this is quick, but I've never felt this way before. And we will not rush the marriage. We will take our time, living in our own households."

"Oh, I had not realized," Edwin said, sounding relieved. "Then you can change your mind."

"Of course I can," Audrey said firmly. "I have learned hard lessons, dear brother. I won't forget them. I'll be sure, this time."

He was obviously trying to sound more lighthearted as he said, "Of course, he is a war hero. That must count for something."

"I am no hero," Lord Knightsbridge said.

Audrey was surprised at the cool tones of his voice, and it made her curious about this new "fiancé" of hers. No one spoke for a moment.

"I—I have to pack for London," Blythe suddenly blurted out.

Her trip had been long planned, and Audrey had totally forgotten. She heard the hurrying tap of her slippers leave the room.

Edwin sighed. "I should get to the hunting party."

"Eat something," Audrey insisted. "You need your strength."

"You've always tried to take care of everyone, sister," Edwin said slowly. "I guess it's time for someone to take care of you."

Audrey bit her lip, then pushed her fork through her cold eggs, touched by the sentiment. But what she wanted to say was—it was time for her to take care of herself.

She felt a hand on her shoulder.

"I'll remain with Mrs. Blake," Lord Knightsbridge said from behind her.

"No, my lord, you must enjoy your morning," she insisted. "I have much packing to do."

He paused. "If you're certain . . ."

"I am."

She heard her father's chair scrape back, and he stomped from the room without speaking. Would he come up with a plan to keep her here, some way to drive off the earl? Audrey felt a bit panicked, wondering how fast she could pack—and then realized Blythe was taking their only carriage to London. They would have to hire one in the village. She mentioned this to Lord Knightsbridge as he and Edwin ate a quick breakfast, and he promised he would see to it later in the morning.

As the earl passed her, following Edwin toward the far door, he took her hand again and brought it to his mouth. "That didn't go so badly, did it?" he whispered.

He still hadn't donned his gloves, and the soft press of his lips was almost shocking. She reminded herself that she was a widow, that she knew the ways of men.

But one night of intimacy with a man who didn't want her had not prepared her for the attentions of Lord Knightsbridge as he put on a show for her family.

"We all survived the telling," she murmured at last.

She shivered as he touched her hair at her temple, then said his good-byes.

She was alone, her hands shaking, her appetite gone. But she nibbled on some of the cold toast and tried to tell herself that it was done, that she could escape.

But she wasn't out the door yet.

Chapter 6

❧

Although Robert was not in the mood to hunt, he could not risk alienating another member of the Collins family, so he walked the woods with Mr. Collins, even as the beaters ran before them to chase out the birds, rabbits, and foxes. He received cautious congratulations from the other young men, and he knew they considered him eccentric or just plain crazy. None of them understood that there was more to marriage than being able to look upon the average debutante for the rest of your life. The surface things faded, especially appearance. He'd seen war damage so many people, yet often, if they were lucky, they were still the same inside.

He shook his head, bemused at his thoughts. He should take his own advice when it was time to find a real bride. What kind of woman that would be? He had no idea, but he should give himself at least a Season to figure it out.

He certainly hadn't gone without women all

these years. British Society flourished in India, and although he'd stayed away from the eligible misses, there had always been an eager widow who appreciated his companionship when he was in Bombay.

When the hunting was finished, he had his horse saddled and rode into the village to the blacksmith's shop, where Mr. Collins had suggested he look for a carriage. One would be available on the morrow, so he resigned himself to another night under Lord Collins's roof. Robert hoped his subtle threats had been enough to dissuade the baron from trying anything to stop their departure.

Audrey's room was a disaster, with clothes sorted into piles everywhere. Molly rushed about gleefully, escorting the footmen as they brought the trunks, talking nonstop until Audrey's head spun.

Molly had taken the news of the engagement with shock and then excitement. After all, Audrey was marrying a handsome earl. It was a fairy tale as far as the staff was concerned, and she had received several offers of congratulations from below the stairs as the morning went on. The housekeeper had actually dabbed at her wet eyes and whispered that it was time Audrey had her own household. Audrey had agreed, and gradually stopped worrying about what her father might do.

Molly had happily decided to accompany Audrey, to "see the world," she kept repeating, even though Buckinghamshire was only the next county. But Audrey felt the same way. She might not be able to "see" it like everyone else, but she had Molly to describe things, and she could experience the world her own way. After all, there were new sounds and smells, things that were very important to her. And she had Molly, for without her . . . Audrey hadn't even considered what she would do if her faithful friend didn't want to go.

By midmorning, the first trunk was packed, and they were sorting through the "maybe" pile for her last trunk.

Molly stopped speaking in mid-sentence, then said uncertainly, "Good morning, Miss Collins."

Surprised, Audrey turned, wishing she could read her sister's expression. "What can I do for you, Blythe? Isn't it strange that we're both packing for a trip?" Oh, now she was babbling. Of course it was strange—Audrey was never allowed to go anywhere. And she certainly hadn't intended to sound sarcastic.

She smelled her sister's jasmine perfume as the woman drew closer.

"I think you're making a terrible mistake." Blythe's voice trembled.

Molly said, "I'll just leave you two—"

"No," Blythe interrupted. "This won't take long, and Molly, even you must agree with me. Audrey doesn't know him. If she won't listen to me, can't you talk sense into her?"

Molly didn't answer, and Audrey thought it unfair to put her maid in the middle. "Blythe, I haven't married him yet. I have time to change my mind."

"But he's a stranger!"

"Every person at dinner last night either knew who he was, or had heard of him. He's not an unknown stranger, anyway. It's not as if he could take me off somewhere. People know what's happening between us." Which was why Lord Knightsbridge had been right, that he couldn't just escort her away. It would have caused not only talk, but alarm.

Blythe still sounded tight with disappointment and anger, but was there also a touch of concern there? Audrey wanted to hope so, but she'd been disappointed so many times before.

"Blythe, I wish . . ." Her words faded for a moment. "I wish this didn't hurt you."

Blythe didn't even attempt to deny it. "Well, it does. It's just not fair."

"I know," she whispered. For just a moment, she wished she could confide the truth in her sister, that she wasn't marrying the earl, but if that knowledge got to their father . . . she'd be trapped there forever.

"How do you make these men feel sorry for you?" Blythe asked in a bewildered voice.

Audrey heard Molly inhale swiftly, and she herself felt defensive. Calmly, she said, "Blythe, do you remember that I was lied to by Mr. Blake? He never felt sorry for me. He used me and betrayed me."

There was a taut silence, and then Blythe suddenly whispered, "You're right. I'm sorry."

That was progress, Audrey thought, beginning to feel hopeful. "And as for Lord Knightsbridge . . . if I thought for one moment he felt sorry for me, I would send him on his way. But why should he, Blythe? Why should my condition matter to him at all, if he has feelings for me? He doesn't owe me anything, especially not pity. I didn't encourage his interest, but I did not turn him away, either. And if he *didn't* have feelings for me, why would he make a blind woman his countess?"

"I don't know!" Blythe cried. "But is it not suspicious?"

Audrey opened her mouth to respond, then closed it. It *would* be suspicious, if it had been true.

But Blythe didn't know that. "I promise I will consider this engagement very carefully. I'll be in my own home, and he'll be in his. I'll meet people from his village, get to know more about him. Will that satisfy you?"

"I—I suppose so."

Audrey heard a whirl of her skirts.

"I need to finish packing," Blythe said.

"Do you have wonderful plans for when you visit Father's sister in London?" It was what she always asked whenever Blythe went away. Normally, it was like rubbing salt in her own wounds, having to live through her sister's adventures—or the brief crumbs Blythe told her. But not anymore.

Blythe didn't answer, and Audrey told herself that perhaps she'd been walking away so fast, she hadn't heard.

Just before luncheon, a carriage drove below her window.

"Molly?"

A moment later, Molly said, "It's the family carriage, Miss Audrey. And I saw Miss Blythe as it went by."

Audrey sighed. "So she left without even saying good-bye."

"I'm sorry, miss."

"Don't be. That conversation might have been one of the best we've ever had. I think she was

honestly worried about me, beneath her anger. I
will write to her when I reach my new home."

My new home, she repeated in her head. It felt
good.

Luncheon was cold meat and sandwiches, so that
the men could get back outside. The afternoon
was for fishing, and Robert might have declined
so that he could help Mrs. Blake, but he thought
his presence in the house would only exacer-
bate Lord Collins's fury. And it had been good to
spend time with Mr. Collins, who didn't seem like
a bad chap. He wanted to get to know Robert, too.
His protectiveness of his sister was very late, but
welcome just the same.

At dinner, Robert made certain he could sit
beside his "fiancée." More of the men spoke to her,
too, as if being a future countess suddenly made
her a person in their eyes.

The evening in the drawing room didn't last
long, as everyone would be getting an early start
home in the morn. When the room was at last just
family and Robert, Lord Collins started to leave.
He hadn't spoken a word to Robert or Mrs. Blake
all evening.

"Lord Collins, may I have a word?" Robert
called, rising to his feet. He noticed Mrs. Blake
stiffen.

Her father came to a stop near the door. "Say it quickly."

"Will Mrs. Blake be able to take her gelding?"

Mrs. Blake tilted her head toward him, but said nothing.

"No, it's my horse," the baron said darkly.

"Erebus has been trained to carry me, Father," Mrs. Blake pointed out. "To train another horse could take years."

"I'll purchase it from you," Robert said flatly, "as my engagement gift to Mrs. Blake."

"Father," Mr. Collins began.

"Fine! Take it!" Lord Collins said harshly and stormed out into the hall.

Mr. Collins gave Robert an apologetic glance. "I'll speak to him." To Mrs. Blake, he said, "Shall I leave you alone with Lord Knightsbridge?"

"Yes, thank you."

Mr. Collins eyed Robert speculatively, then closed the door. Robert sat back down on the sofa beside Mrs. Blake.

"Thank you for thinking of my horse, my lord," she said quietly. "In all the confusion of packing up my room, I never thought of the animal."

"You deserve to have it, for all the reasons you stated. I want you to be comfortable in your new home."

"My new home," she echoed wistfully.

They both heard footsteps in the entrance hall again. Robert had a flash of Mr. Collins's speculation, and suddenly he realized he had to make this look good. He pulled off his gloves, and then cupped Mrs. Blake's face in his hands, leaning close.

She gasped and whispered, "What are you doing?"

He felt the warmth of her breath on his mouth, and was startled by how distracting such a simple thing was. "Your brother looked suspicious," he said. "I believe he means to test us."

"But—"

"Stop talking, or I'll have to kiss you to keep you quiet."

Her eyes went round, her moist lips parted, and suddenly, he *wanted* to kiss her. She smelled of rose water, and he inhaled as if he could fill his entire being with it. But he held back, knowing he had no plans to marry her, however soft and warm her cheeks felt in his hands, however prettily she blushed.

"You have the most beautiful eyes," he murmured, even as he vaguely heard the door open.

Mrs. Blake jumped back.

He dropped his hands and glanced to see Mr. Collins enter hesitantly.

"Forgot my book," the other man said, reddening. "Forgive me."

"Nothing to forgive," Robert said cheerfully, and waited until the other man took a book from a shelf and left the room. He let out his breath.

"A book?" Mrs. Blake said dubiously. "Edwin hasn't read a book since university."

"It was a deception to see what we were doing."

"I don't understand . . ."

Robert smiled at her, but she gave no answering response. He'd never considered how much human interaction had to do with reading the signals from another person's expression and body. "Your brother—or perhaps your father put him up to it—wonders if something else is going on. Mr. Collins wanted to see if we had any passion when we were alone."

Her blush deepened even by candlelight. "But won't that make him think everything between us is . . . physical? That instead of making logical decisions, my heart is being swayed by . . ."

When her voice trailed away, he grinned. "By my expert kisses?"

"Oh please," she said with skepticism.

"Passion is a better reason to marry than something as cold-blooded as money or social status—or power."

"The first two are already proven wrong where we're concerned. I have nothing but a small manor to bring to this supposed marriage." She lowered her voice on "supposed." "But power? What do you mean?"

"There are men who want to control everything around them," he said quietly, thinking of his father. "And a wife should be controlled most of all, because she's an extension of him."

Mrs. Blake pressed her lips together and held herself still for a moment. "You are talking about your parents?"

"Not really. My mother did as she pleased— but she was very careful to be discreet. My father treated everyone as if they were under his power. Another thing you and I have in common. What about your parents?"

"You may be surprised, but I think they loved each other. My mother tempered my father's worst impulses. He was always embarrassed by me, but she made things better. When she died seven years ago . . . he was not the same man. Then again, none of us were the same. She was my champion, who treated me like a normal girl."

"Was Miss Collins jealous of her attention to you?"

"I . . . maybe she was, and I just never realized."

They were still sitting close together on the sofa, their knees brushing. And then Mrs. Blake slid back.

"My lord—"

"Call me Robert," he suddenly said. "No one has done so in years, and I have a sudden yearning to hear my Christian name."

"Very well . . . Robert."

That was dragged out of her so reluctantly, he almost laughed.

"You may call me Audrey."

"Audrey," he repeated. "If I say it's a lovely name, will you blush again? You do it so prettily."

She did blush again, but her words were no-nonsense. "No one can see us now, Lord—Robert, so please do not flirt. It is . . . distracting."

"I'm to play a part, Audrey. It is difficult to put the fiancé aside, and then remember to be him again."

"I may be playing your fiancée, but I expect you to treat me as I want to be treated. Last night I asked you to allow me to handle breaking the news of our engagement to my brother and sister. But you didn't."

"I was trying to be of help," he said, bemused.

"I'm not a doll you need to protect. I knew the situation might be bad, and I was prepared to handle it. Next time, please respect my wishes."

Had he just assumed he knew what was best for her? That wasn't gentlemanly of him, and he didn't like the trait. "I will do my best to agree with your wishes from now on."

"You sound sincere, and I appreciate that. Just remember—I can hear when you're not. People think they're better at lying than they really are."

"How interesting. I will keep it in mind."

She rose to her feet. "We leave just after dawn, do we not?"

"It would be best, considering that a carriage with two extra horses tied behind will have to drive at a slow pace. It will take us near two full days."

"Oh, I had not realized," she murmured, her forehead wrinkled with doubt.

"You can't be nervous to be alone with your fiancé," he teased.

"I'll have Molly with me. We'll be perfectly respectable."

But she still looked nervous, and that amused him.

Audrey ate a simple breakfast as she felt the first touch of the sun's morning rays on her face. She only nibbled toast and eggs because Molly insisted.

Strangely, she was almost too nervous to eat. She was leaving the only home she'd ever known, where she knew every piece of furniture, and every person's distinctive footstep. She was going off into a dark world she couldn't see, in the hands of a man she'd only just met—Martin's friend. Shouldn't she have considered that more closely? she wondered a bit wildly.

No, he was an earl, a former captain in the Queen's army. He would not mistreat her. He said he owed her his assistance, because he felt so badly about Martin's death. She would have to trust in that.

"There you are," Robert said.

"You sound almost relieved," she answered lightly.

"I thought someone might have changed your mind."

She'd certainly been worried her father might try. But she hadn't seen him yet this morning.

"You should eat before our journey," she told him.

"I did, since I had to meet the carriage when it was delivered. The footmen are already loading your trunks."

"Thank you," she said, feeling surprised. It was so rare for someone to do things for her, or on her schedule. She had so much to get used to.

"Audrey?" said her brother as he entered the dining room.

"I'm still here, Edwin. Please share this last meal with me. Is Father—"

"No, he's in his study," her brother said, "and doesn't wish to be disturbed."

If that was how he wanted it, then fine.

"I . . . had some things I wished to say to you," Edwin began, his words awkward. "I was never home much, and I think I was so concerned with myself, I never . . . thought much about you. It was wrong of me, and I ask your forgiveness."

Audrey blinked at the sting of tears. Wasn't this just what she'd wished, to improve relationships with her siblings? It took her leaving to make her brother treat her better, she thought with faint irony.

"I accepted Father's certainty that you could never handle the outside world," Edwin continued, "especially after Blake abandoned you as he did. But that was wrong. I saw how you were with my friends, how—normal everything seemed. Forgive me if that sounds cruel, but I hope you understand what I mean."

Robert said, "Collins—"

"No, Robert," Audrey said firmly. "It is all right." She turned toward her brother. "Edwin, I accept your apology, and I want you to know how glad I am for it. When I write to you, I hope you'll answer."

"I will," he said, relief in his voice. "Now I must go. My friends are just rising and will be departing soon."

"Go. Enjoy yourself, Edwin. We will keep in touch."

When he'd gone, Audrey turned to Robert. "I know what you might have said, that Edwin's words couldn't make up for years of neglect. But I consider his words a good start. And accepting them—forgiving him—is my choice, not yours. Again, you're trying to do too much for me."

"Perhaps you're assuming too much," he said. "You didn't know what I was going to say. Please do me the courtesy of not scolding me unless I need it."

The awkward moment felt strange to her, for everything had been so easy between them so far. "Very well, if I was mistaken, then I apologize."

"*If* you were mistaken?" he echoed.

She couldn't help but smile ruefully. "Ah, these word games we play. Then I apologize with no conditions attached."

"Good. I feel much better. But I want to explain one thing that you should consider. I feel protective toward you as I would toward any woman I had agreed to marry. That is just what men *do*. Perhaps you're occasionally being too sensitive."

She considered that with astonishment. "I have not experienced protectiveness in a long time, my—Robert. I will consider what you've said."

"Thank you. Then shall we go?"

The smile spread so wide across her face, it felt like a flower opening up to the sun. "Yes, oh yes, let us go."

In the entrance hall, Molly called, "Miss Audrey, I have your valise and reticule."

"Thank you. You didn't forget your own, did you?"

The other woman laughed. "No, miss. I have sandwiches in there and your writing paper and a book or two."

"I noticed that the footman could barely lift your trunks into the boot," Robert said.

"I only took what was necessary," Audrey insisted. "I am starting a new life, sir. There are things a woman must have." She was rattling on a bit, and she kept listening for her father's study door to open, but it didn't. "Excuse me." She went to it and knocked, opening it without waiting for a reply. "Father?"

"I'm busy," he called in a gruff voice. "Be on your way if you're going."

She lifted her chin. "I'm going. Good-bye, Father."

When he said nothing, she closed the door again. Neither Robert nor Molly made a sound. Audrey felt embarrassed more than anything, by how little she meant to her own father. Then the anger set in, as she realized that her success could *prove* to him that she'd made the right decision. But in the end, what he thought didn't really matter. He'd treated her like a servant, not a daughter. Let him hire someone else.

"Good-bye, Mrs. Blake," said the housekeeper. "Do enjoy your new home."

Audrey hadn't even realized she'd arrived. "Thank you so much for everything, Mrs. Gibbs. And to all the other servants, too."

Robert put her hand on his arm. "May I escort you to the carriage?"

"You may." She could have done it herself, but it would have taken longer. And she was impressed that he remembered to tell her where the stairs began. People often forgot the most obvious things when dealing with a blind person.

Outside, the breeze was almost warm, for autumn, and she inhaled deeply. This might be the last time she ever smelled these scents, if her relationship with her family didn't improve. But she wasn't going to think that way. Molly told her that the coachman had already lowered the step. Audrey found it, and Robert held her hand as she stepped up inside.

"Molly," Robert said, "take the rear seat with your mistress, and I'll sit across."

"Facing backward?" Audrey teased. "How chivalrous."

"I do have my moments."

She felt a flash of excitement as the door closed, and soon the carriage jerked into motion. "Oh, you have my horse?"

"Tied to the back, on the opposite corner from mine," he assured her.

"Then I'm ready."

It was time to head into the unknown.

Chapter 7

~~~⌒⌒~~~

As the morning went on, Robert kept expecting the carriage ride to grow monotonous, but it never did. He couldn't stop watching Audrey's face. Molly would excitedly describe a thatched-roof cottage or a stone bridge, and it was as if he could see the wonder of the world reflected in Audrey's expression. Molly had obviously spent much of her life in this capacity, and she was good at spotting the tiniest details, from a spotted dog lying beside a child fishing on a riverbank, to the ruins of an old stone wall, "which was surely part of a castle," Molly would insist. Audrey laughed as if this was a game they'd long played.

Audrey must have been nervous before the journey, and maybe that was why they'd quarreled, but once on their way she seemed only full of eagerness and excitement—and relief. When he'd mentioned they'd left her village behind, she'd sagged back against the bench and looked almost bewildered.

"He really let me go," she'd murmured. "I had feared . . ."

But her words had trailed off, and he hadn't pressed for more. He well knew what she feared: a scene, some reason to involve the law. But Robert and his earldom had won the day.

It was amazing to think that the daughter of a baron had never been beyond her own village, never been to London. Part of him wanted to give her some of those experiences—and then he had to rein himself in. He was escorting her to her new home, making sure she was settled, and then his debt to Blake would be repaid.

But would it? he wondered. Would these feelings of guilt finally give him some peace?

"You must think our excitement rather silly, Robert," Audrey said, "especially when you've seen so much of the world."

"And that's why it's refreshing."

"Were you just as excited when you first left England?"

He hesitated. It had been nine years ago, and Stephen Kepple had just taken his own life. Robert had been questioning everything about himself, his motives, his beliefs, his ability to be the earl. But he wouldn't tell her any of this. "I was excited to see lands that weren't green and wet all the time. Little did I know, but India has a monsoon season that makes England's weather look tame in comparison. And don't forget about the six weeks at sea." He gave an exaggerated shudder, then realized she couldn't see him, but he got a smile out of Molly.

The carriage was bouncing on the country roads, making it too difficult for Molly to read aloud for any length of time. So the two of them settled on going over the list of servants at the manor.

"I've been corresponding with the land agent hired by my late husband's estate," Audrey explained when he expressed curiosity. "I'm told a family has been caring for the manor for the last few years. The mother is the cook and housekeeper, the father takes care of the grounds, their son is the footman, and a daughter is the maid."

"Well, that makes it convenient," Robert said. "With none of the Blake family there, it's been like their own home."

Audrey's brow furrowed. "Very true. I imagine we'll all get used to one another."

She was already taking care of the people attached to her manor. Robert didn't even know most of the ones who served him. At the London town house, the only familiar faces had been the butler and housekeeper. He hadn't even been to his country house yet. He and Audrey were almost on the same journey. While she'd be getting to know her new home, he'd be relearning the one he left behind a lifetime ago, one that ran without any effort by him at all. He'd hired the right staff, he told himself. That's what he'd paid them to do. He found himself hesitant about getting too involved—his father had always had that trait. In the military, one allowed the officers to command their regiments, one did not try to do every job. He'd learned his lesson.

"**H**e's fallen asleep," Molly whispered sometime later, and the two women lapsed into a peaceful silence.

Audrey's thoughts drifted, but she was too wound up to sleep. She recalled her earlier conversation with Robert, when she'd asked if he'd been excited leaving England. There had been something in his voice that seemed . . . different. He'd answered lightly about the weather, as if that was all that mattered. She hadn't asked more questions, because there was no point in prying. Yet he knew so much of her life; she couldn't help being curious about his.

Audrey still felt dreamy with happiness and expectation. At last she was free to chart her own course. She imagined the countryside streaming by her, all detailed so lovingly by Molly's gift for words.

She felt the carriage slow and thought it must be noon. They'd stopped midmorn to water and feed the horses, and decided then to take a more extended break for luncheon.

"I must have closed my eyes," Robert said.

She smiled. "So I heard. I hope you found some rest."

"I did, thank you. We've arrived at an inn. Let me get down and I'll assist you."

She accepted his hand, and when she was on the ground, she trailed her fingers along the carriage until she reached the back. Her gelding, Erebus, came near and nuzzled her shoulder.

"You've been so good," she murmured, petting his nose.

She heard their coachman call for grooms to care for the horses, and then Robert took her arm.

"Shall we share a meal?" he asked.

"I'm starving," she agreed.

As they walked, she heard the ringing of a hostler's bell at the gate, and the voices of servants in the stable yard off to the side. There were so many people, she realized.

"I'll rent a private dining room," Robert was saying. "We can relax there."

"No, I'd like to eat in the public rooms with the other travelers. I can't see, but I can hear, and it all sounds wonderful."

He chuckled. "Very well. Take a step up here, and we'll be in the front hall."

"Ooh, Miss Audrey, there's a row of basins and jugs," Molly said. "Would you like to wash?"

"Yes, please!"

Molly chatted on about the cupboard displaying pies and cheeses, and how the next open room was crowded with tables and benches where people were eating.

"This way, ladies."

"There must be a servants' hall," Molly protested.

"You'll eat with us," Audrey said. "We're sharing this adventure together, remember?"

Molly giggled.

As Robert once again took Audrey's arm and turned into the next room, the sounds were overwhelming, dozens of people talking at once. She was suddenly bumped from behind.

"Excuse me, miss!" someone called.

"The waiter," Molly said quietly. "There are so many bustling about."

"He should watch where he's going," Robert said coldly.

"He didn't hurt me," Audrey pointed out.

"Our table has benches, not chairs," he said. "Will that do?"

"Of course." She reached to feel the table, then

let go of Robert to find the bench. She stepped sideways along it, making room for Molly at her side.

And that was when the hushed voices began, spreading out from around them. The travelers around them had realized she was blind.

"You can't be the only blind woman they've ever seen," Robert said crossly.

Audrey smiled. "I imagine most are beggars, and anyone highborn isn't using a public coaching house. They'll become used to me."

The waiter raised his voice, the old trick, and Audrey could feel—and hear—Robert's tension rise. He really was far too protective. This was nothing she had not experienced the time or two she'd been permitted into the village.

And then a baby wailed.

The sudden stab of grief took her by surprise, and she found herself holding still, listening. After her baby had died, she'd spent months wallowing in her sorrow, wondering why God had punished her, when so much had already happened. Gradually she'd come to terms with her loss, but she was never near babies.

"Audrey?" Robert asked.

Hearing the puzzlement in his voice, she put those feelings aside again. "Yes?"

"The expression on your face—" he began, then stopped. "It is none of my business."

She didn't have to answer, because a waiter chose that moment to inform them of the menu.

The meal, veal pies and cabbage, was plain but hardy, and afterward they strolled through the gardens, both vegetable and flower gardens, to stretch their legs and give the horses a chance to rest. But they changed the carriage horses, and soon they were on their way again. The coachman had an inn in mind for the night until an axel broke, jolting the passengers.

Robert cursed their bad luck, but was surprised how unaffected Audrey seemed. She said she was happy for any new experience, and listened contentedly as Molly described the coachman riding one of the carriage horses up the hill toward a manor in the distance. Robert didn't know if he should have gone himself to smooth the way, but wasn't about to leave Audrey. Soon enough, an older-model carriage came trundling down the drive.

As he assisted Audrey from their listing carriage, the coachman said, "Sir Miles Paley and his family live here. They'd be honored if ye'd spend the night while I see to the carriage repairs at the local blacksmith."

When they finally stood in the little entrance hall of the manor, Lady Paley didn't bother to hide her surprise as she studied Audrey. She was a petite woman, with delicate, childlike hands she absently rubbed together. *"You're* Audrey Collins?"

"Audrey Blake, ma'am," she corrected. "My husband was killed when stationed with the army in India."

Sir Miles, tall and slightly stooped, gave a guilty smile. "We all assumed you a reclusive invalid, Mrs. Blake."

Audrey accepted their assumptions with ease, while Robert wanted to bash some heads together. Of course, this wasn't their fault.

And then they turned the full force of their enthusiasm on him.

"Please meet my daughters, Lord Knightsbridge," Lady Paley said with proud formality. "Miss Rachel Paley and Miss Rosalind Paley. Girls, meet the Earl of Knightsbridge, here in our own home!"

Both young women were tall and coltish like their father, almost meeting Robert in height. It must be difficult to find husbands, but his presence unquestionably put that worry right out of their minds.

He smiled politely, then took Audrey's arm. "May my fiancée rest before dinner? It's been a long day."

Surely the coachman had already told them of

Audrey's status, but their faces looked like he'd slapped them with the reminder. He saw Audrey holding back a smile. She'd come in handy—and she knew it.

By the time dinner was served, the Paley family had calmed down, eager to show off their lovely china and silver place settings.

In the middle of an awkward pause, as the family tried not to stare at Audrey eating, Sir Miles said, "You've been long gone from England, my lord, but not on the Grand Tour other young noblemen take. Why the army?"

It was a personal question at the same time as it was an obvious one. He'd answered it with Audrey and her father, but he saw that she was still very interested, by the way her head was tilted toward him. Had she sensed there was more?

And suddenly he flashed back, to when he'd heard Stephen Kepple was dead by his own hand, the stunned, sick feelings that had tightened his gut, the first realization of guilt. He'd wondered if it had been his fault Kepple was dead, even as others told him that Kepple was never strong enough for the risky investments he'd gotten involved in. It was Robert's fault Kepple was even involved, for he'd pretended to be the man's friend, all to get his participation in the early railway deal. And when it had gone bad, everyone had lost money. He would never know if Kepple had realized he'd been manipulated into joining, or if the man had foolishly risked too much of his own money. But none of that mattered, for Robert had discovered he was a controlling bully, just like his father. And he'd had to find a way to change himself, before he had no friends and no self-respect, which had already taken a terrible blow. The army had helped him before it was too late.

Could he say that to the waiting Paley family? No. But he could say part of the truth, and perhaps Audrey would be appeased as well.

"There was a retired army colonel in our village while I was growing up," he said at last. "Originally he helped my tutor teach me history before I went off to Eton, but it was his own stories that I found the most fascinating. He'd been at Waterloo and other famous battles. Everyone respected him, and he knew he'd contributed much to the protection of England. I wanted to feel that way. I was only twenty when my father died, and even though I reached my majority within the year, I never felt like I was the earl."

"Your father's shadow was long," Sir Miles said, nodding with understanding. "It is difficult to follow a great man."

Robert only nodded. It wasn't difficult to follow

his father—it was all too easy to *become* him. He felt ashamed at the thought of his military mentor knowing about the men who'd died because of his rash decisions. "I learned loyalty and duty in the army, and I became a man. There were triumphs and there were sorrows, but I don't regret many."

He glanced at Audrey. *Some,* he thought. *I regret some.*

And now here he was, supposedly engaged to a woman who swore she never wanted to marry again. But he'd seen her expression when that baby had wailed at the coaching inn. Didn't all women wish to be mothers? Or did she think a blind woman shouldn't give birth, and that was another reason she swore never to marry?

They all retired to the parlor together, where the daughters took turns at the piano to show off their skills, and never once did their hosts direct much of their conversation toward Audrey.

Robert had had it. "Please allow me the pleasure of introducing you to my fiancée's talents at the piano."

Audrey blinked those lovely amber eyes at him. "My lord—"

"She is very shy, you must understand," he confided to the Paleys. "But you'll soon see that she's wrong to be worried about her musical skill."

The family looked ready to wince, so their shock as she played the first measure was satisfying to behold.

But it wasn't until they were in the carriage the next day that Audrey let him know what she thought of his own performance.

"Robert, you did not ask me if I wanted to play the piano for the Paley family."

"Of course I did," he said, smiling.

"No, you offered my performance without giving me any say at all."

His smile died as he took in her cool tone of voice, and the way Molly deliberately looked out the window.

"I am not a trained monkey that you can bring out and have perform on command," she continued sternly.

"I wanted them to see the accomplished young woman you are, not the invalid they all assume. Every young lady performs—are they trained monkeys, too?"

"Of course not."

"As an earl, I am often on display," he asked. "I grew up watching commoners deal with my father with some awe. Then I was in the military, where only the experience of my rank and what I'd learned on the battlefield mattered to my men. And now I'm back in Society, where my title alone lets a family push their daughters at me, and ignore you. So do you not think I sometimes have the right to use my title?"

She sighed. "I can grasp your point. But I'm not sure I agree with it."

After that, the day passed slowly, with some tension, as rain drummed on the roof above their heads and made the roads turn muddy. Even Audrey seemed to grow weary of Molly's descriptions of the same rain-drenched gardens, and the chessboard that was the hedgerowed countryside.

That night, they registered at an inn, which had decent accommodations, especially for an earl, as the owner kept repeating in a groveling tone. Once in his room, Robert wasn't even tired as he paced and listened to Molly, through thin walls, describe in detail their room, the paces separating pieces of furniture. When he heard Audrey stumble and laugh at herself, he could only be impressed. Next, Molly read a book aloud.

He ruminated on his earlier conversation with Audrey, where he'd actually complained about the perils of being an earl to a blind woman. Not only did he have wealth and power, he had the ability to do anything he wished. Had he thought the military had shown him all he had to learn? No, there was still so much of life he took for granted, and a blind woman was showing him that.

If they were actually to marry, their quarrels could worsen. She might resent him for being able to do all the things she couldn't, or he might resent her for slowing him down, or making him defensive. Or was he just trying to remind himself he didn't have to worry about such a choice?

Angry with himself, he lay back in the bed and covered his eyes with his forearm.

Audrey was almost ready for bed. She was wearing her dressing gown over her nightdress, and Molly had already brushed her hair out. There were two small beds on parallel walls, a table and two chairs, a chest of drawers, and a washstand. Audrey had paced among the furnishings several times, until she was comfortable. Now she could hear Molly at the washstand, humming softly to herself as she often did.

But Audrey wasn't tired, though she told Molly to blow out the candle. She kept pacing, remembering Robert's description of why he'd entered the military. She'd known for certain he was leaving things out. What about the man who'd killed himself? How did that all fit in? She would have given anything to ask, but not in front of the Paley family.

Her thoughts were disturbed by a brisk knock at the door.

Before Audrey could even speak, Molly said, "Surely it could only be Lord Knightsbridge."

"Perhaps we should ask—"

But then she heard Molly open the door, a startled gasp, and the sound of something heavy hitting the wooden floor.

"Molly?" Audrey cried.

No one answered, though someone breathed heavily. The bolt slid home with a thump to lock them in. She slowly backed away, even as the first fear raised gooseflesh up her spine.

A chair skittered suddenly, and she heard a mild oath. A man's voice, but not Robert's. A thief! She started to shake, but she focused her mind. Had the intruder tripped? Then she remembered that the candle was out, and he couldn't see.

The back of her legs hit the bed, and she dropped to her knees, hoping the man wouldn't detect her location.

He was moving around in the dark. "Where are ye, wench?" he crooned. "I just want yer gold. Give it to me, and I'll let ye go. I don't hurt cripples."

She didn't believe that. Crawling very slowly toward the nightstand, she silently cursed her dressing gown as it tangled around her thighs. She froze when she heard a board creak nearby, felt the breeze of his passing, but he was heading toward the other bed—Molly's bed. Oh, God, let her dear friend be all right, she silently prayed.

At last she reached the nightstand, and using her hand to feel along the top, she discovered the book Molly had been reading from, a hairbrush— and at last the candleholder, which felt as solid as it had looked. Lifting it carefully, she brought it to her lap, and yanked out the candle itself, setting it beneath the bed.

The other bed was shaken violently, then thumped against the floor, as if the intruder searched on top and beneath it for her. What was she supposed to do? If he came at her, she could wave her candlestick about and hope she hit him, but she couldn't plan her own attack.

And then suddenly she remembered that Robert was right next door, the shared wall behind her bed. But if she screamed, the thief would know exactly where she was.

She had to take a chance.

Coming up on her knees, she slammed the candleholder into the wall above her bed, hoping to mislead him, then rolled away toward the table and chairs. The thief swore and stomped toward her.

Chapter 8

Robert sat bolt upright, the thump on the wall next to him practically rattling his bed. And then he heard a scream.

Audrey.

He pulled his trousers on quickly, but that was all he made time for as he ran into the corridor and tried Audrey's door. It was locked, but couldn't withstand his shoulder as he slammed into it. The door opened wide with a bang. The room was dark, but for the faint reddish glow of the coal fire. The oil lamp hung in the hall allowed him to see a man's figure, then the sheen of his wide eyes reflected in the light. Where was Audrey?

As Robert advanced into the room he caught a glimpse of a body on the floor, and felt a shock of fear that surprised him. Then he saw another pale oval of a face peering out from behind the table. It all happened in a flash, for then the thief tried to race past him. Robert caught the man with a hard punch to the gut, then jerked him up by the front of the clothes to shake him.

"What have you done?" Robert demanded between gritted teeth. "If you've hurt them—"

Audrey bumped into them in her haste to get to Molly. Robert waited, holding the man off his toes as he sputtered.

"Wrong room!" he gasped. "Mistake!"

Audrey stumbled to her knees beside her friend. "He hit Molly and went after me for my valuables."

Robert punched him hard across the jaw. The thief sagged, but he caught him up again. "How is Molly?"

The maid moaned, "My head . . ."

"I don't feel blood," Audrey said, "but there's a nasty lump."

With one hand, Robert flung open the door to the small balcony, then tossed the man over the rail. He heard a scream as he hit, then watched him stagger to his feet in the torch-lit yard and hobble into the darkness, dragging a leg behind him.

"Milord?" said another voice in the corridor.

He saw the innkeeper in his nightcap and dressing gown. "I just sent a thief through the window. Find the man with the newly broken leg, and you'll have the culprit. I suggest you increase your security, sir, if women can be attacked in their bedchambers!" He took the candelabrum from the innkeeper's hand and slammed the door in his face.

"You tossed him off the balcony?" Audrey asked in surprise.

He set the candles down on the table. "I did. To deal with him, I would have had to leave you, and he might have had an accomplice in the taproom below."

"Oh," she murmured.

She reached to touch Molly, who'd pushed herself to a sitting position. Audrey put an arm around her.

"Miss Audrey?" Molly said weakly. "What happened?"

"A thief, dear."

"Did he hurt either of you?" Robert demanded.

Audrey shook her head. "You came quickly. Thank you."

Her hair, dark in the night, was caught back in a simple braid, and her golden eyes glowed large and luminous in the candlelight. Without her corset and petticoats, she looked fragile in her plain linen dressing gown. That protectiveness she didn't like about him surged into prominence.

When Molly shivered, he said, "I'll put her in bed," almost glad for the distraction. He glanced around and noticed that both beds seemed to be overly disheveled. "What happened to the beds?"

"He was searching them," Audrey explained.

Her voice seemed a bit faint, her complexion pale, but other than that, she was taking the attack better than most women would. She reached around her, found a table leg, and that seemed to orient her.

She pointed to the far wall. "That is her bed."

Robert lifted Molly into his arms, and she gave him a wide-eyed stare, her face going red as she covered her smiling mouth with a hand. By the time he'd laid her in bed, Audrey was there behind him.

"Let me get a cold compress for your head, Molly."

Reaching with both hands, she found the washstand and the facecloths, poured water in the basin, and brought a damp cloth to her maid.

Molly held it to the side of her head. "I'll be fine, miss, don't you worry."

Though her voice was cheerful, her face showed the strain. Robert knew from experience that her head must be pounding.

He drew Audrey aside by the arm. Now that he was touching her, he could feel the faint trembling in her body. Her free hand reached out as if to steady herself, and touched his bare chest.

She gave a little gasp and whispered, "What are you wearing?"

"Trousers," he said in a husky voice. "When I heard your signal, I came running."

He'd expected her to recoil, but her hand still touched him, right in the center of his chest, and suddenly his heartbeat accelerated, and he was feeling things he didn't want to feel, not for his pretend-fiancée. And certainly not while her maid was present.

He spoke in a low voice without thinking. "You're out in the world now, Audrey, where people will take advantage of you. Are you prepared for that?"

Was he talking about thieves—or himself?

And she still kept her hand in the center of his chest, her lips parted, her breathing fast. He had her by the arm, and her thigh pressed along the length of his, without bulky layers of petticoats between them.

"I—I'll be safe in my own home," she murmured.

"So you're going to stay within those walls, never leaving, just like you were raised?"

She stiffened. "No. I will be like every other woman. I will visit others and have dinner parties and be *normal*."

He let her go. "I do admire you, Audrey Blake. You certainly didn't panic, when many sighted women would have."

And she looked damned good in her dressing gown, too.

He wasn't going to start lusting after Blake's widow. If she ever found out he'd been part of the reason her husband was dead, she'd never treat him the same way again. He'd rather be her hero than the man she despised.

"Promise me you won't open the door again unless you know it's me," he said.

" 'Twas my fault, milord," Molly called weakly, the facecloth still pressed to her head. "I just assumed it was you."

He kept his voice light. "I imagine you won't make that mistake again."

"No." She closed her eyes briefly, and when she opened them, they shined with tears. "To think I could have gotten my mistress killed . . ."

"He wasn't going to kill you," Robert reassured them both, even though he had his doubts. "Just be careful from now on. Do you need me to stay with you?"

"No," Audrey said, her voice back under control. "I will bolt the door when you leave and—oh dear. Didn't I hear you break open the door?"

"You did. We'll exchange rooms so you'll feel safe. I only have one bed, but it's wide enough to hold you both."

Audrey blushed at the mere thought of lying in

the bed Robert had lain in. It was already difficult to even think, knowing he was partially nude, and she'd let herself touch his chest—and she'd kept her hand there, even when she knew what she was doing! He was built so very . . . different than her husband had been.

She'd felt his breath on her face as he'd leaned over to speak to her—good Lord, she was turning into Blythe, all flustered by his mere presence.

And with poor Molly lying there injured!

"Let me help you pack your things," he said.

"No, no, I will do fine. I know where everything is."

"Even the things he threw around the room?"

Now she could definitely hear the amusement in his voice. Did he know how he affected her? Was he secretly laughing that a blind girl would be so foolish?

But no, she didn't believe it of him. He would never make fun of her.

"I think there's a hairbrush under the bed," he said, his voice strained as if he was bending over.

She could hear Molly giggling, and it was such a relief—even if it was at her expense. But of course, Molly could *see* the half-naked earl on his hands and knees.

Audrey bit her lip, for even she could imagine it.

But she couldn't crawl around on the floor with him, so she went to the washstand and drawers and collected their toiletries into her valise. She hastily rolled up her gown and petticoats and tossed them in.

As if he'd never seen a woman's petticoats, she scolded herself. Her face was hot with mortification now, and she was starting to imagine Robert's body over hers in his big bed.

Why was she thinking of that now? She'd just had a shock, for goodness sake, and her wedding night had hardly been the stuff of a young girl's imaginings. But with Robert . . .

"Molly, do not try to stand," he was saying sternly.

"Oh, no, milord, I'm too heavy—"

He was obviously ignoring her. "Audrey, will you open the doors for me?"

She did feel a little tingle of warm contentment that he assumed she could pack up the room and open doors, everything sighted people did. Reaching out with her hands, she found his bare back and quickly pulled away, but not before she could feel muscles move as he held Molly so manfully. She skirted around them, found the door, and opened it.

In the corridor, she hesitated, unable to see if anyone was there. She felt him come up behind her.

It was Molly who said, "I see no one, Miss Audrey."

Audrey turned to the left, walked a few paces, running her hand lightly along the wall. She turned the handle of the next door, opened it wide, then stepped inside and out of the way. She felt some part of Molly brush her arm, then heard the squeak of a bed.

"You should have let me get my things, milord," Molly said in an embarrassed voice. "You shouldn't have to . . ."

As her words trailed off, Audrey understood. Molly did have a tendency to throw her own things about as she sorted through them.

"I'll gather everything," Audrey insisted.

"Oh, miss, I'm causing such trouble! They're on the chair and table."

The maid already sounded relieved. Audrey gave her a reassuring smile and returned to the door. She hit the frame with her toe and winced, but bruises were nothing new to her.

"I'll accompany you," Robert said.

She felt him at her back as she walked the few short steps down the hall, then turned into the room. Had he donned a shirt?

She pretended he had, as she moved from surface to surface, and heard him call out that there was nothing on the floor. She turned—and ran right into him. She would have fallen had he not grasped her upper arms. Once again, her hands were flat against his chest, and she felt the faint brush of hair, smelled the scent of him, so very different from the perfumes women wore.

"You didn't don your shirt," she said between gritted teeth.

"Does it bother you so much?" he murmured. "I did rescue you."

"And I thank you." She tried to keep her hands off his hot skin. "Please let me go."

"We are engaged," he pointed out, his voice wicked.

When that almost made sense, she knew she was going too far. But he released her, and she ignored her disappointment.

"I think between us, we have everything," he said.

"Thank you."

He took Molly's bag from her, and she knew he must already have her own. She preceded him to the door.

Inside her new room, he said, "I've put both bags on the chairs. Can I do anything else for you, ladies?"

"Does Molly look like we should send for a physician?" Audrey suddenly asked, mortified she hadn't thought of it before.

"Oh no, miss, I'm feeling much better."

"The color has returned to her face," Robert said. "I think she is better."

"Thank you, my lord," Audrey said, her voice small.

"Good night. And Molly—"

"I'll never open the door again!" she said fervently.

"Bolt this, Audrey."

She did, and heard him say from the corridor, "Good girl."

She briefly leaned her head against the door, feeling tired and angry and ridiculous. She wasn't a good girl. A good girl would have been unaffected by his touch—after all, they were not truly engaged. But Molly didn't know that.

The other woman sighed and said dreamily, "Oh, Miss Audrey, he is such a man. You must feel so very lucky."

She pasted a smile to her lips before turning around. "Oh, I do."

"Did you know from the moment you met him?"

"Love at first sight?" Audrey shot back, her smile softening into a real one.

Molly groaned. "Now you're teasing me. But truly—was it your first conversation when you suspected you might suit each other?"

Audrey hesitated. "Yes, I suppose it was." Theoretically, that was true—she'd known she had to ask for his help. Maybe she suspected all along that he was trustworthy.

And now he'd saved her life.

"Have you—" Molly broke off, and she sounded most hesitant. "Has he . . . kissed you?"

"Oh, no, he has been most proper," Audrey insisted.

"I am sorry for that."

"I am, too," Audrey said, trying to play her part.

Molly lowered her voice. "But he wants to kiss you, I can tell."

Right then, Audrey almost told her the truth, but something held her back. No one must know, not until she was safe. *I am playing a part,* she told herself again. "How do you know he wants to kiss me?"

"I can just . . . tell. He doesn't have to hide his feelings when he looks into your face, like a man would with a sighted woman. And the way he held you—like he didn't want to let you go."

"I hope so," Audrey had to say, even though it wasn't true. He was playing his part, too.

He'd better be, because Audrey would never allow herself to have more with a man. Not ever again, no matter what he felt like or how he smelled—or how he might kiss.

Not that she was planning to find out.

"**W**elcome to Hedgerley," Robert said, late the next morning.

Audrey clapped her hands together. "My new village—my home."

"Let me describe it to you, miss," Molly said with excitement.

"Are you sure you're up to it?"

Molly had been in pain last night, and Audrey knew she hadn't slept well. She'd dozed the several-hour journey, though, and was sounding better.

"I could describe it," Robert offered.

Both women hesitated.

"You think I cannot?"

Audrey was starting to think he could do anything he wanted—he'd gotten her away from her father, he'd saved her from a thief, and now he'd brought her to her own home.

"Shall we allow it just this one time, Molly?" she asked.

Molly heaved a dramatic sigh. "Just this once."

"With that kind of belief," he began dryly, "I shall commence. I see a village green. And there's a church on the far side with a pointed steeple."

"A green and a church," Audrey said dubiously. "Do not strain your creativity so."

"The straight facts are important in the army,"

he insisted. "But I shall try to go deeper. The church is made of stone, with ivy climbing."

"Better, milord," Molly encouraged.

"I do believe I see the sign of a tavern, which it seems I will soon need the benefits of."

Audrey couldn't help joining Molly in laughter. "You are so easy to tease, Robert. What is the name of the tavern?"

"The Lion and the Hen."

"Now you are teasing me."

"Molly, am I?"

"No, miss, in fact the sign shows the hen with its wings raised, as if it's frightening the lion."

"A strange village you have here," Robert mused.

She loved it already. "What else?"

Too soon they left Hedgerley behind. Audrey could barely sit still as Molly talked about an orchard of pear trees, and a flock of sheep in the distance.

They took a turn down a bumpy lane.

"I see your house, Miss Audrey! It is two stories made of stone, cresting the top of a gentle hill, and the parklands slope down away from it—oh, and there's a stream leading into a pond."

"Can we swim?" Audrey asked excitedly.

"You swim?" Robert's tone was incredulous.

"I do—not that you will see me."

"Your husband cannot see you swim?" he retorted.

She withheld a wince. "Oh . . . I imagine there is so much for me to get used to."

"You were not married long the first time," Molly pointed out. Then, "Oh, so many windows and chimneys. I see a stable in the distance, but not a separate coach house. I imagine there's room for a carriage in there."

So many windows, Audrey mused dreamily. Was she a wealthy woman, then—at least where land was concerned? From what she'd been told, the estate supported itself. There were dozens of tenants leasing good farmland. She didn't care about wealth, as long as the manor and lands were thriving.

It was Molly's turn to sound dreamy. "It is a pretty place to live."

"And ours forever," Audrey said.

"Until you marry," Molly pointed out. "And then perhaps you'll live in a castle."

Audrey smiled stiffly, then turned toward Robert. "Thank you, my lord, for bringing us here."

"You're welcome. I hope it is everything you wish."

There was a thread of . . . something in his voice, but she would allow nothing to spoil this day she'd dreamed of her whole life long. She was the mistress of her own household.

"We're pulling up to the entrance, miss. There's no portico, but a lovely set of wide marble stairs leading up to an impressive door. Oh, it is opening! An older woman is standing there, and I confess, she looks confused."

"She's wondering who her visitors are," Audrey said. "She will be so surprised." And not too disappointed, she hoped. She'd had no time to send word ahead that this little servant family was finally to have a mistress after several years.

Audrey could barely wait while the coachman opened the door to let down the stairs, and Robert climbed out. She reached out for his hand, knew it would be there, and began to descend.

"Does your pretty home have a name?" he asked softly.

He knows how important this is to me, she realized. She gave him a smile. "Rose Cottage."

"A little more than a cottage, Audrey, but a lovely name."

More than a cottage, she thought, almost hugging herself. It could be four rooms or twenty—she didn't care. It was all hers.

"May I help you, milady?" said an unfamiliar voice. The woman sounded older, but respectful. "Are ye lost?"

"No, I am not lost. I regret I could not inform you in advance, but I'm Mrs. Martin Blake, and I've come to take up residence."

There was a stark silence, and Audrey reminded herself that it was a shock. The woman was probably worrying about the state of the house, with bedrooms not aired and not enough foodstuffs in the pantry.

"Are you Mrs. Sanford?" Audrey asked gently.

The woman cleared her throat. "Aye, ma'am, I am. Do forgive me."

"May I present the Earl of Knightsbridge," Audrey said.

"Milord!" the woman said, sounding a bit breathless now.

Had she curtsied? Audrey barely held back a smile, wondering if it had been difficult at her age, or if she was a spry woman. "Fear not, Mrs. Sanford, his lordship will not be a guest, since he lives nearby."

"He's her betrothed," Molly suddenly announced.

There was another silence as the housekeeper took that in. Audrey imagined it changed everything about how the servants might treat her—and she didn't like it. But she had no choice for now.

"And this is my lady's maid, Molly," Audrey said dryly, "she who speaks before thinking."

"I'm sorry, miss," Molly said, not sounding sorry at all. "Shall I lead you inside?"

"Of course. Mrs. Sanford, you would soon realize it, but I find it's only fair to inform you that I'm blind."

Chapter 9

~~~~~~~~~~~~~~~~~~~ ∽OC∽ ~~~~~~~~~~~~~~~~~~~

Robert saw the astonishment that Mrs. Sanford could not momentarily hide, but then she merely nodded, realized her mistake, and said, "Aye, ma'am, thank you for tellin' me."

He almost felt sorry for the woman. She'd received one shock after another. She was tall and robust, with gray hair pulled back in a simple bun, spectacles perched on her nose. She wore an apron tied at the waist of a plain black gown that did not quite hide her broad, working-class shoulders. Hopefully she kept house as if she always expected the mistress any moment, the way all competent servants should. They would soon find out.

And could she cook? His stomach rumbled at the thought. Their dawn breakfast had been many hours ago, and he still had at least an hour's journey home by horse. He needed fortification.

But Audrey could barely contain her excitement, and he knew food was last on her list. Her expressions were so changeable now that she'd relaxed her guard around him. He'd practically been able to see her processing every part of the village as he'd listed the buildings, probably creating her own map in her head.

She traveled a few villages away from home, and it was as if her own world had opened up for her.

"Please come inside, Mrs. Blake," the housekeeper was saying. "There are three steps up."

"Thank you. You will find that I learn quickly, so you will not have to continually explain such things to me."

"My fiancée moved so comfortably around her home," Robert offered, "that I had to be told she was blind."

Audrey gave another of those pretty blushes that set off her golden eyes.

He told the coachman to take the carriage to the stable for help unloading, and to come into the kitchens for a meal and the last payment when he was done.

Once they'd stepped inside the hall, a young man came forward and bowed. Tall like his mother, he wore plain livery of a dark jacket, starched white shirt, and trousers. His blond hair was a riot of curls, and his eyes lively as he glanced curiously at the housekeeper.

Mrs. Sanford gave a brief smile. "My son, Francis, is our footman."

"So I've been told by my land agent," Audrey said.

"Francis, this is our mistress, Mrs. Blake."

Audrey smiled as she chose a direction, but it was the wrong one, and Robert watched the young man send his mother a confused glance as he said, "Pleased to meet ye, ma'am."

Both servants looked fearful, but Audrey only adjusted the direction of her body. "I am pleased to make your acquaintance, Francis. I understand your sister is the maid here."

"One of them, ma'am," he responded shyly, still glancing at his mother.

Did Mrs. Sanford seem to flinch upon hearing her son's words? Robert wondered. Of course, she would not want him to speak freely with their new mistress.

Francis continued, "Shall I fetch her, Mo—Mrs. Sanford?"

"I do not mind if you call your mother the name you always do," Audrey said. "But yes, I would like to meet the rest of your family."

She shrugged out of her cloak, and Molly took it for her, folding both of their cloaks over her arm.

"'Tis a brisk day, Mrs. Blake," Mrs. Sanford said. "Shall I bring tea to the drawin' room while you wait?"

"I don't wish to keep you from your luncheon duties," Audrey said.

" 'Tis no bother, ma'am. If you don't mind plain fare, I have cold ham and carrot soup that I can warm if you're hungry."

"That would be good," Robert said.

Audrey cocked her head toward him, smiling.

Over the next half hour, while they sipped their tea, they met Evelyn Sanford, also as tall as her mother, who blushed profusely and kept tucking strands of blond hair behind her ears. Mr. Sanford, the groundskeeper and groom, was half a head shorter than the rest of his family, but made up for it with a barrel chest and workman's large hands. He was balding on top, with a white fringe that circled his head and puffed over his ears. Robert thought he seemed somehow . . . disapproving of Audrey, but his tone was respectful, if clipped.

"You have an older daughter, I understand?" Audrey asked, holding her teacup between both hands as if to warm herself.

Before Mr. Sanford could speak, his wife entered the room. "We do, ma'am, but she is a widow livin' nearby."

"Oh, I am sorry to hear that," Audrey murmured. "Do send her my sympathies."

Robert had spent too many years learning to

read the faces of prisoners, and it seemed to him that this little family was hiding something, with the way they glanced at each other, and always quickly away from Audrey. In fact, there seemed to be a decided shift in attitude since the family had had a chance to speak alone together.

Or was he being too protective of Audrey, just as she'd accused him? These people were allowed to be dismayed that their cozy family life was about to change.

After a delectable luncheon—thank God—in a sunny dining room that overlooked a terrace, Robert followed Audrey about as Mrs. Sanford led them on a tour of the ground floor. Molly described everything with her usual thoroughness, and Robert saw Audrey's concentration as she tried to absorb all the details.

He did not attend her on the first floor, but was waiting in the study that also seemed to be the library. When Audrey came to find him, he set down the book on London history he'd been reading. She looked much more hesitant than he'd ever seen her, but only in movement, not in manner. She still glowed with the excitement of the day.

"Robert?" she called.

"I'm here."

Her body turned toward him. "Oh bother, I've already forgotten where everything is," she mum-

bled, reaching forward with a hand as she started
to walk.

Robert took her hand and held it between his
own.

"You don't need to do that," she whispered.

"The door is open. Do you want your servants
to see me taking my leave more formally than a
lover should?"

She stopped fighting and let her hand rest
in his. She pressed her lips together, even as he
chuckled.

"No gloves, Audrey?"

"I forgot after luncheon."

"You were far too excited."

"It seems you were, too."

He knew she referred to his hands, but his
mind briefly went elsewhere, his smile fading. "I
don't want to leave you like this," he said at last.

She, too, sobered. "But you have done everything I asked of you—more than even that. You
escorted me to my new home and kept me safe
from the dangers of the road. Why should you
feel unsettled now?"

"Because this household is full of strangers to
you."

"But the land agent said—"

"He's a stranger, too," Robert interrupted. "He
seems to have done his job, at least as far as house-

hold servants go. Everything shines with polish and is well taken care of." But the servants had exchanged suspicious glances with each other and he couldn't forget that.

"I could smell the lemon polish," she said, smiling. "And in the unused rooms, sheets covered the furniture. They're removing all of that now."

"You haven't seen the last of me, Audrey. I plan to visit you most frequently. I will feel better to see you settled in."

"You worry about my blindness," she told him, "but you needn't. My other senses do almost as well, and people reveal much by their voices."

"Tell me what it was like," he said, deliberately delaying his departure. "Going blind, I mean. You must have been so frightened."

He drew her toward a chair, and she accepted his help with a smile.

"It was a long time ago, Robert. I was seven, and so weak with sickness. I most remember being relieved to wake up feeling better."

"And your sight was just gone?"

"Completely, like the sun had blown out. I remember my mother holding me and crying, and though she was relieved I would live, there was great sorrow, too. And fear. She worried that Blythe would succumb as well, but although she experienced the fever, it was never as severe as mine."

"How did you cope, being so young?" Was he trying to torture himself, to feel even more guilty that this woman was alone in the world because of him?

"I was very sad for a long time, of course." Her voice was lower, almost distant. "It is difficult to think of those days, when I was coming to the realization that people would treat me differently. I might have been only seven, but I was smart, and I understood what was happening. My mother was the only one who treated me the same, who did not coddle me or behave as if I should now be confined to bed or a chair by the window for the rest of my life."

"She sounds like a good woman."

"She was, and her death seven years ago was like the light leaving our family."

She sighed and lost herself in a moment of reflection, but Robert had learned patience in the army.

"It was she who suggested I keep the world of sight alive in my mind, to replay the memories over and over, so I wouldn't forget them. What my family looks like, the sun setting, a winter storm."

"That did not make you feel bitter?"

"It did not make it worse," she corrected. "Of course I felt bitter that I would be different, but my mother didn't let me linger long in that. She pointed out that God has plans for people, and we can't always know them."

"A wise woman," he murmured.

Audrey grinned. "She was. And I was lucky enough to have Molly. Finding things in the dark was almost a game between us. Even then, she was my guide in my new world, reading the words I painfully wrote out for my governess."

"You still write?"

"Not often, but I learned to write by guiding my pencil between two pieces of string. I can make myself understood, but Molly is usually my secretary. But what Molly couldn't help me with was the loss I felt being unable to see people's faces. It is shocking how we depend upon that. We adjust everything we say and do because of a person's expression, and I realized that at seven years of age I felt . . . left out. I gradually adjusted, of course, and learned about tones of voice, but it's not the same." She hesitated, then sighed. "I will confess, that part of me feels like that little girl again. I never imagined how much confident knowledge of my home affected me."

"You'll have that again," he insisted. "It will just take time."

She gave him a rueful grin. "You are so certain of me?"

"I am. But now I must go. My steward is expecting me. I have yet to set foot in my country house in nine years. Apparently, there is much I need to do."

"And I am certain of you," she countered.

"Thank you, but men do not need to be so bolstered," he said. "We are confident." He rose to stand before her, took her hand, and bowed over it. "Until tomorrow, Audrey."

"That is not necessary, Robert. You have much to do."

"I decide my own schedule, madam, one of the privileges of being an earl."

"But I will understand if your duties keep you away. You have fulfilled your promise, my lord, and seen me safe. You owe me nothing else."

Don't I? he found himself wondering. Was providing escort all it took to make up for a man's life? He didn't think so.

Audrey stood at the window for a long time, feeling the late autumn sun on her face, as if she could watch Robert ride away. She was surprised by how much she'd come to rely on him in just a few short days, on his solid presence, his confidence, his air of command.

She didn't have any of that herself, as the tour of the house had shown her. She'd once believed she did, but now? Now she'd traveled to places she could no longer picture in her mind, been attacked in her bedchamber, and met servants who didn't seem at all glad to see her. Oh, they were polite, but she felt they were directing their voices at Robert more than herself. She understood why, of course, he being a titled nobleman. They even spoke to Molly, as she explained each room in detail.

And the furnishings in those rooms! They were all hidden traps that could make her look and feel foolish. *Should* she begin to use a cane? No, Robert was right; with practice, she would learn the layout of the house. She was simply still uneasy after the attack at the inn.

She winced, remembering how Molly had made certain the servants knew she was betrothed to an earl. Audrey had known the necessity at her father's home, but she hadn't thought through the consequences here. Did she want to be respected merely because she was supposed to become a countess?

Or should she just announce a change of heart today—right now? Then she'd be here on her own merits, dealing with the servants in her own right.

But she had to discuss it with Robert first. It seemed . . . ungrateful to make a sudden decision without him. She turned to walk toward the entrance hall and bumped her leg, hard, on a low table. Wincing, she put out her hands and began to move about the drawing room again, planting each piece of furniture in her mind's eye. She would memorize everything, one room at a time.

That night, Audrey was relieved to be alone in her bedroom at last. It was the only place she felt safe, since Molly had specifically helped her rearrange the furniture to more suitable, functional positions. And her day? Not what one would call a success.

Molly had spent the afternoon unpacking their trunks, and Audrey had had her first meal alone in the dining room. Though she'd invited Molly to join her, the maid didn't think that set the correct tone for the household, and Audrey had reluctantly agreed.

She'd spent many a meal alone, of course, since she'd seldom been permitted to leave her home. But this was different. Audrey had been left sitting long past when she should, waiting for the meal to commence. Mrs. Sanford had apologized for her tardiness, and Audrey had believed her that she would need a day or two and consultations with Audrey to prepare the right menu.

But was that a reason some of the food was cold? It had tasted fine, but the service left much to be desired. She told herself it was just the first day—and a long one. Molly had already retired for the night, and Audrey would do the same. But first, she stood at the window and imagined where Robert must be—and missed him, even though he'd be gone from her life soon. She couldn't become attached, couldn't let herself care. She was never again going to be at someone else's mercy.

At midmorning the next day, Audrey was in her bedroom with Molly, making decisions about how best to arrange things, when there was a soft knock at the door. Audrey opened it and heard—nothing.

"Who is it?" she asked, controlling her irritation. More than once she'd explained how she liked to be told who it was without asking. But she'd say it again. It would just take a while.

"Sorry, Mrs. Blake, ma'am, it's Evelyn. You have a caller."

"And the caller is . . ."

"The Earl of Knightsbridge, beggin' your pardon. He's in the drawin' room."

She felt a thrill of excitement she had no business feeling. He felt far too protective of her— that was the reason he'd returned. Or he thought she couldn't handle things herself. "Thank you. Please tell him I'll be down in a moment." When Evelyn had gone, she heard Molly chuckle. "And what is that for?"

"You should see your face at just the mention of his name. Go to him, miss. Leave me to all of this. Take a walk and get out of this house."

"But I just got here," she said, feeling tired already.

"I know but . . . it is not the welcoming place I'd hoped for you, miss. We'll work on that."

It wasn't as if Audrey felt like she could terminate the employment of a whole family, not without good cause. But . . . "Oh, very well, Molly."

"Shall I escort you down?"

"No!" she said, too sharply, then sighed. "Forgive me."

"Nothing to forgive, Miss Audrey. No one said adjusting was going to be easy, not for any of us. Now you run along and see that fiancé of yours."

She was expecting Molly's usual dreamy tone when talking about Robert, the one that made Audrey grind her teeth together, but instead, the maid simply sounded tired.

"Molly, you don't sound yourself. Are you feeling well?"

Her hesitation spoke volumes.

"I'll be fine, miss. Just overtired from the travel."

"Then you rest while I'm gone."

"But—"

"I insist, Molly O'Hern."

"Very well, miss," she said, her voice as meek as a mouse.

Shaking her head, Audrey grinned at her before leaving the room. She moved at such a slow pace, it left her frustrated. But God forbid she fall down the stairs and become truly crippled. By the time she made it to the drawing room, she must have left Robert waiting an uncomfortably long time.

"Robert?"

She heard . . . nothing. She said his name again, then stepped into the entrance hall. "Francis?" But the footman didn't answer.

She went across the hall to the study and called Robert's name again. She received no answer, but this time, she heard a noise, and as she slowly moved into the room to investigate, hands held before her, she heard it again. Snoring.

She cocked her head, then turned in the proper direction, trying to sort the correct layout of the room from all the ones she'd been shown. There was a deep chair right—

Her hand encountered a male shoulder, and she gave a little shake. "Robert?"

The faint rumbling died away in a snort. "Audrey? Did I fall asleep?"

She smiled. "You must have. I came as soon as I heard about your arrival. Has it been that long?"

There was a pause, and he said, "A half hour at least."

She groaned. "We will do better next time, I promise."

"We?"

"Never mind." She was not going to complain about the servants! "So tell me, how was your homecoming?"

"The place is the same as I remember," he said ruefully. "Old and formal and run perfectly on schedule."

How wonderful.

"But I'm not complaining. They were happy to see me, and I was glad that old ghosts don't seem to haunt the place."

She wanted to touch his face, to soothe him, but she clasped her hands to keep them still.

"So have you walked the grounds of your estate?" he asked.

"Not yet. We were busy unpacking."

"Then come take a walk with me."

That coincided perfectly with Molly's idea, and she couldn't help smiling. "Let me fetch my shawl. I like to keep one in the entrance hall, just in case."

But of course it wasn't there, and Evelyn rushed back upstairs to retrieve one for her. Audrey knew Molly had put one in the hall, but she didn't say anything.

"Shall we begin?" Robert asked, taking her arm in his.

And her very excitement at just that contact made her feel wary and resigned. This couldn't go on, looking forward to seeing him, being with him—touching him.

But she let him guide her around the park and describe the sheep on a distant hill, the hedgerows separating farmed fields, the garden with the dirt paths.

"I'll have to put gravel here," she mused. "Much easier for me to stay on the path. Do you see Mr. Sanford?"

"I have once or twice. He's in the stables now. Shall we go there and tell him about your plans?"

"Oh, I need to come up with a list first, rather than spring them on him whenever I think of something. But let's see the stables just the same, and you tell me what you think."

Mr. Sanford had a gruff voice that made Audrey feel like he put up with a mistress because he had to. But he seemed to listen respectfully to Robert's military-orderliness suggestions, and they had a discussion about stable management that Audrey listened to, but felt outside of.

Once they were alone again, she said, "Robert, those things could have gone on my list, the one I'm preparing for my discussion with Mr. Sanford."

"Forgive me—was I not supposed to speak to

the man?" he asked, amusement in his voice. "I was a cavalry officer, so I'm considered an expert on horses."

"I want the servants to trust and listen to me, not you. You won't be their master, although we're letting them think otherwise." She hesitated. "This is a valid consideration, and one I wouldn't have to worry about if we call off the engagement now. There's no need to keep up the pretense," she hurried to add.

"That's a mistake, Audrey," he said in a low voice. "Come sit by the pond with me."

"Where we can be alone?" she said just as quietly.

"Exactly."

As they walked, he described the reeds around the pond, the little dock where a rowboat could be tied up.

"Or I could jump off the dock for a good swim," she countered, just to shock him.

"*That* I would like to see." Then he turned her about. "The bench is right behind you."

She sat down as gracefully as possible, then noticed how small the bench was when she could feel the line of his thigh against her skirts. She didn't quite touch him with her own thigh, but if she moved just a bit . . .

Oh, what was she doing? "Robert, the engagement was just to get me away from my family. That's over. I won't even write to them that we have called it off."

"So they can learn from gossip?"

She said nothing.

"And do you know how it will look? Like I used the engagement as a ruse to get you alone, away from your family, for only one reason."

She felt overly warm with a blush.

"And then after a night in the inn, maybe I already took all I wanted."

For a frozen moment, she imagined that, his kisses, the seduction she couldn't resist, his hands on her body. She was no innocent maid—she knew exactly what he meant. Yet the thought of being intimate with him seemed so exciting, even though as a widow she knew the reality of it. The heat in her face spread lower, languorously across her breasts and down her body, full of fevered need and desperation.

That's what it was, desperation, she realized with a start. She was lonely already, lonely and uncomfortable and too needy. But she was under no one's command but her own. Giving in to these treacherous, fleeting feelings would be a disastrous mistake.

But . . .

"You are right, of course," she said at last, embarrassed at how soft and breathless her voice sounded. "I would never want you to seem like an unscrupulous rake."

"I didn't say this on my own behalf," he insisted. "An earl can afford to care little about his own reputation."

She thought of his scandalous past, and the man who'd killed himself.

"But you, Audrey, would be . . ." His voice trailed away.

She felt her lips twist into a wry smile. "A Society widow? Is that not what some scandalous widows do, take a lover once their husbands are gone?"

She'd expected him to laugh, but when he didn't, she grew uncertain. "Robert?"

"Is that what you want, Audrey?" he asked in a husky voice.

She felt the pressure of his thigh, no longer just next to her skirts, but against her own.

"To have people think you a scandalous widow?"

"Surely better than having them think me an invalid, or weak-natured enough to allow myself to be used."

She thought of the servants she was trying to win over, imagined the rumors of their blind mistress they were already spreading to other servants, and hence to Hedgerley, to the people she hadn't even begun to meet yet.

"No," she said at last. "I want to be respected, to become part of the village society, not the fast London Society."

He eased his thigh away. "That's what I want for you, too, Audrey. So we will remain engaged for a while longer. Shall we continue our walk about the grounds?"

He took both her hands and pulled her to her feet, and for just a moment she stood before him, skirts tangled with his legs, their hands joined. The autumn wind tugged at them both, but they heard no other sounds, as if they were alone on the grounds.

Suddenly, she felt him looming over her, bending near.

"But if we're engaged," he whispered, "cannot a fiancé steal a kiss?"

Even as she gasped, she felt the press of his lips against her cheek. His skin was rougher than hers with newly shaved whiskers, but his lips—ah, his lips were soft and warm and lingered a heartbeat too long. She could smell the cleanliness of soap, even beneath the scents of horse and leather from his ride to see her. She leaned into him, unable to help her weakness.

Yet still their hands were clasped between

them, the backs of his hands against her stomach. He felt solid, and she remembered him shirtless in the inn, and her hands on his hot skin.

She swayed, beginning to turn her head into the kiss, wanting more.

But she couldn't want more—wouldn't be so weak.

She took a step back, and the backs of her knees hit the bench hard, but at least the kiss was broken.

She cleared her throat, yet her voice trembled. "So you've stolen a kiss and proved to everyone we're engaged for a reason. Very . . . smart of you."

He chuckled. "I stole a moment of intimacy, but I'm not sure how much of a true kiss that was."

"Enough to seem convincing, Robert. Thank you for thinking of my reputation as an engaged widow."

Now he laughed aloud, and she felt her own smile grow wide. They started back to the house, but her ebullient mood didn't last.

She'd felt some of these same feelings when Martin Blake had first paid attention to her—flattered and embarrassed and too afraid to hope. But they'd all been misconceptions. She'd thought Martin cared for her at least, but their wedding night had revealed her true worth in his eyes. He'd treated her maidenly shyness as an inconvenience, had done nothing to encourage any romantic feelings a bride should experience—or so she'd been told by Molly. After that, she'd known the twin blows of embarrassment and self-doubt, as if she were unworthy of even a husband's attention.

And now to feel such desire again for a man who was openly falsifying their attachment—she was so disappointed in herself.

But she was a woman, and he was a man who knew how to seduce a woman's senses. Was he a rake, then, one of those notorious men who slept with many women, regardless of what the Grand Dames of Society said?

But he'd been gone since he was twenty-one— hardly enough time to be considered a rake. But service in India might have changed him, and not in a good way.

She had to stop these doubts. She'd committed to this course, and she would see it through. He'd be returning to his estate, surely getting caught up in everything an earl had to do. It would be easy to pretend that their attachment was slowly dying.

But not so easy to pretend that she was strong, when she had trouble distinguishing between reality . . . and the fantasy of her own fevered dreams.

Chapter 10

After a detour to the kitchen to discuss the earl's presence at luncheon with Mrs. Sanford, Audrey went back upstairs to see what Molly was up to. She said her name softly, wondering if the maid was still asleep.

In a groggy voice, Molly answered, "I'm awake, miss."

"You don't sound any better," she said with concern, following her voice. She found Molly curled up in the window seat.

"I just don't seem to have any gumption today," the maid murmured.

Audrey reached out with the back of her hand, touched Molly's arm, then skimmed up to her face.

"You have a fever," she said in a brisk voice, although she felt a moment of panic. Molly never got sick.

"No, that can't be," she insisted weakly. "Just give me a moment and I'll be fine."

"Come lie down on my bed. Later, we can have Francis help you to your room."

"The cot in your dressing room would be—"

"My bed."

She was shocked how slowly Molly moved, and she seemed to collapse when they'd reached the bed. Audrey felt a twist of fear deep inside. She was always afraid of fever and didn't want her friend to suffer as she had, those hot, achy days that had blended into one long nightmare she still remembered though eighteen years had passed.

"You had letters you wanted me to write," Molly said, as Audrey tucked blankets around her. "I could do it from here."

She tsked as she shook her head. "That's not important right now. You need to conserve your strength."

"Then let me rest, and you go be with your lord."

Audrey grimaced at that, remembering that she'd been off flirting while Molly was feeling ill. She brought her a pitcher of water and poured her a cup to drink.

"Have you *seen* him, miss?" Molly finally asked.

"Seen him?" Audrey echoed, already making plans to talk to Mrs. Sanford about sending for a doctor. Was Molly hallucinating?

"Like you did with me. Surely he wouldn't mind if you touched his face."

Audrey felt the swiftness of memory, his cheek touching hers. "I—I couldn't impose like that."

"You'll be touching more than his face," Molly said, giving a weak chuckle.

"You're a romantic," Audrey said, trying to keep her voice light. "Now lie here and sleep while I send for the doctor."

"Surely that's too much trouble. Just let me sleep."

And then she did, just drifted right off, which frightened Audrey even more. Molly was one of those women who didn't need a lot of sleep, went to bed after Audrey and was up before dawn. She touched Molly's burning face again.

"Stay strong, my dear," she whispered.

She hurried downstairs as quickly as she could, holding tightly to the banister.

"What's wrong?"

She almost stumbled on the last step at Robert's question. He caught her arm to steady her.

"Molly has a fever, and she's never sick. I must talk to Mrs. Sanford about the local doctor. Robert—maybe you should go before you succumb, too."

"It's a fever, Audrey," he said in a soothing voice. "I've been exposed to far worse in the East. I'll stay and help."

Molly rang for Mrs. Sanford. The housekeeper

sent her son off to the village for Dr. Ascham, who ended up being a young man working with his father. All he recommended was that they bathe her with cold water when the fever was at its worst, and offered small draughts of opium if she experienced any pain. Audrey was frustrated that he could do no more.

To her surprise, Mrs. Sanford insisted Audrey eat the luncheon she'd skipped, and that she'd stay with Molly. The maid was sleeping, so that was the only reason Audrey agreed.

Robert greeted her again as she descended to the entrance hall. "How is Molly? The doctor only said there was little he could do to help her improve."

Audrey had put the earl to the back of her mind, but his concern made her feel better—and then teary-eyed. She cleared her throat and willed herself not to cry. "We just have to wait out the fever. Molly insists she'll be fine. But as you can imagine, I don't like the thought of anyone having a fever."

"Of course not," he murmured, taking her hand in his.

She allowed the comfort for a moment, then said, "Have you eaten?"

"I decided to wait for you."

"Then come, we'll tell Francis we're ready to be served."

She wasn't all that hungry, but it gave her something to do. And Robert had ridden over just to see her—he needed a good meal.

But when she found herself being unusually silent, she realized she could not be discouraged. There was too much to do—and Molly wouldn't be able to help.

As if reading her mind, Robert said, "Molly usually assists you almost as a secretary, does she not?"

They were eating roast venison, and Audrey took a determined bite. "Yes, she does. And she'll worry about that more than she'll concentrate on getting better. I'll be fine." And she was not about to ask Mrs. Sanford for assistance—the woman seemed to have trouble completing her own tasks.

"Perhaps I can be of help," Robert offered.

"That is very nice, but I certainly can't—"

"Why not? I am not needed at my own home, and you can't tell me to go back to London. It's not even the Season. You'll be doing me a favor. It's been so long since I was involved in the daily workings of an estate. We can learn all about it together."

He took her hand again, and she almost flinched at the touch of his bare skin on hers.

"Let me be of help to you."

Because he felt sorry for her? she wondered. After all, she was Blake's poor, blind widow.

Or was he just a man who had no family left, nothing to return home to?

"That is a kind offer," she said at last. "I will accept."

He squeezed her hand and released her, saying briskly. "Good. We will accomplish much together."

She knew her own smile was weak, but couldn't help it. Hours together every day, just when she was trying to make it look like their engagement would eventually end?

There was no help for it. She had to learn the workings of her new estate, and she needed eyes to help her. She'd fought the feeling of dependency so long that it was frustrating to accept it once again. She was used to moving fluidly, confidently, through her home, but every room in Rose Cottage seemed to have tables in odd places. As for the people, she was already working on memorizing the sound of their footsteps—that would help her know who was around her.

And Robert? His presence was a temporary convenience until both she and Molly were back on their feet.

She heard the footsteps before anyone even spoke. It was surely Evelyn.

"Mrs. Blake?"

And she'd been right. Feeling a touch more confident, she said, "Yes?"

"The land agent, Mr. Drayton, has arrived. He says you sent for him?"

Audrey turned toward Robert. "I requested a meeting. I didn't realize he'd come so quickly. I have so many questions about the estate."

"Are you ready?" he asked.

She heard the determination, even eagerness in his voice. She smiled, and did her best to put her concern for Molly aside for the moment. "I'm ready."

Robert left before dinner, almost as if he were just a neighbor who kept dropping in. Audrey wasn't sad this time, now that she knew he planned to return. Oh, what did that say about the state of her attachment to him? she asked herself, even as she slowly climbed the stairs to visit Molly in the servants' quarters in the attics.

She had to admit, Robert had had questions for the land agent that she would never have thought of—how many sheep did they plan to drive to market this month, the state of the recent grain harvest, the strategy for the spring planting. They hadn't even begun to discuss tenants, but that could wait for another time. Mr. Drayton had seemed genial enough, although a bit too glad to have the Earl of Knightsbridge to explain things to. Audrey would be patient, and allow him to become used to dealing with a woman. For now, Robert was the bridge between her and the people who worked for her. And soon she wouldn't need that bridge anymore. She'd be her own . . . island.

A pathetic comparison, she thought, even as she reached the top floor. To her surprise, when she went to knock on Molly's door, it was already open.

"Hello?" she said warily. "Molly?"

"She's asleep," said a young man.

"Oh, Francis, I didn't realize . . ." Her voice trailed off in confusion.

"I offered to sit with Molly while me mum prepared dinner. She's been asleep the whole time."

"That was very nice of you." Audrey moved farther into the room, heard the young man step to the side as she approached the bed. She laid a hand on Molly's forehead and winced. "Still so hot," she murmured. "Please tell your mother to send up a dinner tray to me here when it's ready, and also some ice from the icehouse."

"Yes, ma'am."

The ice and some broth for Molly's benefit arrived quickly, but a dinner tray never did. Audrey spent an hour using cooling cloths on Molly's forehead, neck, and arms, over and over again. She wasn't even hungry by the time she felt she'd done all she could.

Molly woke briefly, took a few sips of broth, but was never quite herself. It was frightening not to hear her amusing comments about whatever state Audrey was in.

When someone knocked on the door and stepped inside without introducing themselves, Audrey was too weary to pay attention to footsteps. Sighing, she said, "Yes?"

"Me mum sent me to sit with Molly, ma'am," Evelyn said. "You should rest."

"Thank you." Whatever Audrey had to say about the servants, she could not doubt their kindness toward her maid. "I'll return in a while."

But she couldn't sleep, although she tried. Her thoughts whirled in fear for her friend, and at last she decided to do something constructive. With no prying eyes to watch her, she began to go through the rooms on the first floor again, getting an understanding of what each bedroom contained. She moved with hands outstretched to feel each piece of furniture, and cement its place in her mind.

To her surprise, in the bedroom closest to the servants' staircase, she found nursery furniture—a cradle, low tables and chairs, and several toys.

Nothing was dusty, although whether that was from good cleanliness or recent use, she didn't know.

She stood among the trappings of a baby, and thought again of hers, who'd been born dead. It had been almost two years. Why now was her grief so easily awakened?

Perhaps . . . the wounds were still raw because her own child would have given her life meaning, someone to love and nurture—someone who loved her for herself and wouldn't care that she was blind.

At last she left the nursery and closed the door behind her, trying to think of closing off the painful emotions, as well. This was a reminder of the pain she never wanted to feel again, the grief from caring too much. Living on her own and the pride in her accomplishments would have to sustain her.

At last she returned to Molly's room and relieved the reluctant maid. Audrey dozed in a chair by her side, to be there whenever Molly needed a sip of water, a blanket, or just companionship.

For several days, Audrey focused on Molly, to the exclusion of all else. She had Francis take a note to Robert, asking him not to visit so he wouldn't become ill. No one else had sickened, but she didn't want to take any chances.

There was an hour or two, in the dead of night, when Molly barely seemed to be breathing, and Audrey wept at her side, begging her to hold on, to fight to be well.

At last Molly's fever broke, and Audrey had cried over that, too. She was still very weak, sleeping much of that day, her rest deep and genuine. She would have a long recovery—but at least she would recover.

Audrey went to the dining room for her first formal meal since . . . since Robert had last visited. The food was cold and late, as if the truce between her and the servants was over now that Molly would live.

Audrey went into the kitchen afterward, and when she called Mrs. Sanford's name, found her and Evelyn in the adjoining scullery washing pans. Audrey could hear the sloshing of water, smell the strong soap.

"Mrs. Sanford, I'd like to speak with you."

"Ma'am, when I'm done, I'll—"

"Evelyn can finish. Please follow me to the study."

She listened as the housekeeper followed, her steps deliberate and heavy. Audrey took a seat behind the desk, then asked the woman to sit opposite her.

"Mrs. Sanford, much as I've appreciated all the help given Molly and me during her illness, I'd like you to concentrate on your duties now, and that includes the preparation of meals. You've only added two people, occasionally three. I cannot believe it is difficult to cook for us."

"No, ma'am," she said impassively.

"Will things be better in the future?"

"Aye, ma'am."

"Then tell me about the nursery on the first floor."

Her pause seemed overly long, and Audrey cocked her head with interest.

"There's always been a nursery here, as far as I know, ma'am."

"The room felt like it had been used more recently, with toys left out."

"Aye, when my daughter visits, occasionally she lets her boy play there. I can make sure it doesn't happen again."

The words seemed pulled from her throat, and Audrey couldn't understand it.

"Mrs. Sanford, why would I wish your daughter not to visit you? Did I ever give you that impression?"

"No, ma'am." Her tone was still wooden.

Audrey didn't think it was time for last measures, so all she said was, "Then let us try to better manage this household together. I look forward to meeting your other daughter. You may go."

She sank back in her chair, unable to decide whether to be offended or suspicious or exasperated. She'd always gotten along well with her servants—better than with her own family! She was determined to do the same at Rose Cottage.

Robert didn't want to disturb the household, so he let himself in the front door without knocking. It had been three days since he'd been here, and he couldn't take the suspense any more. Was Molly on her way to recovery?

Would Audrey see him?

He'd never met a woman he couldn't stop thinking about, and now he had. Of course, her entire situation was so unusual—naturally he'd be concerned about how she was getting on with the servants. She'd been trying to keep her difficulties from him, he knew, so he hadn't intruded. She was so proud of being able to do everything herself.

He hadn't let himself think that she might have taken ill as well.

He heard a sound in the drawing room and went toward it. At that moment, Francis entered the hall and drew up short on seeing him. Robert held a finger to his lips; Francis's gaze darted to the drawing room. He bowed and withdrew.

Robert moved carefully, stopping in the door-

way. Audrey was alone, moving from one furniture group to another, exploring her world by
touch. He experienced a profound relief and gladness that she was well. Standing still for several
minutes, he watched the concentration on her
face, the delicate way her fingers moved over each
carved detail of woodwork. Satisfaction enlivened
her expression as she touched the piano, and he
knew how important music was to her.

Then she suddenly stilled and cocked her head.
He knew he'd made no sound, and in the army,
he'd been known for his ability to move stealthily.

"Robert?"

He shook his head in amazement. "Tell me that
was a guess."

She smiled, and now he could see the faint
shadows beneath her eyes. She was working so
hard, and his admiration only grew.

"Let us say . . . an educated guess," she said.
Her head dipped, and she murmured, "I am sur-
prised by how much I can sense your presence.
It must be from spending several days together."

He was taken aback that she'd admit such a
thing. He didn't want to know she was so attuned
to him.

But he was attuned to her. He kept remembering the soft sweetness of her cheek when he'd
kissed her there, the way he'd almost turned his

head to make the kiss more—and thought she'd almost done the same.

Just a momentary whim on both their parts.

He studied her in the morning light; she looked . . . fragile, as if she'd lost weight. "How is Molly?" he asked.

Her smile held relief, and it filled him with the same.

"Oh, she is better. I am so sorry I did not write to tell you. The fever only just broke and . . ."

"And Molly usually writes your letters, I know."

Audrey smiled.

"I'm glad for her," he said, moving toward her, "but you should have taken better care of yourself. I wasn't certain if I'd find you in your own sickbed."

And then he touched her face, cupped her cheek, needing to feel her health, needing to comfort. She closed her eyes and gave a soft sigh, even as she nestled her cheek deeper into his hand. They stood together a long moment, and he felt the peace that had been eluding him for days.

She was well, he told himself. He didn't have to worry anymore.

She stiffened and stepped back, pressing her lips together in the semblance of a smile. He knew how she felt—that he was touching her when no one could see them, when he had no right.

"And what brings you to Rose Cottage today, my lord?" she asked in too cheerful a voice.

"You, of course. I did promise to assist you however I could. Don't tell me you've gone to visit all your tenants without me, or made a triumphant appearance in the village."

She laughed. "No, nothing like that. I've been here sitting with Molly. What have you been up to?"

"I've been receiving the first congratulatory notes about our engagement. They are all expressing surprise, for they've never heard of you."

Her lips parted in shock, and then she covered them with her fingertips. "Oh no," she murmured. "I am so sorry. And when they find out I'm blind—"

"You know I don't care about that. And why are you sorry? The engagement was my idea, and it was bound to become common knowledge."

"But you do realize how it *became* common knowledge," she said, reaching behind her quite accurately for a padded chair, and sinking back into it.

"Servants talk."

"Oh, not just servants. My sister went to London, and it's not even the Season. What else would she have to do but spread the gossip that she would soon be sister-by-marriage to an earl?"

"Aah," he said.

"You sound amused."

"I am. And remember, she's not the only one who left your house for London."

"My brother's friends," Audrey agreed, shaking her head in bemusement.

"It doesn't matter."

"But it is an inconvenience to you, Robert, and I never wanted that."

"The engagement wasn't your idea, remember?" He pulled up a chair and sat before her. "I knew what I was getting into."

"Days have passed now, Robert," she said, lowering her voice. "It's time to end this farce."

"It's too soon. I will not harm your reputation, so stop asking it of me."

"Very well," she said, her nose tilted in the air.

Something out of place caught his eye, and he glanced past her. "There's a coal bucket—empty it seems—on its side in the middle of your carpet."

She winced. "I forgot to pick it up. That's what I was looking for when you came."

"You are not the only one who can interpret voices, madam. Now tell me the truth. I may be ignorant of household duties, but I know the maid takes away the coal bucket when she's done."

"Not always."

"You're right—she could forget. You tripped, didn't you?"

She sighed. "I'm all right."

He rose to his feet. "It's time for me to—"

"No!" She reached for him, and he caught her hand. "I am dealing with this, Robert. This is not any easier for me than it is for them."

"They're *servants*," he said angrily. "They surely know what they're doing. I've always believed that, unlike the rest of the army."

"What do you mean?"

She gave his hand a tug, and he reluctantly sat back down. "In the army, the assumption is always that uneducated people are unintelligent."

"They just haven't had the same access to knowledge that we've had," she said, her expression bewildered.

"We both know that, having grown up with servants. But as an officer, I'd often be ordered to oversee soldiers doing the simplest tasks around the encampment, as if they were incapable of digging holes by themselves."

"But they knew you were watching, Robert. It's different here, because I can't *see* them. But I can comprehend the results. And the other thing that's difficult to reconcile is how helpful they all were when Molly was at her worst. It was like we put aside our problems to assist her. We took turns in the sickroom. The Sanfords are the only reason I slept. So let me deal with them and discover what's going on."

"Then how can I help you?" he asked.

"Well, I just happen to have a list of my tenants and where they live. I'd like to visit them, but I need a driver. Can I trust you with my life on these country roads?"

He rubbed his hands together. "Now this I can do. I even drove a wagon through the Afghan mountains once, when there weren't enough healthy soldiers."

"I'm hardly a lumbering wagon, but I am useless cargo."

"Useless?" He shook his head. "These tenants owe their livelihood to you."

"To my dead husband's estate, you mean."

"To you. After all, you could turn them all out and convert their farms to sheep pasture, if you *really* wanted to make a profit."

She gasped. "I would never!"

"I know that, but they don't. Let's go introduce you."

Chapter 11

Robert drove the little curricle, hood down, and the autumn sun shone down on them. Audrey wore a bonnet to shield her face, but he was glad to see color return to her pale cheeks.

"So what does it look like?" she asked with quiet excitement. "This estate of mine?"

He grinned. "Very well-maintained and picturesque."

"You mean quaint and countrified compared to your noble castle," she said dryly.

"Now don't say that. I own a manor, too."

"*A* manor?"

"Very well, I own several, some of which are in Scotland, and I haven't seen them."

She winced. "My, how above it all you are."

"That is unfair," he said mildly. "I did leave England at the age of twenty-one. Before I was twenty, I was at the mercy of my father's schedule. He believed in delegating only when he absolutely had to."

"I imagine people think I should be doing the same," she mused. "I do have a land agent."

"And you're letting him complete his duties. You're simply overseeing him."

"Is that what you do?"

"Not exactly. My steward and lawyers have been overseeing the various land agents of all of my properties. To be honest, I don't even know how many I have. That is what I'm home to rectify," he added. "In India, it was too difficult to make day-to-day decisions when the mail roundtrip takes at least twelve weeks."

"Your steward must be happy you're home."

"I'm not so certain of that. Remember I told you my father needed to be in control at all times? And I showed those tendencies before I left. I imagine all my servants and men of business are waiting to see what I'll do now that I'm home."

"We're in the same situation, you know."

"It's good to have someone who understands how awkward all of this is."

She smiled and lifted her face to the sun again.

"If I'm taking Molly's place," he said, "am I supposed to tell you you'll develop freckles doing that?"

She gave a little groan. "No, never that. I already have freckles, and they're not from the sun. They're—"

She broke off, and he saw her face go all blotchy red before she turned away.

"You're going to leave me like that? Where are the freckles?"

She lifted her chin. "None of your business. A gentleman wouldn't ask."

"I'm a soldier. We're a crude lot."

She ignored him, and he shook his head, smiling. She was far too easy to tease. Several peaceful minutes passed, where they listened to the birds, and he pointed out natural landmarks, a winding stream, a copse of trees sheltering a fox.

At last she asked, "Robert . . . do you think my tenants *want* to meet me? Am I making a mistake?"

He put his free hand on hers. "Not at all. This is a small estate, and you'll all be living near one another. I believe it's good for people to know they can come to you with questions. That's one thing the army taught me, to take care of the men below me, to understand my responsibilities."

"But I thought your father steeped you in your responsibilities whenever you weren't in school?"

"But not the same way. I don't think employees and tenants were real *people* to Father. They were chess pieces to be manipulated, like he was a god. One can make bad decisions when one doesn't consider how the people themselves will be affected."

And he'd been heading down that path, too. Investing had been a game to him, a new way to liven up what he thought was a boring life. Before he was even twenty-one, he'd been bored by gambling and much of Society, since he hadn't been planning to marry right away. There were women, of course, but not the kind of women who cared about him, and wanted to be cared for in return.

"Ah, I think we're approaching the first cottage," he said, relieved to put the memories behind him.

"What does it look like?" she asked.

He could hear the trepidation in her voice. Cottagers often had terrible conditions in which to raise their children. But these were decent. "Thatched-roof, brick walls, and it looks as if they have at least three or four rooms inside."

She let her breath out slowly. "Oh, that's a relief."

"I can see a little kitchen garden behind, flowers growing in front."

"Even better."

"There's a goat tethered in the back."

She laughed. "And I hear chickens in the yard."

He jumped down, then reached up for her. She held on to the back of the bench, searching with her foot for the step down.

"Lean out to me. I'll catch you."

She frowned. "If you'll just guide my foot—"

"You don't trust me? Your own fiancé?"

She tilted her head toward the cottage, and he knew she was wondering who was observing them.

"There's a little boy standing in the open doorway, thumb in his mouth. He's watching us quite solemnly."

She scrunched up her nose, and he laughed aloud.

With no warning, she leaned out from the curricle. He caught her waist in both hands, holding her suspended for an extra moment, so he could stare up at her face against the bright, cloud-dotted sky.

What was he doing?

Easing her down onto her feet, he resisted the urge to hold her close. She wasn't his fiancée, much as they were pretending it for the world. She was a woman who'd been badly hurt—who never wanted to marry again. And he was a man who didn't know what he wanted, didn't know if he could ease back into his old life without easing back into old ways.

Keeping his voice low, Robert said, "A woman just came through the door, wiping her hands with a towel. She's waiting near her son, hand on his shoulder, watching us as solemnly as he is."

"We've probably frightened her. Take me to her, please. Don't forget one of the baskets."

She'd put several on the bench where a groom

usually sat, a gift for each family, she'd explained: breads, tarts, jams, and meat pies from the kitchen at Rose Cottage. He'd seen Mrs. Sanford's face when she'd been told what Audrey wanted—her expression had gone from pleasure to such a look of pain, he'd wanted to demand the truth of what was going on. But he'd bowed to Audrey's wishes and kept his mouth shut.

Now he guided her through the little gate and past the late-blooming flowers, just as the woman stepped forward, putting her son behind her protectively. Robert didn't tell Audrey that. "She's straight ahead of us," he murmured.

"Good morning," Audrey said cheerfully, facing in the right direction. "Are you Mrs. Telford?"

"Aye, ma'am," she said, her expression wary and resigned all at the same time. Her hands were reddened from hard work, and her dark hair was caught beneath a plain cap.

"I'm Mrs. Blake, the widow of Martin Blake, and now the owner of Rose Cottage. I wanted to introduce myself, since I'm now in residence for good. I've brought you a gift."

She held the basket out before her. The little boy darted around his mother and came forward, eyes alight with interest, reaching for the basket. But of course, Audrey didn't see him, and didn't lower it to his level.

Mrs. Telford glanced sharply at Robert, the question in her eyes. He nodded, and a look of pity briefly overcame her wariness.

"I can't reach it!" the boy cried.

Without a moment's hesitation, Audrey lowered it to him, smiling when he pulled it from her hands. "What's your name?"

"Billy."

"It is a pleasure to meet you, Billy. Now show this to your mother," she urged. "You'll want to share with your whole family."

"'Tis very kind of you, Mrs. Blake," the other woman said.

"Your family's hard work is in those breads, Mrs. Telford, and I wanted you to know how much I appreciate it. And please allow me to introduce the Earl of Knightsbridge, our distant neighbor."

He bowed, but couldn't miss the way Mrs. Telford's expression turned to awe, and her shoulders, at first so straight with pride, now stooped forward as she tried to curtsy awkwardly. It reminded him too much of the way his father expected people to treat him—the way Robert had once assumed even his business partners should behave.

She pulled the little boy to her side so quickly, he dropped the basket, and a jar of jam rolled out. Robert went down on one knee to retrieve the jam and put it into the basket. Smiling, he handed it back to her and finally won a tentative, disbelieving smile in return.

"Is your husband at home?" Audrey asked, unaware that anything had happened.

"No, ma'am. He's buying supplies in Hedgerley."

"Then please tell him that anytime he has questions, he can always come to me. I know you've been dealing with Mr. Drayton, but I'm available, as well."

Suddenly, the little boy's voice piped up. "Mummy, the lady doesn't look at us."

Mrs. Telford shot a horrified glance at Robert, but it was Audrey who dropped to one knee this time, at the boy's eye level.

"I can't look at you because I'm blind, Billy."

He gaped at her. "You can't see at all?"

"No, not since I was seven years old."

"I'm six."

"You're very smart for your age," she answered.

Watching her, Billy stepped sideways, and although she certainly heard him, Audrey didn't turn her head.

"I'm right here!" Billy called, as if delighted in a new game.

"Billy!" his mother scolded. "That is teasing the nice lady."

Audrey straightened. "I don't mind, Mrs. Telford. Children have questions. I'd rather they ask me than treat me like I'll break."

"Thank you, ma'am. And the treats look real good."

"You're welcome. I'll give Mrs. Sanford your compliments. And please offer my regards to your husband."

Mrs. Telford sank into a better curtsy this time.

"It was a pleasure to meet you," Robert said.

She blushed and managed her first smile.

Once he'd helped Audrey back into the curricle, and they were on the road again, she grinned up at him.

"That went well, didn't it?" she asked.

"It most certainly did. You won them over with your charm and sincerity."

"She didn't take my blindness too poorly, but what else would she have done with the Earl of Knightsbridge standing guard over me?"

"You inflate the effect of my presence."

"I don't think I do, but thank you. So can you see the next cottage yet?"

For the next couple hours, Robert had the privilege of watching Audrey introduce herself to her tenants. The families often greeted her with more enthusiasm than her servants had. He almost hated to be introduced because it spoiled the day for him, distracting attention away from Audrey.

She didn't seem to mind. Several tenants brought problems to her attention, a leaking roof, a dispute over boundary lines, a bachelor farmer about to take a wife and wanting to be placed on the list for a larger cottage. She listened gravely and promised she would consult Mr. Drayton and have the problems taken care of. And since she was used to memorizing the layout of so many rooms, Robert had no doubt her well-trained mind would not forget each problem.

"All of our baskets are gone," she said, as they drove away from the last little cottage. "Should we go home now?"

"I can see the village just ahead." He saw the uncertainty pass over her face. "Have you visited yet?"

"I have not. I was so busy unpacking, and then Molly became ill."

"I think we should have our luncheon there. It's been a long time since I've been 'seen.'"

"That is important," she said solemnly. "Your people would like to know of your return."

"I think they already know. And they most likely know you're my fiancée," he added, still watching her.

She swallowed. "You don't have to do this, Robert. We're not really engaged, and even more people will eventually know I cried off."

"Do you think I care about gossip?" he asked quietly. "I have been the subject of it before. Our engagement is for a good reason. First you'll be known as my fiancée, and then you'll be known as the woman who figured out I didn't deserve her."

Her smile gradually widened. "Well, if you put it that way . . ."

"Then you're game?"

"I'm game. Shall we visit all the shops?"

"Every one of them."

She gave a merry laugh, and it rang out behind them as he urged the horses onward. Because they drove a carriage without a coat of arms, no one took much notice of them at first, except as strangers. But after Robert reintroduced himself and his fiancée to the butcher and then the grocer, word must have spread out before them, and the bookstore owner was already outside his door waiting for them.

Audrey knew she was only along for the ride, but she vastly enjoyed it. Much as Robert was a kind man, she heard the confidence in his voice as he spoke to people, the understanding that he'd be respected, even obeyed. It was an unconscious thing among the nobility, she decided, a way of being raised that set them apart. She wanted to resent it, knowing she'd always had to obey the men in her life, but today that voice, that earl, was helping smooth her introduction to her new neighbors. Though she felt foolish being introduced as his future bride, there was a warmth of belonging she'd never felt before. She certainly didn't trust it, of course, knowing she could only rely on herself. But for now, she'd take strength where she could get it. By the time the villagers heard she was no longer engaged, hopefully they would know her well enough to sympathize rather than pity.

The vicar introduced himself and promised that his wife would come to call soon. The milliner suggested ribbons to go with bonnets, and Robert bought her some.

At the White Horse Inn, he didn't even try to suggest a private dining parlor, and she was glad. They introduced themselves to the innkeeper, and the dining parlor grew crowded with people who might not normally have a late luncheon. She could hear the chatter and the whispers, felt themselves the object of speculation—and she didn't hate it. Perhaps people ought to be more aware that just because a woman was blind didn't mean she couldn't live a normal life.

After the innkeeper himself waited on them, Audrey sat back and teased Robert: "You must enjoy how easily people do what you want."

He said nothing for a moment, and her smile died.

"Robert?"

"It is not always a thing I want," he said, regret in his voice. "Not here. It was too easy to be swayed by it, to feel the power of my position. I thought the army beat that out of me, but apparently not enough."

She leaned forward, "Oh, no, I did not mean it that way. You smoothed the way for my acceptance—that's what I was talking about. Growing up as I did, my family helped to create my inner doubts. I felt confident in my own home, but that was it. And here, now, I need to emulate you, so don't regret your belief in yourself."

"I have confidence in you, Audrey. You'll discover strengths in yourself you never knew existed. The army showed me that. Moving to a new village, a new home—they're your own private battle to overcome."

"A battle," she mused. "So was this my first foray into enemy territory?"

"Or perhaps meeting and negotiating with possible allies."

She laughed. A man approached the table to talk with Robert, and she listened politely, wondering what all these people saw. She knew what she *felt* when she was with him, his charm and confidence and humor. It was a dangerous combination, one that drew her more than she felt comfortable with.

She mustn't start relying on him too much. He was taking Molly's place temporarily—she had to remember that. But would she and Molly have been greeted so eagerly by all the villagers? No.

It was almost . . . fun to be the pretend-fiancée of an earl.

Chapter 12

By the time they returned to Rose Cottage late that afternoon, Audrey was anxious to see how Molly fared. Robert was waiting to help her from the carriage, and this time she didn't think twice about leaning into his strong hands, resting her own on his wide shoulders. He swung her down before him, and her thighs and stomach brushed his. She gave a little gasp of shock, of embarrassment, but he didn't let her go. Unless she pushed herself away, she couldn't keep her breasts from brushing his chest.

"Robert," she began, surprised to feel a shiver move through her.

"I'm your fiancé, remember," he said in a low, rumbling voice. "We've just spent the day together in front of people, where I could look at you and not touch. How would I be expected to resist your delicate waist in my hands?"

"You are teasing me," she whispered, biting her lip. "I have heard stories of men who try to seduce women."

He let her go. "I don't mean to tease you. I'm trying to help you. Bridegrooms are *supposed* to show desire for their fiancées."

She nodded, but couldn't speak, and their leave-taking was more strained than normal. *Bridegrooms are supposed to show desire for their fiancées*, she thought. But her first groom had misled her—every experience she'd had with a man had been false. And she'd gone along with Robert's false engagement.

So why couldn't she stay distant and unemotional?

Sighing, she went up to Molly's room in the attics and found her dozing, Francis watching over her. He excused himself, his voice humble, and left the room.

Audrey was considering him when she heard Molly murmur in a hoarse voice, "He's a nice young man. He doesn't say much to me, but he has a comforting way about him."

Audrey sat down on the edge of the bed, knowing her smile must be foolishly wide. "You sound better."

"Then tell that to the rest of my body, for I feel like I've taken a beating. It's a good thing you can't see me."

"Why? Have you been studying yourself in a mirror already?"

"No, but I saw Francis wince."

Audrey chuckled, then couldn't resist touching Molly's forehead. "Hmm. I think you're still a bit warm."

"The doctor visited today, and he said that was normal, that it'll be days before I'm up and about. Days! I told him I'd prove him wrong."

"No, you won't. I'll see that you stay right here."

"You won't 'see' anything."

"Oh, yes, I will. I have spies, you know."

"I think only one spy. You have him quite dazzled, I believe."

Audrey stiffened. "Francis?" she said, knowing that wasn't whom she meant.

Molly gave a tired laugh. "Now don't you go fooling yourself. I was trying to sit up just now and saw you two out the window."

Audrey, hesitated, hating to lie, but feeling trapped. "Robert is . . . flattering."

"Why do you seem unhappy about that?"

She decided to give a measure of truth. "I have only been under the control of other people. Before I marry, I need to be on my own for a bit."

"It seems he's letting you. He brought you here to live alone, didn't he? Or is he pressing for a wedding date?"

"No. Sometimes I think the pressure is all from myself." Audrey found herself straightening Molly's blanket, and then urging her to take another sip of water. "Are you hungry?"

"Francis said he'd have Evelyn bring me broth. Feels like that's all I've had for days."

"It is." Audrey took her hand, felt the delicate bones. "You're wasting away. I'll see if Mrs. Sanford will prepare you something else."

Molly yawned. "I think I'll go back to sleep until then."

"You do that, dear."

Audrey slowly made her way down the servants' stair to the kitchen. "Mrs. Sanford?"

"Aye, ma'am?"

She could hear the woman rolling something out on the big wooden table that took up the center of the kitchen. She gave her Molly's request, and the woman snorted.

"I've nursed many a sick child, Mrs. Blake," the housekeeper said, "and they all want more than's good for them."

Audrey thought about the child she'd never had the chance to nurse, and then let it go. Mrs. Sanford couldn't know the unwelcome memories she stirred.

"Is there a stool I may sit upon?" Audrey asked, thinking that the woman might relax more in her own domain.

"Of course, ma'am."

She felt one pushed against her skirts. "Thank you. What are you making?"

"Tarts. The earl likes them. And we've run out."

Of course she'd want to prepare his favorite foods. "I cannot begin to express my thanks for those baskets you made for the tenants. They were so appreciative."

"I'm glad."

"Everyone seemed very nice. Has there ever been trouble with the tenants?"

"Not this group, ma'am. Mr. Drayton has done a fine job of findin' married folks, and those with a history of payin' their own way."

"The cottages seem to be a decent size and well maintained."

"The old Mr. Blake saw to that. Thought contented people did better work. Caused some uproar in these parts when other landowners were offended, but he didn't care. He used to put on a feast every year, too, for all the tenants, but that stopped after his death, many years ago."

"A feast?" Audrey echoed, intrigued. "That sounds lovely. I'll have to discuss it with Mr. Drayton." They hadn't gone over much of the finances yet. But a feast might go a long way toward smoothing things over with both her tenants and her servants.

"Have you worked here long?" Audrey asked.

There was a momentary silence, and she knew Mrs. Sanford was debating carrying on their conversation.

"Since I was a girl. And when I wanted to marry, old Mr. Blake brought on my husband."

"That was very kind of him."

"I know it's not done in other houses," she began defensively.

"I don't care how others run their homes. I will not turn you out because you're married, not as long as your work is satisfactory." She didn't say anything else, hating to leave a threat hanging, but knowing she had to. "Your oldest daughter did not wish to work here?" she continued when the silence lengthened.

"She did, ma'am, but then she decided to marry."

Audrey could hear the rolling pin hitting the wooden table hard, as if Mrs. Sanford was really emphasizing her work—or emphasizing how busy she was, too busy to talk.

"I haven't met her yet. Will she be coming by the house?"

"Mayhap. She's busy with her boy."

"Let her know I'd like to meet her, please. I'll leave you to your cooking and look forward to dinner. I'll eat with Molly."

She'd almost reached the door when Mrs. Sanford said, "Ma'am?"

"Yes?"

"You always take good care of Molly, like she's more than a servant."

"She is, to me."

"I—appreciate it."

"Um . . . thank you." Audrey left the kitchen, feeling bewildered and unsatisfied. There was a mystery she needed to discover, and it wouldn't help to let her whole staff go for their insolence. And Mrs. Sanford's words made Audrey hope for the future. Or was the family's conduct because of *Mr.* Sanford? She seldom encountered him, since he only did occasional work inside the house. Perhaps she would have to make an effort to converse with him. She'd been meaning to ride Erebus . . .

Robert arrived home just as dusk was settling over the land like a gray cloud, and fog darted its fingers around trees and hedges. Knightsbridge Hall stood sentinel, its hundreds of windows still shimmering with the last of the setting sun. It was a rectangular mansion, with a courtyard in the center for unloading passengers. There was a family wing, a bachelor wing, servants' wing, and gilded public rooms in front that would have done the Queen proud.

And he was the only one who lived there. He almost found himself wishing for poor relations who needed to be housed. There were dozens of servants, of course, and they were good people. But he could already see that he would be spending more time in London—until he had a family of his own to liven the place up.

Again, he realized the similarities between Audrey and him. She was alone in a house of servants, too, but it was how she wanted it. She wanted independence and freedom, and she had Molly, of course, her dear friend.

Robert had his own friends, the same ones he'd bonded with in India—Blackthorne and Rothford—but both of them were trying to make amends to the families of the other two soldiers who'd died in that dreaded battle. He was looking forward to hearing their stories, but he knew it might not be until the opening of Parliament in January.

There would be other friends from his youth, now gentlemen and peers in their own right, to reestablish ties with. He had much to look forward to.

But now? All he wanted to do was be with Audrey, where he felt useful and needed. It was time to visit his own tenants, but would that even be the same without her? He liked being her eyes, helping her to see the world. Because she'd been so sheltered, she had the wonder of a child.

So he spent the next day on a tour of his own large estate. He couldn't even meet a quarter of the tenants in one day, but it was a start. He came away with a clearer understanding of what had been going on the last nine years, and some changes he wanted to make, enlarging cottages and improving the lives of his farmers. There was enough of a demand for housing that he could build more homes, as well.

But there was so much he didn't know! He'd spent years being in command, and now to come home and simply allow others to oversee everything was just wrong. Surely he could find a medium ground, where he had his hands on the reins, but allowed his people to do the work he'd hired them for. Visiting with the tenants made him see that people wanted to know he cared, that he was involved.

Throughout the day, he'd found himself thinking about what Audrey might say, how the people would react to her warmth and caring. He wondered what she was doing, if she spent the day nursing Molly or exploring her home. He had been trying to keep an emotional distance between them, but it just wasn't working.

Robert's good intentions faded when he saw Audrey the next morning. Once again, the door was unmanned, and he walked into her entrance hall unannounced. He would have tracked down Francis, but knew she wouldn't be pleased at his interference. He found her in the study reading one of her embossed books. He was five steps inside before she gave a start of surprise.

"So much for your vaunted ability to tell people apart," he teased.

"Good morning, Robert," she said, slowly smiling her pleasure.

And it was pleasure. She was happy to see him. "So maybe we need a signal so you'll know it's me."

"You could knock," she answered dryly. "In some cultures, that is the signal someone has arrived."

"We could have different signals for different things," he said, ignoring her common sense. "The 'I need to talk privately' signal, the 'Someone's coming!' signal."

He came around the desk until he was beside her. She looked so flustered at his approach, rising up as if to meet him partway. And instead that brought them face-to-face, and before he knew it, against all resolve, he leaned in and kissed her.

Her lips were sweetly parted, so still at first that he knew he'd shocked her. He pressed several gentle kisses along the full lower curve, gradually deepening until he could just taste the warmth between. He cupped the back of her head, tilting her, and with a breathless moan she opened her mouth to him.

He explored her, gently teased her tongue until she met his. Then the kiss turned bolder, more passionate, and he couldn't get enough of the taste of her. He felt the press of her body against him, and even with all the clothes separating them, it was alluring and encompassing and all that mattered.

He knew with a certainty that he wanted her to be a scandalous widow and take him as her lover.

Audrey was lost in the heat, the urgency, the sensations of Robert taking possession of her mouth, her very will. She could feel the long press of his body against hers, the power, the forceful-ness that made refusing unthinkable.

She broke the kiss then, suddenly frightened at how easily he swept away all her restraint, all her promises to never need another man.

"I—I can't," she whispered. "Please don't ask me to."

She was still in his arms, and he didn't let her

go as he said in a hoarse voice, "I didn't intend this to happen but I did enjoy it. Will you accept my apology?"

"Perhaps . . . perhaps if you would release me first."

And then he did, and she had to put her hand against the desk to hold herself upright, as if she could no longer stand without his support.

She didn't need anyone's support, she told herself. But it was more difficult than she'd imagined, playing the role of his fiancée, pretending to be drawn to each other, and not making it happen for real.

He'd promised to take Molly's role in her life, and when he wasn't there yesterday, she'd felt almost helpless, something so alien to her nature. She was seeing how much she depended on Molly—on another person—to guide her through the sighted world. And it was frightening to know she could never have full independence because of her blindness.

But she couldn't use him to bring back her confidence. Only she could do that for herself.

"I don't know what you're thinking, Robert," she said at last, when all she could hear was his ragged breathing. "But I've told you I won't play the scandalous widow to your rake. I am not interested in an affair."

"I know," he murmured, "and I didn't mean to try to convince you. Hell, I don't know what I was trying to do. I just saw you there, looking sweet and irresistible, and I kissed you. And then I thought, What would be wrong with an affair?"

"No. Now sit over there," she said, pointing to the other side of the desk. "Let's keep some distance here."

"Is that for my benefit or yours?"

He was teasing her again, and she tried to relax. "Yours," she answered firmly.

"I am just a man, Audrey, no paragon."

"No one is perfect," she said, sighing as she sat down. "Least of all me. Just to prove how not-perfect I am, shall I tell you what happened yesterday?"

"What happened?" The amusement was gone from his voice.

"Do not over-worry. I started out the day surprisingly well. I met with Mr. Drayton, and we discussed the problems my tenants brought forth. We even discussed the finances, and my ability to hold a feast to celebrate a successful harvest and get to know everyone."

"Will it be possible?"

"It will. I would have liked to invite the poor of the parish, but he says that would put too deep a strain on us this year. But maybe next."

"And this is why you're not perfect?" he asked, bemused.

"Oh, no, let me tell you about my next idea." She put a finger to her lips, then rose, circled the desk and went to shut the door.

"Now who's scandalous?" he asked.

"We're engaged. Just listen." She returned to her leather chair. "I decided it was time to get to know Mr. Sanford better. I seldom actually see him, and when I do, his voice sounds so gruff and . . . disapproving. I don't need his approval, mind you, but I would like harmony in my home, and I thought if we had some time together . . ." She sighed. "It was a good idea, but not very successful. I decided to have Erebus saddled and take my first ride."

"Without Molly or me?"

"You sound indignant, Robert. Why is that?"

"I wanted to be with you your first ride through your new estate. But I imagine you don't want to hear that."

"No."

"So what happened?"

"Did you know the stable dog had puppies?"

"What does this have to do with Mr. Sanford?"

She smiled at the bewilderment in his voice. "Just be patient. So I had Francis guide me to the stables and leave me in the hands of his father—who was not happy to be saddled with me."

"He is your employee," Robert said tightly. "The fact that he shows such hostility toward you—"

"Is curious, don't you think?" she interrupted. "It just doesn't make sense. So I had him saddle Erebus, and he was going to lead me about, to exercise the horse, of course, but also so Erebus could begin to learn the grounds. He's a very smart horse—did I tell you that?"

He sighed. "Finish the main story first."

"So impatient!"

"Which is one of the reasons I kissed you."

She didn't want to be reminded, because the memory of it made her lose all rational thought. So she ignored him. "I didn't see the dog, of course, and I'm assuming he didn't either. But the dog is very wary guarding her pups, and when we got too close, she set up a vicious barking, startling poor Erebus. I guess I'd never realized my horse had never been around dogs, because he reared and I fell off."

"You fell off?"

She could hear him getting to his feet and coming back around the desk. She held up a hand before he could get too near, although already her heart beat a little faster. "Stay back. I'm fine."

"Well you didn't wince when I held you," he admitted.

"Stop reminding me of that improper moment!"

"I can't help it. I'm just a man, Audrey."

"So you keep saying. But I am not a siren who lures men, so there's no cause—"

"You have not seen yourself," he said softly. "You are quite beautiful."

"My husband flattered me, too," she said dryly. "And it was all to have his way."

"I'm telling you the truth."

"To have your way."

He didn't answer for a moment. "Truly, Audrey, you are unharmed? Nothing bruised?"

"Oh, I have bruises in places you will not be seeing."

"Next to the mysterious freckles?"

She bit her lip to keep from laughing. She would not encourage him. "Mr. Sanford sounded just horrified after I fell. He hadn't meant that to happen, of course. A suspicious person might think him lying, but . . . I don't think he was."

"You are not suspicious enough."

"I have changed their lives and made the future uncertain for them. I will be patient. As for my poor horse, Erebus didn't know what to do with himself. He kept nudging me with his nose. I think he was trying to apologize."

"Or trying to get away from Sanford. Did the horse seem neglected?"

"Heavens, no. He was his usual temperament,

though glad to see me, of course. Your horse has been in the stables every day. He is well, is he not?"

"He is, but I'm a visiting earl, not the unwished-for blind mistress. Promise me you'll be careful, Audrey."

"I will."

"And next time wait for me."

"Or Molly."

"Oh very well. Were you going to ask me what I was doing yesterday?"

"Of course."

He told her about visiting his tenants, and his plans for more cottages.

"That sounds wonderful, Robert!"

"But I missed having you with me."

She ignored the serious tone of his voice. "And how would that have looked? Like you couldn't be apart from your blind fiancée. I'd look helpless and you'd look weak."

"You're wrong, but let us agree to disagree. So what can I do to help you today?"

"I'd like to read through the household ledgers, without Mr. Drayton looking over our shoulders. If you would do me the honor of reading aloud, I can hear the expenditures of the estate in detail. I need to make certain we can continue to sustain ourselves, because, as you know, I bring no money myself, and all that's left is what little is held in trust."

"So where do I find these ledgers?"

"They should be here in the study—somewhere. But there are a lot of books. I imagine they're near the desk . . ."

She listened as he began to search. "They were quite large and leather-bound when I looked at them with Mr. Drayton."

After a few minutes, he said, "I don't see them. Could he have taken them home?"

"He keeps his own copies, which he brings every time to make sure they match. I guess he could have taken our copy accidentally. But the books are so heavy, how could he not have known he carried two?"

But they didn't find the ledgers, nor were they with Mrs. Sanford's kitchen account book. Was this just another attempt to fluster her? Audrey couldn't help thinking.

Francis appeared in the kitchen and intoned, "You have a visitor, Mrs. Blake."

Audrey perked up—her first visitor, if one didn't count Robert. Perhaps the vicar's wife was making an appearance already.

"It is your sister, Miss Blythe Collins, and her lady's maid."

Audrey came to a complete stop just as she was

beginning to cross the kitchen, and Robert ran into her from behind, catching her arms in case she stumbled forward.

"Your sister?" Robert asked in surprise. "Isn't she supposed to be in London?"

"She was. I have no idea what is going on. I hope nothing is wrong."

Chapter 13

As Robert followed Audrey into the entrance hall, he worried about how the arrival of her judgmental sister would affect her. In Rose Cottage, Audrey was the mistress, but her sister's presence might bring back memories of the woman who was never even permitted to leave her home.

A young servant wearing a shawl and lace cap sat on a bench near the front door, and when she saw him, she blushed and looked at her fingers twined together.

"Shall Miss Collins's maid go to the kitchen?" Robert asked Audrey.

Audrey paused and sent him a thankful smile over her shoulder. "Charlotte?"

The girl stood and bobbed a quick curtsy. "Aye, Mrs. Blake."

"Lord Knightsbridge is correct. The housekeeper, Mrs. Sanford, will find you a room and show you about. The kitchen is back through this hall."

"Thank you, ma'am," Charlotte said, and quickly left the room.

Audrey squared her shoulders and moved briskly into the drawing room, showing no hesitation. "Blythe?"

Robert paused in the doorway to take everything in. Miss Collins stood in the middle of the drawing room, wearing a bright green gown with a matching shaped jacket for warmth during travel, and a little hat perched on the top of her piled brunette curls. He thought she looked nervous upon first seeing Audrey, but when she caught sight of him, she gave that "confident-in-my-beauty" smile, and he found himself distrusting her motives before she even opened her mouth.

"Audrey, this is a lovely home," she said politely, guardedly.

"I'm glad you came, Blythe." Audrey reached out her hand, and Miss Collins took it. "Why didn't you tell me you wanted to visit? I thought you were staying in London."

Miss Collins shrugged, glancing at Robert again. "It's not the Season yet, and so many people aren't in Town. I made my rounds and then . . . I wanted to see the house you inherited. Rose Cottage is the name?"

Audrey smiled and nodded, as if she'd never

had a problem with her sister. Robert suspected that Audrey would do anything to improve her relationship with Miss Collins. He felt a rise of anger on her behalf, that she would have to be so desperate for her family's approval. But was that all it was? He had no family at all but distant cousins, and would give much to have the companionship and shared past of close kin. Perhaps Audrey wanted to preserve that, rather than take whatever abuse her sister handed out.

Robert would make certain that Miss Collins understood that he would not tolerate poor treatment of Audrey.

"Are you just stopping by," Audrey began, "or might you visit for a while? You'd be my first overnight guest."

Miss Collins glanced at Robert with speculation. "Lord Knightsbridge did not stay?"

What did the woman think they were doing, conducting an open affair? Not that Robert would have minded for himself, but he minded on Audrey's behalf.

"My home is only eight miles away," Robert said coolly. "It would be inappropriate for me to spend a night here, do you not think?"

Miss Collins's eyes widened. "Oh, forgive me. Of course you're right. But you're *engaged* now, and I thought Audrey might wish for your help."

"We do much together, it is true," Audrey said, before Robert could answer. "He has been a good friend, especially since Molly's illness has confined her to her room."

"I'm sorry to hear about Molly's illness, and hope she's recovering, but *friend*?" Miss Collins said with interest.

"Shouldn't those about to be married do well to be friends?" Robert asked dryly.

Audrey tilted her head toward him, and he already knew her particular warning look. She wanted to handle this, and she didn't appreciate his interference.

Sometimes it was damned annoying to be involved with an independent woman. It made him not want to find his own wife.

But a lover, on the other hand . . .

"Please sit down, Blythe," Audrey said warmly. "Robert, please ask Francis to bring a tea tray to stave off our hunger before luncheon."

Robert stepped out the door and relayed the request to Francis, then returned. Audrey and Miss Collins were seated side by side on the sofa, so he took an upholstered chair across the low table from them.

"London was quite boring," Miss Collins said, heaving a dramatic sigh.

As if Audrey had any idea what London was

like, Robert thought angrily. This wasn't going well already. It was amazing how the passing of just a few days made him even more defensive and irate on Audrey's behalf.

"I'm sorry to hear that," Audrey murmured. "I know how much you usually enjoy it there."

"Yes, well, it gave me such a good opportunity to see your inheritance. I know how excited you always were. Could it possibly have lived up to your expectations?" Miss Collins asked, her voice laced with doubt.

He admired Audrey's forbearance more and more as she remained the gracious hostess.

"It has been more than I ever dreamed," Audrey said quietly, hope evident in her shining expression. "I feel like this inheritance is Mr. Blake's gift to me, an apology, the chance to start my new life."

"But you won't be here long," Miss Collins pointed out. "Soon you'll be the mistress of Knightsbridge Hall."

Robert awaited her response to *that* one, lobbed as if from a mortar and targeted precisely.

"We haven't set a wedding date yet," Audrey said, without even a momentary hesitation. "And this will be one of our properties, as well, and my dower property, so I want to see it thriving."

"Already planning for my death?" Robert asked with faint sarcasm.

To his surprise, it was Miss Collins who answered.

"Every woman must be prepared for that, my lord. Our father would never dream of allowing a marriage contract that did not grant Audrey protection in her elderly years."

Surprised and bewildered, Audrey thought upon her sister's words, even as a tea tray was set before her and she began to pour. It was true, her father wanted to make sure she was taken care of, and she'd always assumed it was because he wanted more property to control. But did he actually care about her future after he was gone? It was a novel concept.

"I do not need Father's assistance in the contract," Audrey said, holding out a cup and saucer to her sister, "since I am a widow who can retain her own lawyers. But I appreciate your sentiment, Blythe, and I agree with you." To change the subject, she said, "Lord Knightsbridge tells me our engagement has become common knowledge in London."

"Was it a secret?" Blythe asked.

Audrey could hear her surprise, and knew she had to tread carefully. She offered Robert his cup, then poured her own. "No, it was not. We were simply surprised he had received congratulations already."

"I mentioned it at a dinner party," she admitted. "People were taken aback that, so soon after returning to England, Lord Knightsbridge would commit himself."

Audrey heard the suspicions Blythe didn't bother to hide. Now that Blythe no longer thought she could win Robert for herself, she was not being as careful around him.

"Were they surprised you had a sister?" Robert asked coldly.

Audrey caught her breath. She tried to picture Blythe's expression, but all she saw was the innocent little girl who'd once been her doll baby. "Robert—"

"No, Audrey," Blythe interrupted. "He has the right to say that if he cares about you. Yes, my lord, my London friends have always known I have a blind sister. What was so surprising to them was that you would offer marriage, when you'd only just returned, and it was obvious you had not known her in your youth."

Audrey's cup rattled briefly in the saucer as she lifted it to her mouth. Was Blythe worried about her, rather than simply jealous? Audrey wasn't such a fool as to forget the jealousy, but maybe her sister had more complicated emotions than she'd ever suspected. It gave her such a spark of hope that they could one day have a sisterly relationship, but she tamped it down, knowing it was too soon.

"Do you believe your sister unable to inspire my respect, admiration, and love?" Robert asked sharply.

"Perhaps you have other motives," Blythe countered.

"Blythe, I have no great dowry or beauty, and I am blind," Audrey said firmly. "I'm not sure there can be other suspicious motives. So let us put this argument behind us. Would you like a tour of my home before luncheon?"

"That would be lovely," Blythe said stiffly.

As Audrey rose, she felt Robert touch her arm, and knew he was offering his guidance, but after their kiss and his open offer of a love affair, she was afraid she'd blush or stammer or forget herself, simply at his touch. So she concentrated on counting her steps, and touching the occasional piece of furniture as they moved from room to room, and prayed the servants had not left something out of place. More than once, Blythe fell into her old habit of constantly warning Audrey about anything in her vicinity, as if Audrey usually blundered over everything. Of course, she'd recently blundered over a coal bucket and fallen off Erebus, things she wasn't about to mention . . .

But Blythe did ask interested questions

throughout, and Audrey found herself relaxing. When Blythe was shown to her room to change before luncheon, Audrey left Robert in the study and went to look in on Molly.

When she tried to feel Molly's forehead, she touched her shoulder instead. "Ah, you're propped up a bit higher in bed today," Audrey said, feeling even more relieved.

"It makes my head pound, but I want to be up and about as soon as I can."

"So anxious for me to work you to the bone?" Audrey smiled, sitting on the edge of the bed.

"Anxious to see what your sister is up to."

"News travels fast."

"Francis came to tell me."

"Did he now?" Audrey asked, amused.

"This isn't a good thing, Miss Audrey," Molly said, her voice serious. "Why is she here, when she never had much use for you before?"

"She said she wants to see my home."

Molly made a dismissive sound.

"It's a good thing I don't hold you to a maid's subservience," Audrey said dryly. "But also . . . she seemed concerned about Lord Knightsbridge's motives, as if she might be trying to put her jealousy aside."

"You be careful, miss. Miss Blythe has only ever thought of herself, and didn't care how she hurt you. I can't believe that'd change so suddenly. I'll talk to Charlotte and see what she knows."

"Thank you for your concern, Molly, but since I've decided to take chances with life, this is one I can't let pass. If my sister and I could have some sort of real relationship . . ." She let the words die as her throat tightened.

"You have a new relationship now, miss," Molly said with kindness. "You'll soon have a husband and family of your own."

Audrey barely withheld her own dismissive sound.

Luncheon was strained, Audrey thought, and it was crazy that both Robert and Blythe found themselves angry on her behalf. It was all such a new experience for her. She didn't know how to handle it, except to charge forward as if it didn't bother her. She talked about her tenants, and asked both Blythe's and Robert's opinions of having a meal for them.

It wasn't until they were served custard for dessert that Robert gave a sigh and said, "I've held my tongue throughout, because I know you like to handle things yourself, Audrey. But Miss Collins is being a good sport about the fact that Francis didn't see fit to give her any forks, even when she subtly reminded him."

Hot with embarrassment, Audrey turned toward her sister. "Why wouldn't you tell me this?"

"I didn't think it very important. The poor young man was obviously nervous about serving an earl."

"He's been serving me for days," Robert said dryly. "I think he was nervous for another reason, one which Audrey wishes to handle on her own."

"What is going on?" Blythe demanded.

Audrey took a moment, still rather shocked that her sister hadn't complained—loudly—about the servants' neglect. "I . . . don't really know. The servants seem to have a reason to wish me gone, and are doing little things to annoy me."

"Such servants deserve to be let go," Robert said.

"But it doesn't make sense," Audrey insisted. "They're a family—it would be terrible if all of them were asked to leave. They could very well starve."

"Unless they've been hiding money away all these years," Robert pointed out.

"I can't believe that. What money? The land agent has shown us every penny spent—"

"And now the ledgers are missing."

"This cannot be a conspiracy," Blythe said.

Her voice was full of an amusement that didn't quite ring true, Audrey thought.

"And why do you say that?" Audrey asked.

"You've introduced me to them. With my own eyes I could see their helplessness. Maybe they're *afraid* you're going to let them go, and are making mistakes because of it."

"Just because I'm blind doesn't mean I can't understand that something is wrong. I won't let such behavior continue in my own household. But your reason has merit."

"Well, it is your decision, of course," Blythe murmured.

Was her sister backing down from an argument? What was wrong with the world?

"Do you have plans this afternoon?" Blythe asked.

It took Audrey a moment to leave her concerns temporarily behind. "Nothing that cannot wait."

"I would like to see your gardens. You know how I adore arranging flowers."

You do? Audrey almost said, and stopped herself. It was a feminine pastime, and perhaps Blythe was still playing up to Robert.

"I'll leave you ladies to the gardens," Robert said. "I have ledgers to look for."

When he had left them, Audrey took her sister's arm to go outside. She did not remember the last time she'd had to do so. She'd known her way so well around their childhood home.

And as if Blythe were thinking the same thing, she said, "And where is your ever-present Molly?"

"She came down with a terrible fever several days ago."

Blythe's arm tensed within Audrey's. "You had mentioned her illness, but I hadn't realized it was serious."

"Don't worry, she was the only one to take ill, and she is recovering well, just still too weak to perform her usual activities."

"Then who's your unofficial secretary?" Blythe asked.

Audrey hesitated. "Lord Knightsbridge graciously offered his assistance."

She felt Blythe lean forward, heard the sound of the door opening, and then the cool breeze and the sun on her face.

"If you need your shawl . . ." Audrey began.

"No, I'll be fine." Blythe's voice seemed a bit strained. "This man seems too good to be true."

"I sometimes think that myself," Audrey admitted.

"I talked to people in London about him." Before Audrey could respond, she hastily said, "Oh, look, you have so many azaleas and rhododendrons."

"But not in bloom at this time of the year. Why did we really come out here, Blythe? Was it simply to be free of Lord Knightsbridge?"

"Don't you want to know what people are saying?"

Audrey hesitated. "No. Gossip is never a good—"

"Gossip is unfounded rumors. Facts are . . . facts. Here, sit down. There's a bench right behind you."

Audrey felt it with the backs of her knees and sat, letting go of Blythe's arm. "Why do you care who I marry, as long as I'm no longer embarrassing you? Or will my being a countess embarrass you even more?"

She wasn't going to be a countess, of course, but she wanted to hear the truth from Blythe's own lips.

"You've been used by a man before," Blythe said coolly. "I didn't think you wanted that again."

"He's not using me—in fact, I—" She stopped, biting her lip at what she'd almost revealed.

"You what?"

"We have not set a date, Blythe. I am being patient and learning all I can, and at the same time, I'm enjoying the first freedom of my life. Why are you trying to disrupt that?"

"Disrupt—I'm not!" She sounded honestly bewildered. "But just like Lord Knightsbridge told you about the servants' treatment of me—because *you* wanted to know—I have to tell you this. He's been gone almost his entire adult life, Audrey, and no one really knows him."

The wind whipped a curl free, and Audrey caught it behind her ear. "But I'm learning to know him. Doesn't that count? Maybe I'm the only one who wants to." She thought of his kisses, and his honesty about wanting her as a lover. My heavens, he could have his pick of any woman. She didn't have to see his face to know that he desired her—

But she was conveniently available to him, and he'd already admitted he wanted to help her. She didn't want to send him away.

"How can you forget about his partner who killed himself?" Blythe demanded. "Did you ask him?"

"No," Audrey admitted, "not yet. It is so very painful, I imagine."

"Maybe it isn't."

"Blythe," she said her sister's name sharply. "Thank you for your concern, but I am handling everything as I see fit."

"Including marrying a man you don't love—again."

Audrey stiffened. "If an earl asked you to marry him, you'd jump at the offer. I know you too well."

Blythe said nothing.

"Me taking a risk is different, though, isn't it?" More silence.

"Let's walk, shall we? And we can pretend everything between us is fine."

They walked down a path, and Audrey estimated they were heading toward the pond.

"There's a man in your gardens," Blythe said at last.

"Mr. Sanford, the groundskeeper. He is married to the housekeeper."

"Your little servant family, that's right. I imagine he must be a helpful fellow. He's following us about in case we need assistance."

And Audrey felt a chill that had nothing to do with the approach of winter.

Chapter 14

They were called back inside by the arrival of another guest, and Audrey wouldn't have been surprised if it was another member of her family. Instead, it was the vicar's wife awaiting her in the drawing room.

"You already went into the village?" Blythe asked Audrey with surprise evident in her voice as they walked through the house.

"I did. People went out of their way to be kind." She did not say that it had been Robert's idea to go so quickly, and he who escorted her.

In the entrance hall, Audrey spoke to Francis about having tea sent in, and then without holding her sister's arm, entered the drawing room.

"Mrs. Blake," a woman's voice intoned in a nasal manner, "it is a pleasure to make your acquaintance."

Audrey could hear the interest the woman didn't bother to hide. "Mrs. Warton, it is surely my own pleasure. I enjoyed my conversation with your husband several days ago. May I introduce my sister, Miss Blythe Collins?"

"How do you do?" Blythe asked.

"Quite fine, thank you," said Mrs. Warton.

"A tea tray will be arriving shortly," Audrey said. "Would you care to sit down?"

"I am already seated, Mrs. Blake," Mrs. Warton said, sounding almost immediately as if she regretted the words.

And Audrey liked her for it. "You'll have to excuse me. I make those mistakes often."

"If you do not mind my saying, my friends in Hedgerley were speaking quite openly of their delight in meeting you," Mrs. Warton explained.

"People don't know what to expect of a blind woman," Audrey admitted. "Isn't that true, Blythe?"

She knew she caught her sister off guard, and felt glad and guilty at the same time. Why should she feel guilty? Blythe was always worried about what people would say if they took Audrey into their own village.

"It is true," Blythe murmured, adding nothing else.

"Some can be so sheltered," Mrs. Warton said. "It is good to shake things up a bit."

Audrey's smile widened. She already liked this woman.

"Ladies?"

She heard Robert's voice coming from the door-way. "Lord Knightsbridge, I am so glad you could join us. Allow me to introduce the vicar's wife, Mrs. Warton."

"A pleasure, my lord," the woman breathed, her voice dipping as she most likely sank into a curtsy. She sounded both awed and amazed, as if she hadn't quite believed that the earl had graced their village.

The tea arrived at that moment, and Audrey took her time serving everyone. She knew she was on display, as she would always be, and didn't mind the attention.

"Mrs. Warton," Audrey began, "I mentioned to your husband that I would enjoy becoming involved in philanthropic endeavors in the village. Can you tell me what programs the church hosts?"

Mrs. Warton enlightened them for long minutes about the Female Aid Society and the Soup Distribution Society. Audrey wondered if Robert was nodding off, although he asked polite questions about the scope of their charities, and Mrs. Warton's opinion on how best to expand their coverage through other villages near his estate. There was even a group who knitted for newborn babies, something Audrey could do to give her a purpose in the evenings after she'd ended things with Robert, and she was alone.

As Mrs. Warton departed, she promised to invite Audrey to her next women's society meeting.

Audrey sat back down, satisfied.

"You will soon be behaving like an old married woman," Blythe commented dourly.

"Doing works of charity?" Audrey said in surprise. "I'll enjoy helping my new parish. I wish I could have done more when I still lived at home."

Blythe ignored that. "I have letters to write before dinner. If you'll excuse me, Audrey, Lord Knightsbridge."

And then she was alone with Robert, and that morning's scandalous suggestion about an affair might as well have been shouted in the room again, for how much it had dwelt on and off in her mind through the day. She felt the sofa sag as he sat down beside her.

"Now don't get all stiff with me, Audrey," he said, his tone full of amusement. "*I* don't think you're behaving like an old married woman."

She sighed. "I do not care what my sister thinks. She does not have to live here and get to know people. This is the best way."

"She's used to Society and balls and dinners."

"Exactly."

"Which she left behind to come here."

"It *is* curious," Audrey murmured, then added even more softly, "She might hear us."

"Then I'll close the door."

He left her side so quickly, all she could say was, "But Robert—"

"Engaged, remember?"

She heard the lock click, and regretted the sharp little thrill that danced its way right up through her body. He was going to try to convince her to be his lover again—how would he do it?

But instead of romantic persuasion, he said, "Mr. Drayton stopped by while you were in the garden. I asked him about the missing ledgers, and he swore they were always in your study, and that he hadn't accidentally taken them."

"That doesn't help us," she said glumly.

"He seemed . . . reluctant to discuss all of this, which I found unusual."

"Perhaps because Rose Cottage isn't yours?"

He chuckled. "I am an earl, Audrey, and engaged to you. Of course he would discuss it with me."

"Of course," she answered dryly.

"He went on about several new tenant openings, and the autumn activity on the farms, but . . . I felt like he was distracting me."

"How strange," she said, now thoroughly distracted by the mystery herself.

"I admit, he might have felt defensive, as if I were questioning him, when really, I was simply trying to get to the bottom of this mystery. He showed no hesitation about letting me peruse his copy of the most recent ledger, and I saw nothing to make me suspicious about the last few months. But of course, maybe the real ledger and the copy are a little different."

"Did he know you suspected that?" she asked.

"No. I have no cause to believe foul of him, and he's done excellent work these last few years with the estate."

"I imagine you let him know you quite admired his dedication and service," she said, hiding a smile.

"It's always important to praise your men."

"Your soldiers?" she teased.

"He works for you, hence, he's quite like a soldier. Praise for a subordinate was not something I saw growing up."

Smiling, she said, "A subordinate—you mean a servant."

"Or man of business, but yes. My father believed in authority and dominance, not in praising people for the work they were supposed to do regardless."

"And you saw that in yourself," she reminded him, feeling Blythe's curiosity as her own.

"I did. I am grateful that the army showed me another way."

The sofa dipped a little more, and then she felt his breath warm against her ear as he softly spoke.

"I could praise your beauty," he murmured.

She shivered, excitement like a fluttering bird longing to be free. "That is not an accomplishment I can claim as my own, so no need to praise me."

"I can praise your talents."

He lifted her hand and slowly removed her glove, each tug making her tremble the harder.

When he had her fingers bare, he kissed each one. "These fingers caress the piano keys lovingly, bringing forth beautiful music."

She laughed softly. "I have not even had a chance to practice since we came here."

"And the piano stands quite forlorn. Do not ignore that part of yourself."

"I must be blushing by now."

"Pink cheeks, the brilliant shine in your golden eyes, that comes from you."

He placed a soft kiss on her neck, just beneath her ear, and with a gasp, she bent her head to offer more to him. Her lips had been so sensitive to him—it was amazing that even her neck prickled with sensation at his touch. When he gently bit her earlobe, she shuddered.

He took her face in his hands and tilted her

toward him. She was ready for his mouth this time, and enjoyed the masterful way his tongue explored her mouth, then met her own. She gasped and moaned, then found herself slowly falling backward on the sofa as he leaned over her. They continued urgent kisses, while his hand moved from her waist and slowly up her bodice, cupping her breast through the corset, such a scandalous thing.

She enjoyed the naughtiness a moment too long, then broke the kiss with a gasp. "It is almost time for dinner. A servant could come looking for us any moment."

He pressed kisses down her throat, dipping his tongue in the hollow at its base. "I locked the door."

"But that is so suspicious."

"We are engaged—"

"We are not!"

"Then let us be lovers."

"No, please, I cannot think about such things now."

He rose away from her, drawing her back upright by both hands.

"My glove?" she asked, feeling for it all around her.

"On the floor." He put it into her hands. "I have not lost hope that you will change your mind."

"I cannot tell you what to think," she said shakily, rising to her feet and then catching the back of the nearby chair to steady herself.

Putting his arm around her waist from behind, he pulled her up against him and whispered into her hair, "Your body wants me."

"Then thank goodness my mind rules my body."

He chuckled, then released her. "I will leave you to your sister's company this evening, as I have an early meeting tomorrow."

"You will not come?"

"Is that regret I hear?"

"I—I only wish to plan my schedule."

"Liar," he whispered, and kissed her cheek. "I will come to you, but I don't know when."

"You are busy, Robert. I do not need to be coddled."

"I have taken Molly's place, and I will not let you down."

"I do have letters to write . . ."

"My tutor used to claim I had excellent penmanship, probably far superior to your sister."

"I would never ask Blythe to write my letters." And that seemed so sad to her.

He must have realized it, for he said nothing for a moment.

"Have a good evening, Audrey."

And then he was gone, and the room seemed so empty without him. She tugged her glove back on, buttoning it at the wrist, trying not to think of his mouth there. Oh, she had to stop this longing.

She considered the piano, so neglected, the perfect thing to occupy her mind. Seating herself on the bench, she lifted the cover and played several chords. The instrument wasn't exactly in tune, but close enough. She started playing, and lost herself in the beauty of such pure, blissful sound. She didn't know how long she played, but when at last she paused between songs, she heard soft clapping.

"As beautiful as always," Blythe said.

Audrey heard honesty rather than jealousy, and smiled. "Thank you. Before he left, Robert mentioned I had not played since we arrived."

"And it's obvious, because as I came downstairs, Mrs. Sanford and both her children were standing in the hall, entranced."

"Oh." Audrey bent her head, surprised. Music had always separated Blythe and her.

"And then I stepped inside, and for just a moment, I saw you as others must when you play, because it seemed as if you were not blind." And then in a contemplative voice, "I have no real memory of that."

"You were but two when we both took ill."

"I remember being very, very hot."

"I, as well. What else do you remember?"

Blythe said nothing for a moment, and Audrey wondered if she'd gone too far. Her sister was always a woman who lived for the future, and what it might hold for her.

"Nothing," Blythe said woodenly. "I was two, as you said."

But for a moment, Audrey thought she'd been about to say something else.

When Robert arrived at Rose Cottage midmorning the next day, Francis told him that Audrey and her sister had gone to Hedgerley. Robert couldn't be surprised that Blythe would need something to do. Why hadn't she escorted her sister to their own village? Audrey seemed to want to put it behind her and start anew, but Robert wasn't so forgiving. He worried that Miss Collins would fall into her old family patterns and try to control Audrey's every move.

Gray clouds overhead threatened rain, but that didn't stop him from leaving Rose Cottage. As he rode down the country lane, the dark clouds scudding away, he remembered the sweet smell of Audrey's neck, the blush that had swept her face and down beneath her bodice. He'd longed to explore, though one touch of the forbidden had made her stop. But he'd gone a step further, and if he'd been patient . . .

He urged his horse into a trot, the better to put such rousing memories aside.

He was almost relieved when it was difficult to find the sisters. No crowds gathered somewhere to stare, no fuss being made. But the first time he'd escorted Audrey there, he'd seen the looks, heard the whispers, and worried that it would be far worse when he wasn't there to deflect it.

He found the women at the millinery, where Miss Collins was trying on hats, looking in a mirror and discussing a purchase with the fawning owner, an older woman corseted into too tight a gown.

As Robert closed the door behind him, he saw Audrey seated on a stool, her face lifted to the sunlight streaming between parting clouds through the plate-glass windows. Her fingers touched a selection of ribbons.

She cocked her head toward the door, and as he walked toward her, her expression brightened. "Lord Knightsbridge."

It wasn't a question.

He grinned and lifted her gloved hand to kiss the back. "Mrs. Blake."

She blushed prettily and drew her hand back as if their affection should be private. "I am surprised you joined our ladies' shopping expedition."

He glanced at her sister, who gave him a polite smile, then returned to the adoration of her mirror. To Audrey, he said, "I was concerned Miss Collins might fall back on old habits in the village and forget all about you. Is she helping you to select a bonnet, too?"

"She asked, and I said she could go first."

He released the breath he didn't know he'd been holding. "Very well, then." It seemed positively unmanly to be concerned that a woman might not be able to shop.

Audrey smiled at him, then, a secret smile that said she understood him. He felt revealed to her in a way he'd never expected with a woman—especially a blind woman. It wasn't a comfortable feeling.

"I admit," Audrey continued in a lower voice, "that I have been using this day to see if my sister really means to change her treatment of me."

"And so far?"

"So far, so good. We do have firm disagreements on how a lady should spend her day. I delayed our departure this morn so I could consult with Mrs. Sanford, leading my sister to say I am too concerned with details rather than enjoyments."

"You spent your life concerned with the details she ignored," he said stiffly.

Audrey sighed. "Managing our household gave me some measure of control in the little world I had been permitted. Now I have the freedoms of a larger world, and I find I still fall back on my old, managing ways. But I am coping. You are not to worry about me," she admonished in a mock stern voice.

He had made it his duty to see her happy and contented, and he was concerned that the arrival of her sister would make things worse.

As Audrey took her turn trying on bonnets and hats, Robert watched her force happiness on Miss Collins, who still seemed reserved and tenuous, as if she expected people to shun them because of Audrey's debility.

Late morning, he escorted them through a stiff wind to a coffee house that faced the village green. While their hands curled around steaming cups of coffee, warming them from the inside out, Audrey smiled at her sister.

"Thank you for helping me to choose a bonnet. I do believe a new one makes me feel prettier."

"You're very welcome," Miss Collins said, her gaze contemplating her coffee.

Audrey took another sip and let out a sigh. "That tastes good. I like the fact that I can come into the village and enjoy such things. Blythe, since you think my concern for charity is too obvious, can you think of other ways I could better involve myself with the village and its people?"

Miss Collins set down her cup and it rattled the saucer. She glanced at Robert a bit wide-eyed, obviously surprised and flustered.

"I imagine," she said slowly, "that you should entertain. And then they will reciprocate."

"Very true," Audrey mused. "Once they get to know me, my opinion will have more merit. I would really like to discuss housing. From speaking with my tenants, I do see a need for more building of humble, yet sound, housing."

"Audrey, we are women," Miss Collins said, her expression bewildered. "Why would you think the men would care about our opinions on anything other than dinner parties and children and the running of households?"

Robert could tell Audrey hesitated to say the truth, that she'd spent too many years powerless in her home, and wouldn't live that way any longer.

"Blythe, I am a landowner now, and my concerns are for many more people than myself. I know this world is slanted toward men, but if I have good ideas, why should they not listen?"

"Speaking as the only man at this table," Robert

said dryly, "I find myself understanding Miss Collins's concerns. Many men do not want a woman's opinion."

"And are you one of them, my lord?" Miss Collins demanded.

A little protective toward Audrey. A good sign. "I should hope my assistance in escorting Mrs. Blake to her home, and being available for support rather than domination, has proven my restraint."

Miss Collins didn't look reassured. So she didn't trust him, and he didn't trust her. Interesting.

He turned to Audrey. "I did learn something from my steward this morning. While I was gone, there was a need for humble cottages for short-term agricultural workers. Because of this, some cottagers were forced to move into the village and are now living in the close quarters of rooming houses. I know this is the way of the world, but I don't like it. Perhaps we can discuss the building of more cottages with parish magistrates."

Audrey smiled. "I'd like that!"

He thought Miss Collins might have wanted to roll her eyes.

"Excuse me, Mrs. Blake?"

A matronly woman with a reticule clutched beneath her ample bosom approached. Robert rose, and when she looked up at him, her lips parted until she collected herself.

"Lord Knightsbridge," she said, giving a little curtsy.

He bowed. "Ma'am."

"I feel very forward introducing myself to you."

"Oh, allow me," Audrey said. "You're Mrs. Edgeworth, are you not?"

"I—you remember!" Mrs. Edgeworth said, her expression one of surprise.

"I remember meeting you at the grocer's. You have a distinctive voice, ma'am. Please allow me to introduce you to Lord Knightsbridge, and to my sister, Miss Collins."

"Your sister! How wonderful to have family nearby."

"If only she could be closer, but I am happy regardless."

"Well, Mrs. Warton mentioned visiting you, and I thought how wonderful it would be to introduce you to more of our parish. Might I send you an invitation to tea?"

"I would love that."

"Then I will not keep you. It was a pleasure meeting you both, Lord Knightsbridge and Miss Collins."

And with a little bobbing nod of her head, she turned and left the coffee house.

But after she'd gone, Audrey's smile faded.

"Is something wrong?" Robert asked.

"I hope her invitation is for after Molly is well. I don't wish to inconvenience Mrs. Edgeworth by making her have to take care of me."

Miss Collins looked troubled, and Robert was glad she didn't speak and reveal that to Audrey.

"It will work out," he insisted. "I will go with you if Molly cannot."

But it was the wrong thing to say.

"I do not want people to feel beholden on my behalf," she said, frowning. "Soon they will all treat me like an invalid, if I cannot be seen to stand on my own."

"Maybe you're expecting too much of yourself," Miss Collins said at last.

Robert grimaced, even as Audrey reddened.

"I expect *much* of myself, Blythe," she said coolly. "If I didn't, I would still be sitting with a blanket on my lap in the corner Father put me in."

"I didn't mean . . ." Miss Collins trailed off.

Robert thought that she did mean it, but hadn't quite understood how it would hurt Audrey.

"I think it's time to go home," Audrey said, carefully placing her napkin beside her coffee cup.

Chapter 15

⸻⸺◦◦⸻⸺

Audrey was very disappointed in herself during the short carriage ride home. Robert rode his horse beside them, and she wondered if her pique had driven even amiable Robert to seek some time away from her.

She was starting a new chapter in her life, and her plan had always been to leave the old one behind. Molly's illness had made her realize how much she really depended on people. To hear Blythe's belief that Audrey should not expect so much of herself? It was frustrating and sad and—

Oh, she didn't know what. She didn't *want* to be so dependent, had thought the freedom of living in her own home would change everything. But that couldn't happen, could it? Not really—not ever.

And now she was depending on Robert as much as she'd ever depended on Molly, and because his kisses and praises flattered her, she'd thought it was different. But was it?

Yet . . . she was a woman, and females were powerless in the world—except for Queen Victoria. How could she expect herself to be different, and how could she expect *Blythe* to be different?

"We're almost home," Blythe said softly. "Rose Cottage looks pretty up on the hill."

Home. And Audrey would do well to remember and be grateful.

"Thank you, Blythe. I want to apologize for snapping at you. You were trying to make me feel better, and I took out all my frustrations on you. My limitations are not your fault."

"That is kind of you."

For a moment, Audrey thought Blythe would say more, but she didn't, and soon Audrey could feel the sway as the carriage rounded the drive.

When the door opened, Blythe said, "Good day, Mr. Sanford."

Mr. Sanford? Audrey thought. Why hadn't Francis met them? "Mr. Sanford, is something wrong? Has Molly relapsed?"

Audrey felt herself the center of attention, knowing that Blythe stared at her, and perhaps Mr. Sanford and Robert, too.

"No, ma'am," Mr. Sanford said in his rumbling voice. "My pardon if I startled ye, but I just spotted a flock of pheasant down near the pond. Lord Knightsbridge had asked about the shootin' hereabouts, and I thought he'd like to give them a go."

Audrey felt the tension of the morning drain out of her, leaving her exhausted and a bit embarrassed. "Oh, of course. Robert, you should do that. You are a guest here, after all. And you can tell me how good the hunting conditions are."

"Our brother might like to know that," Blythe suggested.

Audrey smiled at her, feeling forgiven.

"Mrs. Blake," Mr. Sanford said, "why do ye not join his lordship? Both of ye ladies. Molly tells me wife ye haven't had yer normal stroll. She worries about ye. And she packed a picnic meal."

Who worries about me—Molly or your wife? Audrey almost said aloud. His invitation was very strange—including the picnic meal. She told herself not to be suspicious—maybe the groundskeeper was simply trying to be more friendly.

"I will give it some thought, Mr. Sanford. Lord Knightsbridge, might I speak to you in private?"

"I'm going to my room to rest before luncheon," Blythe said. "Shall I take your new bonnet inside?"

"Thank you," Audrey said, handing over the box.

Robert took her arm and led her away from the carriage, which she could hear jingling as the Collins coachman drove it away.

"Is something wrong?" Robert asked quietly.

"I find it . . . peculiar that today Mr. Sanford wants me to accompany you shooting, and yesterday, Blythe thought he was following us about the garden. His kindness has always seemed grudging. So this invitation makes me feel that he wants me away from the house."

"Wait—you thought he was following you?"

"Blythe said he was."

"He could have been concerned about your progress around the estate. Neither you nor your sister knows the grounds."

"We would hardly hike in any wooded terrain," she said dryly. "I have simply begun to feel that their poor behavior as servants is more of a distraction to hide something else, something important enough to risk being let go, rather than just being directed personally at me. Would you do me the favor of letting him guide you this afternoon?"

"Of course. But if he wants you away from the house, there could be something going on right now."

"I don't get that feeling, do you? Or is there something in his expression I can't see?"

"No. He did allow Miss Collins to leave without looking too worried."

"Then you go with him, and I'll discover if something's going on inside." She could sense his hesitation. "Robert, I will be fine. I do not fear anyone means me harm."

"Very well." He raised his voice. "Sanford? Do you have a gun I can use?"

"Aye, milord."

"Then go prepare it, and after I escort Mrs. Blake to the house, I will return."

At the door, she insisted he go back. "I'm fine within, Robert."

"This isn't going to take long," he insisted.

"You're such a crack shot, you'll have all our pheasants killed in no time?"

"Audrey—"

"Just go," she said softly, patting his arm before he released hers.

She felt him kiss her hand.

"Take care," he warned.

When she was alone in her entrance hall, she stood still, listening. Francis was obviously not there, and she couldn't hear his sister cleaning in any of the nearby rooms.

And then she heard a child wail from the back of the house.

For just a moment, she stiffened, swept up again in that old grief, that feeling that a part of life had passed her by—the painful part, she reminded herself. She didn't want this stab of pain any more.

But the pain receded, and she realized who the child must be—the Sanfords' grandchild.

Why would Mr. Sanford try to keep her away? It made no sense—unless he wanted his wife free to enjoy the child without having to work, as she would if Audrey were home. Of course, Audrey would allow her some personal time. But maybe they didn't know that.

Feeling better, she walked toward the rear hall, hand outstretched so she wouldn't miss the doorway. As she walked quietly, she could hear the murmur of women's voices, then the fretful child forcefully saying, "No!"

Audrey had to smile. She stepped inside the kitchen, and almost all sound ceased.

"Mrs. Blake, you've returned," Mrs. Sanford said.

The child gave a squeal, as if someone had picked him up.

"I have. I would enjoy meeting your guests."

"Of course, ma'am. May I introduce my daughter, Louisa Roebuck, and her son, Arthur?"

"How wonderful to meet you," Audrey said. "I'm glad you were finally able to visit."

"Th-thank you, ma'am," the young woman said in a timid voice. "I didn't mean to be intrudin'."

"No intrusion at all. I'd been wondering when I would meet you. How old is your little boy?"

"Two years old, ma'am."

Two years, Audrey thought, keeping her smile in place. That was how old her own son would have been. Every so often, she would think on the date, and wonder what he would have been doing, had he lived.

The little boy gave another squeal.

"Please, I hope you are not holding him back on my account. Does he want to explore?"

"We're teachin' him the dangers of the kitchen," Mrs. Sanford said. "And he's not payin' much attention."

Audrey laughed. "He sounds like any child. I heard his 'No!' from down the hall." She turned toward where she thought the young woman was sitting. "I would like to express my condolences on the death of your husband, Louisa. I well understand your grief at his loss." But did she? She hadn't loved Martin. Perhaps this girl knew more about love than Audrey ever would, since she'd never been that close to anyone—and didn't plan to be, ever.

She heard Robert's wicked voice in her mind, remembered his touch, and then banished the thought quickly.

"Thank you, ma'am," Louisa said.

She spoke so softly that even Audrey with her sensitive hearing barely heard it. "Well, I'll leave you to your visit. Stay as long as you'd like,

Louisa." Now the Sanford family should know they had nothing to fear from her. Maybe things would be better.

"But your luncheon, Mrs. Blake," the house-keeper began.

"You enjoy your meal together. Just send up a tray for Molly and me to her room. Is Evelyn with her?"

"I'm here, ma'am," the maid piped up.

Audrey had more than once asked the servants to always tell her who was in the room, but she would let it go, since Louisa was visiting.

"I think Francis was going to check up on her before trimmin' the lamps," Evelyn continued.

Francis and Molly seemed to have quite the friendship, Audrey thought, amused. She left the kitchen and ascended to the servants' quarters. She heard laughter, Francis's in the corridor, as if he stood in the doorway of Molly's room.

"Mornin', Mrs. Blake," he said cautiously.

"I think it might be almost afternoon, Francis," Audrey said cheerfully. "How is Molly doing?"

"I'm well!" Molly called. "Too well to be trapped up here."

"The doctor will be the judge. Francis, your mother will be preparing a luncheon tray for Molly and myself. Please bring it up when it's ready."

"Yes, ma'am."

She heard his big boots clomping down the stairs.

"So how was your expedition?" Molly asked.

Audrey briefly told her about buying a bonnet with Blythe, and a future invitation to tea.

"A success then!" Molly said with satisfaction in her voice. "I'm not surprised."

"But then I arrived home." She explained about Mr. Sanford's peculiar behavior, and finding the Sanford grandchild. Lowering her voice, she murmured, "It was as if they didn't want me to meet their daughter."

"That doesn't make sense," Molly insisted. "Although come to think of it, Francis hasn't mentioned her at all."

Audrey bit her lip, trying to hide a smile.

"Now don't give me that look," Molly said. "He's a nice, friendly man who makes the hours up here not so dreary with his brief visits."

"Then I'm glad for you. But I think, now that I've met and accepted Louisa, perhaps my servants will at least realize I mean them no harm. I've told them she could visit anytime, and now maybe they'll believe me." She gave Molly a smile. "Are you hungry? They'll be bringing up a tray soon that we can share."

"I could eat in the kitchen," Molly grumbled. "I've started standing up, just to test my legs."

"And how are they working?"

After a faint pause, she said, "Better."

"Hmm, why do I not believe you?"

"You could at least let me begin to write for you."

"Lord Knightsbridge has volunteered."

"Now that's a fiancé," Molly said with admiration.

He was far too wonderful to her, Audrey agreed silently. And too dependable.

"I'll let his lordship take over for me another day or two," Molly teased.

Audrey wasn't sure how much longer she could let that happen.

At dinner that evening, Blythe pleaded a headache and retired to her room, leaving Audrey to entertain Robert. He had Francis leave the serving dishes, then close the doors behind him.

Audrey felt a little thrill at being alone with him. "That's not very nice of you."

"We have much to discuss," he insisted. "We didn't have a chance while I was writing your letters—not that there were many."

"Just to my father and brother," she insisted.

"And short ones at that, although I do understand." He paused. "You had no female friends to write to?"

"None," she said, keeping her voice brisk and impassive. "But that is about to change. I've already met Mrs. Warton and Mrs. Edgeworth. Louisa Roebuck is about my age, although it might be inappropriate to cultivate her friendship. But she is a widow, too."

"Louisa Roebuck?" he asked blankly.

"Oh, I forgot to mention it while we were writing letters." She lowered her voice. "Or to be more accurate, I chose not to mention her until I was certain we were alone. Mr. Sanford was trying to distract me from his widowed daughter and grandson. I believe they might all have worried I would punish them for seeing her."

"Do you think that's what all the fuss has been about?"

Audrey hesitated. "I don't know. Today's attempt at distraction made some sort of sense, but causing trouble for me? I don't know what purpose it serves."

"To drive you away?"

"By now they must know I won't go."

"Unless they escalate their attacks."

"Attacks? This is not a battleground, Robert," she said, shaking her head.

"They're making it into one," he said coldly.

Just hearing his tone of voice made her not want to get on his bad side. But the fact that he was so concerned on her behalf gave her a feeling of safety she'd never known before.

It was temporary, she reminded herself sternly. She had to discover her own safety.

"You'll be happy to know your missing ledgers turned up."

"Where?" she demanded.

"In your study, beneath a stack of books. I know they weren't there before."

"How frustrating! Did you have a chance to glance through the most recent one?"

"Yes, and if memory serves, at least the last few pages seemed identical to Mr. Drayton's copy. It may have simply been another prank to annoy you. But we'll do a more thorough comparison the next time he visits."

"Speaking of pranks, you said your shooting adventure went well, but did you mean it?"

"It was fine. Mr. Sanford was knowledgeable of the grounds and the hunting. It appears it really was just a ruse to keep all of us away. I don't like it. Why is this daughter so fragile? Did she seem morose?"

"No, simply shy, and embarrassed that her little boy was misbehaving. The next time she visits, I'll make more of an effort to converse with her."

"If they let you," he mused darkly.

But she didn't want to consider that. "I'm going

to discuss in detail with Mr. Drayton the idea of having a feast for my tenants. Can you think of some suggestions?"

She could tell he didn't like being distracted from his concerns, but soon he was just as involved in the idea as she was.

But her own concerns continued to simmer.

The next day, Audrey received an invitation for tea at Mrs. Edgeworth's. On the following day, she and Blythe went at the appropriate hour. Blythe had been quite insistent that Audrey didn't need Molly or Lord Knightsbridge, and Audrey told herself she was like any normal woman, attending an event with her sister.

It was actually a good feeling, and so rare. She didn't know what was going on with Blythe's conscience, or how long her sister intended to visit, but Audrey wasn't questioning it.

Robert had had to go to London on business, so it had been a quiet few days without him. Blythe still seemed to think Audrey's days could be spent in ladylike relaxation and pastimes, and Audrey was feeling a bit frustrated with her. Didn't her sister realize that someday she'd have her own household?

Mrs. Edgeworth lived in a little stone house within the village boundaries. Audrey already knew from Mrs. Sanford that the woman was a widow who considered herself one of the village matriarchs. She was stern but fair, and tireless in her volunteer work. She sounded like the perfect person for Audrey to get to know. There were four other ladies in attendance: Mrs. Warton, the vicar's middle-aged wife; her daughter, Miss Warton, newly engaged, whose voice rang with happiness that still sounded surprised about her good fortune; Lady Flitcroft, the wife of a local baronet, who was so quiet Audrey often forgot she was in the room; and Miss Yardley, a young friend of Miss Warton's, who was mostly focused on her coming-out next Season in London.

Audrey had sensed their curiosity as she and Blythe entered the parlor, but they'd seemed eager to know her. Her status as the blind future countess must be very intriguing. She hoped to win them over as herself, so that when she broke off the engagement, they'd be sympathetic friends.

When Mrs. Warton went off to see why the sandwiches she'd ordered hadn't arrived, and Blythe was speaking to Miss Warton on her other side, Audrey spoke to Miss Yardley, seated to her left.

"I'm sorry that Mrs. Warton is embarrassed by her servants," Audrey said, shaking her head. "We can be so dependent on them. At least I am, although I imagine that is obvious."

Miss Yardley lowered her voice and seemed to lean nearer. "If you don't mind a little gossip, I am very curious about your servants."

"Why is that?" Audrey asked politely.

"I heard that Louisa Sanford is trying to say she went away to be married."

"I've been told her name is Louisa Roebuck," Audrey said cautiously.

"My mother's housekeeper claims that is all fiction to try to protect her reputation. She was never married!" Miss Yardley's voice was breathless with the intrigue.

The tea seemed to settle uneasily in Audrey's stomach. "You are claiming the child is illegitimate?"

"My housekeeper insists it is so! She says Louisa was always fast, and sadly reaped what she sowed. She should have left Hedgerley permanently, but apparently Mrs. Sanford didn't wish to force her, so she returned with this fiction of a dead husband."

"That is very sad," Audrey murmured. "I hope it is not true."

Miss Yardley, probably sensing that Audrey wasn't going to add any gossip, turned to the lady on her other side, leaving Audrey to think troubled thoughts.

Was this the secret that the Sanfords had

been hiding, their daughter's shame? By driving Audrey away, did they think they could move Louisa back to Rose Cottage with them?

After light sandwiches, iced cakes, and more discussion of the Female Aid Society's next fundraising dance in the local Assembly room, Audrey and Blythe rode home in the curricle. Blythe had been delighted to drive, and Audrey found herself teasing that someday Blythe would have to let *her* drive on a flat, open road.

They spoke briefly about the various guests, and Blythe seemed more cautious than Audrey about Audrey's acceptance.

"I know they probably stared at me," Audrey said. "I don't mind, since their behavior put me at ease. Though you had difficulty accepting my blindness, others might be able to see past it."

And then Blythe burst into tears, and Audrey wondered if she was going to have to take over the reins anyway.

"I'm sorry," Audrey said. "Do dry your eyes, Blythe. We're putting the past behind us, remember? I should not have brought it up."

But although Blythe was able to finish driving home, she was not to be consoled that day, and fled to spend the rest of it in her room. This sensitive side to her sister was new, and Audrey didn't know what to make of it.

She played mournful tunes on the piano and tried to consider what she should do about the rumors concerning the Sanfords' oldest daughter, and wished she could discuss it with Robert. She missed him far too much for a woman who firmly believed she could live without a husband. Was it her place to confront them, so they knew what people were saying? Or perhaps they didn't care, as long as they misled *her*, the woman who had the power to let the entire family go. Then, how would they support their grandchild?

By nightfall, she'd decided to do nothing—their shame wasn't her business, and perhaps the gossip wasn't even true. Yet, it would make more sense, why they were trying to mislead her . . .

Wouldn't it?

Chapter 16

Before dinner the next day, Audrey waited in the drawing room for Blythe, feeling chilled from the dreary, misty rain that had fallen all day. She may not have been able to see it, but the steady patter of rain was like someone strumming every last nerve. The dampness seemed to seep into the house. She'd been warm in Molly's bedroom, where Molly had begun to write the invitations for the new annual tenants' feast. It would take several days to do, since Molly still needed to rest after an hour of writing.

But since Audrey had come downstairs, she'd begun to shiver. With a sudden determination to prove that she wasn't helpless, she knelt before the hearth and felt the empty coal grate. There was a bucket of coal nearby, and plenty of kindling. So she began to pile the kindling, and with a match, encouraged a steady flame, feeling the heat with her hands, trying to judge it. The kindling had to be hot enough to spark the coal. Eventually she shoveled on small coal chips and waited for their ignition, feeling even that little bit of warmth.

"So you're doing the work of your servants now?" Robert suddenly asked.

She gave a start and had to put out a hand to keep from toppling into the coal grate. "My word, Robert, what happened to our signals?"

"I didn't think we ever settled on one."

"There was that handy invention, the knock," she said dryly.

But even as she tried to be calm and sarcastic and oh so above it all, her heart pounded at the sound of his voice, and she felt all warm and happy inside.

Oh, this wasn't good. She was getting too caught up in him, too used to his help, his presence, his sensual attention.

She swallowed. "I didn't want to bother the servants as they prepared for dinner. I tried to do this myself."

"Not bad," he said, coming to stand above her.

She could almost feel the warmth of him, the vibrancy, as he stood beside her, his limbs so near.

"I think the coal chips are hot enough to add larger. Shall I?"

"No," she said, taking up the little shovel again, and by the sensation of warmth, adding more large pieces. She heard a few fall off, but that didn't matter. At last, she stood up, dusting her hands against each other, knowing she would have to wash up before dinner. "How was London?"

"Still rather sparse. But your sister seemed to put word in the right ears, for everywhere I went, people asked about our engagement. You are the mysterious woman no one has ever met, and you swept aside my normal soldier's caution."

"Powerful, aren't I?" But she couldn't help her laughter.

"One of my distant cousins wanted to host an engagement party."

Her laughter died. "Oh, my. I'm so sorry."

"Don't be. It's the first time we've ever taken notice of each other. And, of course, I am an earl, and to host such an event would be quite the accomplishment."

"You're so cynical. Perhaps he just wants to get to know you, since you've been gone nine years."

"Maybe."

She heard his approach, and suddenly, she wanted to forestall however he might attempt to weaken her senses. "The servants tried another little trick."

"Doing what?" he asked flatly.

"They said there was no milk for breakfast, that the dairymaid had been having problems with our cows."

"Audrey—"

"So I went out to the dairy barn myself, only to hear that the dairymaid had sent in the pails before dawn, as she did every morning."

"Damn those Sanfords."

She laughed. "I'm starting to find it all amusing. So I told them they must have misplaced the pails, and please make certain I had some at lunch. They'll have to try harder than that."

"You almost sound like you're enjoying this little competition."

"It's a challenge I mean to win."

"Hold still," he suddenly said, from much closer.

She gave a little gasp as he cupped her face with one hand, and used the thumb of his other to wipe down her cheek.

"Coal dust," he murmured.

He didn't move away, and she stood there, her face so warm, cradled in the strength of his rough hand. Without even knowing what she meant to do, she slid her hands up his chest, then neck, until she felt his rough cheeks.

"Let me see you," she whispered.

"Of course," was his hoarse answer. "But how?"

"Like this."

Beneath her exploring fingers, his cheekbones were high and proud, and the hollows below showed his lean face. His chin was square and blunt, and his lips, which had felt soft against hers, had a full lower lip, and a more narrow upper. His nose was as lean as the rest of his face, with a little bump near the bridge.

"You broke your nose?"

"Not all by myself."

She smiled, even as she continued her exploration. She was gentle moving over his closed eyelids, felt the blunt, manly shape of his brow and the silkiness of his hair falling forward over it.

"You are very handsome," she murmured, still letting her fingers trail through his hair above his ears, then sliding back over his scalp and to his neck again.

"Can you imagine what I look like, from a simple touch?" he asked.

"I think so. But I've always been able to imagine you. It's your voice, so very evocative, so . . . different."

Robert didn't have to imagine at all. He could drink in the beauty of her, even as he held her face in his hands. Her full moist lips were meant for his kisses, and those eyes might not see him, but they decorated her face with golden light, the light of her gentle spirit within.

He kissed her then, each of them holding the other's face, their bodies swaying against each other, each brush of her breasts against his chest sending a hot wave of desire straight to his groin.

"Oh, I'm so sorry!"

He lifted his head to see Miss Collins standing in the doorway, her gaze taking them in before turning aside.

Audrey stepped away so quickly, he had to grab her to make sure she didn't send her skirt sweeping across the coal grate.

"I'm not going to fall," she said crossly, her face red with embarrassment.

"I—I should have knocked," Miss Collins said, "but the door was open."

Robert gave her a smile. "It was simply the kiss of an engaged couple who'd been separated too long."

"I'm sorry three days was too long for you," Audrey said with faint amusement.

He grinned down at her. "It was too long for you, too."

Miss Collins frowned as she stepped farther into the room. "Audrey, what is that dirt across your skirt?"

Audrey winced. "It must be coal dust."

"Did you fall into the hearth?" Miss Collins asked, her voice rising in worry.

"Not at all. I started the coal fire myself and couldn't see where I knelt."

"But that is the servants' duty," Miss Collins said in bewilderment.

"And I can do it almost as well. I enjoyed the challenge."

"And the dirt?" her sister continued.

"I don't always have to be a burden," Audrey said, brushing past Robert and heading toward her sister. "Excuse me while I change."

"I never said you were a burden," Miss Collins called.

To her credit, she sounded forlorn. Perhaps there really was hope for Audrey and her sister to become closer.

Miss Collins came back inside and went to the window, looking out as if she could find the answers to all her problems in the misty rain. Or else not wanting to face him.

"Lord Knightsbridge, did you get wet on your ride over?" she finally asked.

"My cloak kept the worst from me. And I'm used to dealing with the weather."

"Ah, I had almost forgotten. Was there even snow in India?"

"Worse snow than England usually sees, at least in the mountains of Afghanistan."

The silence lengthened again.

"What do you think of this situation with the staff?" Robert asked in a low voice.

Miss Collins glanced at him over her shoulder. "You mean their furtive behavior? It's almost as if they meant to hide the baby from us. Considering they don't know of Audrey's grief after her own died, it doesn't make sense."

He must have gaped at her, for her eyes went wide and she covered her mouth.

"She never told you," Miss Collins whispered. "Oh, heavens, what have I done but reveal secrets that weren't mine to reveal?"

"She lost a baby?" It was as if the earth moved under his feet, changing everything he ever thought he could do for her. "Tell me."

"But I shouldn't—"

"You already did, and unless you want me to tell her exactly where I found out, you will finish explaining this to me." He walked toward her, each syllable emphasized with his footfalls.

Miss Collins squeezed her eyes shut. "It must have been too painful for her to speak of. She grieved far worse for the baby than she ever did for her husband."

"She was with child when he left."

She nodded, her head bobbing even as the first tear spilled down her cheek.

"Tell me everything," he ordered, in the voice he used when he expected to be obeyed.

Miss Collins swallowed. "She found out just

after Mr. Blake left. After word of his death, she went into labor early and the babe was born dead. A little boy . . ." She trailed off for a moment, then seemed to rally as she looked him in the eye. "My father was relieved. His attitude . . . it sickened me. I admit I was uncertain about Audrey's ability to raise a child, and there are always those who believe a blind woman could also give birth to a blind baby, but . . . her grief was terrible to witness, and for some time, I worried over the state of her health and mind."

Robert found himself sitting down heavily in a chair, his hands moving through his hair to clasp his bent neck as he stared at the floor. Miss Collins's words pounded into him as if they were blows landed from a boxer.

"I think this house saved her, in some sense. She began to concentrate on Rose Cottage, and her future independence, and even when Father refused to permit her departure, she never gave up."

She paused a long moment, as if waiting for him to speak, but he had no words.

"She must not have wanted your pity," Miss Collins continued in a low voice.

Pity? Robert felt far more than that—guilt, gut-clenching guilt that a decision he'd help make to release prisoners, a decision against the orders of his commander, a decision he just assumed was right and just, had not only taken the lives of three good soldiers, including Audrey's husband, but had caused the death of her unborn child. He couldn't make that right with just an escort to her new home and some shaky estate advice. My God, he'd only been doing what was convenient for him, as if he knew best—another trait of his father's.

No, he'd give her what every woman deserved— marriage, and the chance to have another baby.

He would bring admiration and desire to this marriage, not pity, and *tonnish* marriages often began with less.

"My lord?" Miss Collins said in a hesitant voice.

He lifted his head, filled with a sense of purpose he hadn't felt since he'd sold his army commission. "Yes?"

"Are you going to tell Audrey you know about the baby?"

"No. I want her to tell me herself."

"Oh." She looked relieved, even as she used her fingers to dab at the corners of her eyes. "Whatever you think best."

They spent several minutes in silence, Miss Collins staring at the window that ran with rivulets of rain, and Robert sitting still, seeing nothing as he tried not to imagine Audrey's grief.

When Audrey returned, he felt in control again,

certain that he was at last doing the right thing. He smiled at her, warm with the knowledge that he'd never let her go. The hard part was going to be convincing her that they should make their engagement real. He had time to proceed slowly. After all, she opened to him more and more with every kiss and caress.

He met her halfway across the room, taking her hands, startling her.

"Sorry," he murmured, raising her gloved hands to his lips.

"I haven't been gone that long," she said with amusement.

"It seemed long." And that wasn't a false statement. His whole life and purpose had changed since she'd been gone, and it felt good.

"I imagine you're hungry," she said. "Shall we go in to the dining room?"

He was becoming used to the three of them eating together like a family. As he helped each of them into their chair, and then took his own, he said, "I found I couldn't wait to be back here sharing a meal with the both of you. The dining rooms at Knightsbridge Hall are cavernous and full of echoes, and I have no one to talk to."

"Oh, that sounds lonely," Audrey said.

"Does it?" He tried to put meaning into those words, knowing he couldn't say, because of Miss

Collins, that he had thought Audrey wanted endless evenings alone.

She blushed as she took a sip of her wine, as if maybe she understood his point, yet determination lifted her chin. She'd worked too hard for her approaching independence to care about meals alone. And she'd have Molly—he could see her mind working. But Molly might want a life, too. Robert had heard about Francis mooning over her.

"You must admit," Audrey began, "that you missed peace and quiet when you were in the army."

"Sometimes. But I'd like voices and laughter in my home, and right now there's only the silent servants and me."

"Soon there'll be Audrey," Miss Collins pointed out.

"Yes, and I'm glad," Robert said quietly.

Audrey shot him a quick, bewildered look. She didn't know where he was going with this.

"Audrey has always been in my life," Miss Collins said quietly.

Audrey and Robert both turned toward her.

"I don't remember much before the scarlet fever, but I think you held me all the time." Miss Collins wasn't looking at either of them, her head turned just to the side.

"I taught you to walk," Audrey whispered.

"Your first baby smiles were for me. I remember what they looked like, so sweet and loving."

A single tear ran down Miss Collins's cheek. "I used to feel so guilty that I survived the scarlet fever unscathed."

"Blythe, no! I was so glad of your healthy recovery."

Miss Collins gave a bleak chuckle. "And that made it worse, at least when I was old enough to understand everything. One can only feel guilty for so long, and then one feels . . . angry about it. And suppresses all the guilt anyway."

Robert knew *his* guilt was deserved, and Miss Collins's guilt wasn't, but he understood her better now.

"Blythe," Audrey began quietly.

"No. I don't want your sympathy or your understanding. My behavior doesn't deserve that. I—I don't even know why I told you all this. It doesn't change the past. I—I don't feel particularly hungry right now." Gracefully, she rose to her feet without looking at either of them, and glided from the room.

Robert turned to Audrey, whose head was bent, her palms flat on either side of her place setting.

"Are you all right?" he asked.

She shrugged. "I never knew how she felt. That confession . . . it changes so much."

"You're lucky, you know."

Her smile was faint. "I am? Not according to Blythe."

"I'm not talking about your eyesight. But you have a chance here to make things right with your sister. I would give anything to have that with my brother, dead at fourteen."

"You were . . . twelve, were you not, when he died? What would need to be fixed in such a young relationship between brothers?"

"I told you we were competitive in our school-work, but that doesn't truly explain it. My father always expected the best from us, and I'm assuming he made certain our tutor understood this, and perhaps even feared for his position if we were not exemplary in our studies. Father, of course, wanted us to go off to Eton so he could be proud of our superiority. But our tutor took this to heart, and chose the worst way possible to increase our studies—he pitted Neil and I against each other in everything, and the one who lost out to the other on even the smallest assignment was punished. Competition turned to anger then to hatred. Even at Eton, we had nothing to do with each other, and I felt like he set his friends on me. Whether that was true, I don't even know. And I'll never know. That's the point. I'll never be able to relate to Neil as an adult, to love him as a brother should. But you have that chance, and Blythe is obviously struggling with the past and how to make things better, just like you are."

"You're very wise, Robert," she said softly. "I am sorry for your childhood—for both our childhoods."

"You and Blythe might never have the kind of full respect you want. At least you and I have that for each other."

She looked confused. "I . . . yes, I agree."

"A lot of marriages begin with less than that."

She frowned. "What are you saying?"

"That I want to make this engagement real. I would like to marry you."

She laughed, ending it so abruptly she almost snorted.

He smiled, not taking offense. "You think I'm teasing you."

"And it is quite the joke."

"I'm not teasing. I would like to marry you. We've worked well together these past weeks, and we always have something to talk about. And then there is passion, of course." He took her hand. "When I'm with you, all I can do is think of kissing you."

"Robert, stop," she insisted, pulling her hand away. "The whole point of accepting your help was so that I could live on my own. I am not marrying any man, ever again."

Or bearing such terrible pain—he could hear those unspoken words, now that he knew the whole truth.

"I know why you're saying this," she said, her voice growing sharp. "You pity me, because you think I'm ineffective with my servants."

"That isn't true at all. I see how you consider the servants a challenge to be overcome and won. That is your choice."

"Robert." She shook her head. "You don't even realize what you're saying. You just don't want Society to know you didn't marry the blind girl when you'd promised."

"I don't care what Society thinks of me."

"You talked about being lonely—you won't be that for long. Just wait until the London debutantes discover you're on the market again. You'll be swarmed with invitations."

"Do you think I'm interested in young women fresh from the schoolroom, with no experiences in life? The first thing that goes wrong, they'll flounder. Whereas you are made of stronger stuff. You're a survivor, Audrey, and I can't think of wanting more in a wife."

"Say what you want, Robert, but this is a whim. We'll pretend you never said these things."

"I can't pretend I don't feel this." He got to his feet and pulled her up and into his arms, capturing her mouth in a kiss more bold and urgent than he'd ever allowed himself to show her.

When she moaned, he felt the first flare of satisfaction.

Chapter 17

Audrey was swept up in the urgency of his kiss, heard a gasp at the door, and then heard it shut, but that all seemed distant and unimportant.

Against her mouth, Robert whispered, "Do these feelings mean nothing to you? Are you trying to deny that we're drawn to each other?"

"I—I—" She could barely think, barely remember to breathe. Her head whirled with the passion that made her throw her arms around his neck and hold on as if she depended on him to even stand.

Then the room seemed to spin as Robert lifted her off her feet and set her on the edge of the table, bending over her until she was flat on her back. He stood between her thighs, only their garments separating them. He kissed his way down her neck and to the edge of her bodice, his tongue dipping between her breasts. She didn't know she could feel such passion and desire, for her husband had never even tried to fan those flames.

And then she felt Robert's hands moving beneath her skirts, trailing up her calf that was only covered by the sheerest stocking. It made her squirm, but it didn't tickle, not exactly. And her squirm made her rub her hips against his, and he groaned. She knew what he wanted, what a man wanted to do with his . . . hips.

His hands moved higher, both of them now lifting her knees, spreading her thighs, placing her feet on the table for support. For a wild moment, she wondered if he would try to take her right on the table. Would she be able to stop him—did she *want* to stop him?

Her skirts and petticoats fell around her hips, and his big hands rested on her knees.

"Robert . . ." Her voice was a whisper, and she couldn't think of any other words.

He began to caress the inside of her thighs across the fabric of her drawers, sliding ever closer, an inch at a time, to the intimate depths of her. She felt . . . hot and aching and desperate for something she had no name for, had never known she could even want.

And still his hand kept moving, until her breathing was ragged gasps and her legs trembled. Those magical fingers met in the center, the most private part of her. Nothing had ever felt so sinful, so wondrous. And then he slid his finger inside the slit of her drawers and felt the wetness of her.

She clamped her hand over her mouth to smother what might have been a scream.

She felt him looming above her, his fingers still teasing and circling and probing inside her. His hair brushed her chin, his tongue slid down the short length of her cleavage. When he put his free hand in her corset and pulled down, she felt her right breast spill free from restraint. And then his mouth was there, drawing her nipple into its hot recesses, licking her—

And she came apart inside in a tiny explosion that rocked her into a shuddering, seething mass of heat and pleasure. With a groan, she felt the satisfaction move through her, turning all her muscles into useless tissue. Robert's hot breath fanned her nipple again before he kissed it, and it made her tremble with another arrow of scorching pleasure.

He slowly straightened, and she felt his hands slide back up her thighs, pulling her layers of skirts up and over. Her feet seemed to fall bonelessly to the floor. He took both her hands to pull her upright.

She'd lost the capacity for speech, not knowing

whether to be embarrassed or grateful for an experience her own husband had never even tried to give her on their wedding night.

Or she could be angry.

Robert didn't do this just to pleasure her, to give her a gift.

"That wasn't fair," she whispered through clenched teeth.

He drew in a sharp breath. "What are you talking about? I wanted to make you feel good, to show you what we can share forever."

"No, you wanted to get your own way, to *control* me."

"I did not—"

"You used my body against me, knowing I couldn't even begin to understand what you were doing."

"You were married once."

"And you surely guessed from all I told you that Martin was not a man who cared to show me any kindness once he had what he wanted—and no pleasure either."

"I didn't know," he said quietly.

"Maybe not. But this was still badly done of you. I don't want another man who thinks he can control me—or abandon me in some drafty castle."

"Abandon you?" His voice rose in anger. "I am not Blake."

"And I won't be a countess in a castle, when I can barely move around this small cottage unassisted."

"That's not true. You're doing fine on your own. You're just letting this situation with your staff unnerve you. If you'd just let me be your husband, protect you and care for you—"

"I don't want to be taken care of!" she interrupted. "Do you not see what you're trying to do?"

"I'm trying to propose!"

"And I'm saying no. Please step away from the table." She rose up, mortified that her legs felt shaky and not her own. He'd done that to her, made her body more his than hers, since he knew what to do with it, how to coerce and seduce her. "I need you to leave, Robert."

"Audrey—"

"Just . . . give me a few days. I need to think, and I can't do that right now."

"Very well," he said stiffly. "You think about what I said, what we feel for each other, how things could be between us."

"Oh believe me, I see how things could be," she said bitterly.

He sighed. "Don't, Audrey. Don't turn a thing of mutual pleasure into something sordid."

"You did that, Robert, not I. Please go now."

She heard the doors of the dining room open,

felt a current of cooler air, and heard his footsteps fade away into the front of the house.

She couldn't cry. Except for during Molly's illness, she hadn't cried since she put the death of her baby behind her, forbid herself to wallow in self-destructive grief.

But oh, she ached inside with confusion and pain.

Was Robert just trying to show her how he felt in a way he couldn't say with words? Before coming to Rose Cottage, she had only known one other man unrelated to her, and his words and caresses had been lies. How was one to know the difference?

She'd asked Robert for time to think, and that had been the right thing to do. She had to wait for this passion and grief to leave her, so that she could consider everything rationally.

But inside, she felt . . . different, changed, new to herself. And she wasn't certain this knowledge was a good thing.

Audrey didn't sleep well that night. Too many times, she awoke with Robert's scent in her nose, or the memory of his hands working magic on her body. Lethargic and sad the next morning, she was frustrated with her mind and body for being unable to forget, and craving that sensation again.

Hard work would make her forget, and she didn't need Robert for that, or even a pair of working eyes. She decided to inspect Evelyn's cleaning, and could tell with her nose and fingers that at least the dirt was swept up and the furniture polished.

While she was in the middle of lifting a corner of the drawing room rug to feel beneath, she heard the light tap of Evelyn's shoes.

"Ma'am, is somethin' wrong?"

"Just doing a little inspection, Evelyn," she said pleasantly. "Should I have a reason to be concerned?"

"N-no, ma'am," the girl answered.

Audrey frowned. "You don't need to fear me, Evelyn, you know that, don't you?"

"Y-yes, ma'am."

The maid's nervous behavior lingered in Audrey's thoughts as she went into her study and found the most recent ledger. Robert had gone over it, but she wanted to hear the numbers herself. It wasn't that she didn't trust him where her household was concerned; she simply wanted to rely on herself.

She took the ledger up to Molly's room, and she could tell by the maid's voice that she was standing at the window.

"I'm up and about more and more, Miss Audrey," Molly said.

Her happiness was almost contagious, and Audrey found herself smiling for the first time all day.

"You are so anxious to begin work again?" Audrey asked.

"It's not work when I help you. What do you have under your arm, miss?"

"The current household ledger. I know Robert looked it over, but I would like to hear the expenditures myself."

"I don't have a table, miss, but come sit with me on the edge of the bed, and we'll see what we see."

Audrey listened as Molly slowly read through the story of the household, from grocer to butcher to oil man. As the maid read through the servants' wages, Audrey found herself frowning.

"I could swear Mrs. Sanford's wages are thrice the amount Mr. Drayton read aloud to me."

"It's not my place to say, Miss Audrey, but I did think her wages quite high for the housekeeper and cook of a small manor house."

"But the point is, I believe Mr. Drayton misled me."

"But . . . you said Lord Knightsbridge looked over these accounts just the other day."

"He wouldn't know a servant's wages," Audrey said distractedly. "He has men of business who handle all his accounts."

Molly said nothing, as if she knew Audrey had to think through all this herself. But Audrey couldn't think—her mind was churning with confusion. Who was trying to deceive her? Mr. Drayton? The Sanfords? What was going on?

She was standing before she even realized it.

"Miss Audrey? What do you mean to do?"

"Find out the truth," she said coldly, then left Molly's room.

She found Mrs. Sanford alone in the kitchen, making preparations for luncheon.

"Good mornin', Mrs. Blake," the woman said.

Audrey thought the housekeeper's voice sounded cautious, but then maybe she knew something important was happening just by Audrey's expression.

"Mrs. Sanford, we need to have a frank discussion."

"Yes, ma'am?"

But she could still hear a rhythmic scraping, as if the woman was stirring something in a bowl, and her temper snapped. "Please stop what you're doing at once!"

The bowl hit the wooden table. "Aye, ma'am. Please forgive me."

"But for what shall I forgive you? I was just going over the household ledgers. Perhaps you can tell me why your wages are thrice what they should be?"

There was such total silence that Audrey could hear a distant church bell in the village though the windows were closed.

"Mrs. Blake, I assure ye that I am worth—"

"Please do not give me assurances of your skill. And regardless of what you and your family have been doing to annoy me since I arrived, I can tell you know what you're doing. That does not account for your wages. I demand to know the truth, right now, or I will at last be forced to terminate not just your employment, but that of your entire family. And the fact that you risk this tells me there is something serious I'm not aware of."

And then she heard Mrs. Sanford give a suppressed sob and blow her nose in a handkerchief. Audrey felt a tinge of sympathy, but she forced herself to put it aside.

"Tell me the truth, Mrs. Sanford. We can deal with it together."

"Nay, Mrs. Blake, I don't think that's possible," she said wearily.

She heard a creak, and imagined the woman slumping onto a kitchen stool.

"So you won't confide in me?" Audrey asked, feeling just as weary.

"Nay, I didn't say . . . I didn't mean . . . oh, dear, this is so hard to say. I'd hoped you'd never need to know, never need to be so . . . hurt."

"*I'll* be hurt?" Audrey said with confusion, putting a hand on the kitchen worktable as if to find something solid to hold on to. "Just tell me, Mrs. Sanford. I need to know the truth."

"The extra money is for me daughter, Louisa," the woman whispered, and her voice cracked at the end. "She . . . she used to work here as a maid. But she can't anymore. The babe—" Another sob seemed to clog her voice.

Audrey said nothing, waiting with barely leashed patience and a growing sense of unease.

"Mr. . . . Mr. Blake said she was to have the money," Mrs. Sanford admitted brokenly. "That's all he would give her."

And then Audrey realized what the woman had been dreading to tell her, and it crashed over her with waves of pain and betrayal—but not shock. No, she couldn't be shocked anymore by anything her late husband had done.

Including father a child on an innocent, young housemaid.

The babe, little Arthur, was Martin's bastard, and he was the same age as their own child would have been.

Martin had said good-bye to *two* women before going off to war, she thought bitterly.

But was that the whole truth?

"Mrs. Sanford, did my husband force his attention on your daughter?" she asked with quiet resignation.

"I wish I could tell ye yea," Mrs. Sanford said with her own bitterness. "But Louisa was a foolish girl with stars in her eyes, far too flattered that a gentleman would be noticin' her. She admits, to her lastin' regret, that she allowed it all to happen. But—she cannot regret little Arthur. He is such a good boy, Mrs. Blake," she said pleadingly. "He bears no blame in this."

"Of course he doesn't," Audrey snapped. "And I wouldn't blame *him*, or take out my anger on him—or on your daughter. Mr. Blake was not a kind man. He used me for my dowry, and he used your daughter for his pleasures."

She could hear the cook's quiet weeping.

"We've been so frightened," Mrs. Sanford said raggedly. "We didn't know what ye'd do if ye knew the truth. We tried to . . . make ye leave your own home, and the shame of that will be with me forever."

Her sobs grew louder, and Audrey winced as footsteps tapped quickly down the hall.

"Mother?" Evelyn cried. "What is it? What has happened?"

"Is it Louisa or the babe?" Francis demanded.

The back door opened, leaving a whiff of brisk autumn air and decaying leaves as Francis called for his father across the yard. Feeling suddenly so tired, Audrey reached beneath the table until she found another stool, then sank onto it and bowed her head.

For a moment, they seemed to ignore her as they gathered around their mother. The door opened again, and boots clomped across the kitchen floor.

"Mrs. Sanford, stop this weepin'," her husband commanded, not unkindly. "What has happened?"

And then there was a silence, as if they all realized that Audrey was still sitting there.

"She knows," Mrs. Sanford murmured, her voice hoarse now. "She knows everythin', how her husband betrayed her, and how we did the same with our lies."

The renewed silence was stifling with old grief and rising fear. Audrey couldn't bear it anymore.

"What my husband did is not your fault," she said heavily. "I regret that you've born the burden of his thoughtless selfishness. I'm relieved that he at least tried to provide Louisa with the money she needs to support little Arthur. That will continue, of course, as will your employment, if you all promise never again to lie to me."

Mrs. Sanford started to weep again, and she could hear Mr. Sanford clearing his throat several times.

"Mrs. Blake," he said huskily, "we don't deserve yer kindness, but we appreciate it."

"What is going on?"

Audrey heard her sister's bewildered voice, and the servants went quiet once again. "I'll speak with my sister," she said, rising her to her feet. "Go on with luncheon preparations, Mrs. Sanford."

"Thank ye, ma'am," the woman said.

The sincerity and relief in her voice finally made Audrey give a faint smile. She walked toward the front hall, knowing Blythe followed her.

"Come into my study, Blythe."

She shut the door behind her sister and leaned against it, closing her eyes, feeling like she could slide right to the floor with sad weariness. But at least she had the truth now, and she could find a way to deal with it. She told Blythe all about Louisa and little Arthur.

When she was done, Blythe breathed, "Oh my."

"I'm glad I can't see the pity on your face. You warned me about Martin. I didn't want to listen. I was dazzled by his courtship."

"You wouldn't see pity," Blythe insisted, "but anger and sadness. Any man could marry a woman and do what Mr. Blake did. It wasn't because you were blind."

And then they were hugging, and Audrey felt

a fierce gladness and even disbelief that she was clinging to her sister of all people.

"It's a good thing you have at last found a man worthy of you," Blythe said.

Audrey gave a bitter laugh as she stepped back. She didn't even hesitate with her next words. "That's the sad thing, Blythe. Our engagement is fictitious, all a sham to get me away from Father's house."

Blythe gasped. "But . . . I don't understand."

"I don't want to marry again, not ever," Audrey said fiercely, knowing after today's revelation it was even more the truth. "I won't be any man's wife again, I won't be under someone's power. Doesn't this—this new secret of Martin's prove that my course is right?"

"Was this false engagement his lordship's idea?" Blythe demanded, sounding bewildered.

"As Martin's fellow soldier, he wanted to help me, and this is what I asked for, his escort, protection, and advice until I could set up my household. The engagement was the only way he felt we could leave Father's household without too much resistance." She hesitated. "Do you . . . do you hate me for the lies?"

"Hate you? How could I hate you when only lies would let you live your life the way you wanted? I never helped at all—no, no, I helped *drive* you to such desperation!"

"You had no power over Father either."

"But I could have supported you, tried to convince him." Her voice went ragged with emotion. "Instead I thought you couldn't possibly be alone. Maybe I was putting my own weakness on you—oh, I don't know. But it was wrong of me, Audrey, and I regret it so terribly."

And then they were hugging again, and Audrey felt the sting of tears she hadn't imagined in such a long time. Happy tears, if one could claim any happiness in this terrible debacle of a day.

Then Blythe straightened and put both hands on Audrey's shoulders. "But as for Lord Knightsbridge—Audrey, you haven't seen what I've seen, the way he looks at you. He truly cares about you. And . . . you've kissed him, when it couldn't matter to anyone but the two of you. He's been here for you almost every day."

"Because he feels like he needs to take care of me," Audrey said bitterly. "That's pity, Blythe."

"Pity? Was it pity when our mother watched out for us, taught us, protected us?"

"She was our *mother*."

"That was love. Why cannot Lord Knightsbridge's protection of you be love? Do we not want to help those we care for?"

Audrey found herself swallowing at the hurt that was like a lump in her throat. She didn't want to believe it could be love, couldn't bear that her resolve to be independent could harm Robert. "No, Blythe, he doesn't love me, and I don't love him." Saying that aloud felt like she spoke thickly, with ashes in her mouth, and she didn't know why that suddenly frightened her. "He feels pity, I know he does, because now that he's seen how much help I need, my problem with the servants, he's decided we really should marry."

Blythe was strangely silent.

"Then you agree with me," Audrey continued.

"No, no, I'm trying to understand it all. He's actually proposed marriage, and you turned him down—a man who cares for you, an *earl*, for heaven's sake?"

Audrey groaned. "You know I don't care about titles! And you shouldn't either."

"Don't be so hasty dismissing his proposal. I know you care for him, too. Admit you feel more for him than you ever felt for Mr. Blake."

"It is different. Robert and I have been . . . friends."

Blythe snorted.

"I don't wish to discuss this anymore." Audrey crossed her arms over her chest and pressed her lips into a thin line.

"Oh, very well, Audrey. But you think things through carefully before making any decisions."

"I already refused him and asked him to leave me in peace for a few days."

Blythe gave a groan. "You foolish girl!"

"I have more important things to deal with than one man's pity."

"The Sanfords' grandchild."

"Yes, that little boy, who is my husband's son."

"His bastard."

"That is such an ugly name for an innocent child. His birth is not his fault. I—I don't know if there is something more I should do about all of this."

"Do? Audrey, the boy is being provided for by Mr. Blake's estate. You are taking care of his entire family by allowing them to keep their employment, even after their trickery and lies. What more can you possibly do?"

Audrey didn't know, but there was something in her subconscious, something that wouldn't let her go, bothering her all the rest of the day. She had dreams that night of her dead child, the first time in well over a year. In her dreams, he wasn't too tiny, without the breath of life. He was a laughing, playful toddler, teasing her by hiding, so smart that he already knew of her blindness, and thought it only a part of her, the mother he loved, not a pitiable flaw.

The revelation of little Arthur reminded her in

a more powerful way what her life would have been like had her own child lived.

She let the terrible pain of her loss remind her of all the reasons she was never going to put herself in such a position again, never going to love or risk such grief again. She wasn't going to marry Robert.

Chapter 18

❧⟋∿❧

As Rose Cottage came into sight the next day, Robert rode with even more determination. He damn well wasn't going to cool his heels another day, regardless of what Audrey thought she wanted.

Because she was wrong.

He understood that she was frightened, that Blake had hurt her terribly—that Robert had, too, helping to cause the death of her husband and her unborn child.

But he damn well wasn't trying to control her, and he was offended she thought he was. Touching her, pleasuring her, had been one of the best experiences of his life—and she'd tried to turn it into something sordid.

He intended to show her she was far from the truth. Somehow he would convince her that they should be together.

When Francis let him into the entrance hall, he thought the young man looked a bit pale, and didn't seem to want to meet his eyes.

"Please wait in the drawin' room, milord," Francis said. "I'll tell Mrs. Blake ye've arrived."

She made him wait a long time, and when at last she swept in, as regal as a queen in flower-sprigged white muslin, indignation still hid behind her cool expression.

To his surprise, he had to mightily resist the urge to sweep her into his arms, to take up where they had left off, to prove to her with his body that they belonged together.

"Lord Knightsbridge," she said, hands clasped before her. "I didn't think I would see you for at least another day."

Using formal titles, was she? "Good morning, Audrey."

She only bowed her head.

Clenching his jaw, he plunged on. "I thought the invitation from Lady Flitcroft would change your mind."

Her expression shifted to one of confusion. "Invitation? I received none."

It was his turn to be confused. "Why would I receive an invitation from a woman I've never met, if it wasn't because of my engagement to you? She can't simply be attempting to move up a social circle."

"The woman is incredibly shy. I had tea with her several days ago." Then she hesitated, and an expression of understanding briefly crossed her face. "Excuse me for a moment."

He was left standing there alone, but not for long. Her sister ducked inside almost furtively, staying near the door.

"Good morning, Miss Collins," he said.

"Please call me Blythe, my lord."

"And you shall call me Robert, since you will soon be my sister."

She arched a brow. "That's not what Audrey tells me, but I would not believe you right for her if you didn't have confidence in yourself."

"She told you she'd changed her mind about marrying me?" he asked, not surprised, but only further convinced of the rightness of his cause.

She lowered her voice. "She told me it was never an engagement at all. I just want to tell you not to give up, that I believe she doesn't know her own mind."

He slowly smiled, hope swelling his chest like pride. "Thank you for the encouragement."

She nodded, then peered over her shoulder. "I must go!" She ran across the hall and ducked into the dining room.

A moment later, Audrey returned. "I discovered that Lady Flitcroft was given the impression by her servants that I would not attend a dinner."

"Who would do that?"

"My servants. But we have come to an understanding. I discovered what was going on, confronted them, and we are now going forward with trust."

He frowned. "There is a lot you're not telling me."

"You're not my fiancé, Robert. I only have to tell you what I feel you need to know."

He fisted a hand in frustration against his thigh, then let it go. This little war between them would be a series of skirmishes, not one large battle. And he could be a patient man. "Very well, then back to this evening's dinner party. Will you be my guest, and show your neighbors that you're perfectly capable of eating a meal with them?"

She hesitated, not very successful at hiding her warring feelings. He could tell she wanted to attend, but also wanted to distance herself from him. He wasn't going to let that happen.

"Very well, I accept your invitation."

"Then if you don't mind, I will ask Francis to press my attire for the evening."

"You were so confident, you brought a valise?" she demanded.

"I knew you wouldn't make me ride all the way home regardless. Now is there a way I can be of assistance today?"

"No, thank you. Pretend you're a guest. Perhaps Mr. Sanford will take you hunting."

"Or you and I could fish together."

"Fish?" She wrinkled her nose. "I have a feast to plan for my tenants. Please excuse me."

"Wait." He caught her arm.

She froze, her head tilted down as if she was frowning at his touch.

He didn't let her go, only leaned down until his mouth was almost against the hair near her ear, and he could smell the scent of roses. "I cannot forget how you felt in my arms, how you tasted, how you found your pleasure with me."

He felt her shudder, knew with relief that she wasn't unaffected.

"Robert, you must stop trying to force me to feel more for you than I want to feel."

She pulled her arm free, and he let her go.

"I don't have to force any emotion from you, Audrey. It's simply there, just as it is for me."

"But that doesn't mean I wish to act on it. Pleasure is fleeting, but pain and grief never go away, nor do regrets from impulsive actions."

He stood still long after she was gone, reflecting on the truth of her words in his own life. He regretted so many things he'd done, wished desperately that Audrey hadn't born the brunt of those impulsive mistakes.

But he couldn't wish that all of the past hadn't led him to this moment. She'd become central to his life, and that realization seemed monumental, mystifying. He didn't want to lose her.

Robert told himself to be patient. He'd known she wouldn't fall into his arms due to her own pride and the grief that must surely have threatened to overwhelm her. But he'd been hoping for a spark of longing, the one that had kept him up all night, hot and unsatisfied and desperate to have more of her.

It had been there, that answering spark, even though she wished it gone. *Patience.*

That evening, Audrey sat in the Collins's carriage beside Blythe, her head tilted away from Robert, who was seated across from them. She kept accidentally brushing against his big feet, his lower limbs, and just the touch made her blush and be grateful for the low lantern light.

She'd been nervous all afternoon as Molly had helped her dress, even nestling tiny pearls in her hair. But she hadn't paid attention to her gown, and didn't even realize it might look different until Blythe had earlier given a little gasp, and waxed enthusiastic about how wonderful she looked.

And then Audrey had happened to touch the bodice, and realized it had a lower décolletage than she remembered, and suddenly knew impudent Molly had been busy with her sewing needle. She'd been about to run back up to her room to change, but Blythe had insisted they'd all be late.

Thankfully, Robert hadn't remarked on her gown, except to say that she was lovely, but she was very conscious of every draft, and kept her cloak firmly closed from the moment she'd donned it.

Why had she never noticed how much room Robert took up in the carriage?

"We're almost there," Blythe said at last. "I can see the house lit up within the trees. Very pretty."

"Very countrified," Audrey amended dryly. "I know you have seen many more grand homes in London."

"Perhaps, but that doesn't mean I don't appreciate the care a family takes with their home and their pride being able to entertain their neighbors."

Audrey barely kept from gaping. Was this mature young woman truly her sister? For after they arrived, Blythe remained at her side, commenting quietly on things that happened, making certain she knew every raised stair in her path, every person in the drawing room who was brought forward to be introduced.

Audrey was no fool—Robert was the main draw here, the earl returned from foreign wars a hero, so rich and powerful and handsome. And she could not miss how kind he was to everyone, how he downplayed himself in favor of learning about every guest, how he never failed to include her in each conversation.

When a young man tried to draw a resisting Blythe away to talk, Audrey had insisted she go, knowing Robert would assist her and not cause her any disappointment.

Not here in public, anyway. He was gracious throughout the meal, making sure he sat at her side, but she'd already ruined Lady Flitcroft's seating arrangements just by her unexpected attendance. The lady herself, so soft-spoken, seemed to sincerely regret that she hadn't given more thought to their comfort—to the needs of a blind woman, Audrey knew, but she understood and took no offense. In fact, she was grateful. Every hostess took care of her guests' needs, whatever they might be. She wasn't so special, being blind. She was becoming used to the thought that people would watch her every move. Robert told her where everything was placed on her plate, as if he'd been paying close attention at each meal they'd shared.

After dinner, the guests returned to the drawing room, where the rugs had been rolled back, and the furniture pushed against the walls—or so Robert told her.

"Find me a suitable chair, Robert, and you go ask the ladies to dance. They will be thrilled."

"I don't wish to be gotten rid of so easily. Did you never learn to dance?"

She hesitated, feeling a momentary excitement that she quickly dismissed out of habit. "I had some formal training for a few months before my blindness, but that was all."

Audrey hadn't realized Blythe was nearby until her sister said, "Do not listen to her, Robert. She and Mama used to dance together all the time. I would watch them."

"Blythe," Audrey said in warning tones.

"Oh please, the musicians are warming up a waltz. Robert can guide you through it. Surely they waltzed at parties in India?"

"They did." He spoke in measured tones, as if he were trying not to sound victorious.

Audrey gritted her teeth—and then truly looked into her soul. Was she going to sit in a corner asking for sympathy just because she didn't want to risk being made a fool? Or was her concern more about being held in Robert's arms and fighting away all the emotions and passion his very touch inspired?

She had to conquer that, and delaying it would only make everything worse.

"Very well, I shall dance," Audrey promised coolly. "Thank you for the invitation, my lord."

"Oh good!" Blythe said, her voice practically gleeful. "And I promised this dance to the vicar's son. He is quite too kind and good for me, but he looks like he can dance most excellently. Have a wonderful waltz!" Her slippers tapped quickly as she moved away.

Even as Audrey smiled, she heard Robert chuckle.

"I quite like the woman your sister is turning out to be," he said.

"As do I. Miracles truly happen."

"Then I'll keep hoping."

She ignored him, pretending she didn't understand what he meant. And then he took her gloved hand in his as the opening bars of the music swelled.

"You're trembling," he murmured.

"It's not as if I have ever danced in public before."

"You will master this as you master everything you attempt. I have never admired anyone more in my life."

She knew he was exaggerating, but could not stop her blush. "Robert, this flirtation will get you nowhere."

"Speaking the truth is always to be commended. Now come into my arms, Mrs. Blake, and relax."

As if she could possibly relax, with his gloved hand holding hers, his big palm in the center of her back, each subtle pressure moving her about. She stumbled over his foot once or twice, but he held her up so effortlessly, she wasn't certain anyone would have noticed her mistakes.

"Relax," he breathed. "Smile."

A genuine one came to her, and he gave her hand a squeeze.

"Feel the music," he said. "I've heard you play, and music is in your very soul."

She did relax then, letting him sweep her away into a swirl of dancers. She felt the very movement of the air as the women's swirling skirts passed her by. She was dancing, actually dancing, in the arms of the most handsome man in the room, surely. She felt like every other woman at that moment, no different, no better or worse. She was dancing, trusting in Robert's every movement.

Until the music seemed to fade behind her, and a cool evening breeze raised gooseflesh on her bare arms.

"Robert, where are we?"

"It was overly warm in there. I thought you might appreciate a moment to collect yourself after your first successful dance."

"But where are we?"

"The terrace. It's lit with torches in the corners, but there are suitable shadows where an engaged couple can quietly . . . speak."

"Quietly speak?" she echoed dryly. "And what would you like to speak of?"

"Are you enjoying the evening thus far?"

She put her hands on the stone balustrade and tried to imagine the dark night, and perhaps the moon peering down on them. It could be a peaceful scene—but she did not feel peaceful with Robert's sleeve brushing her.

"The evening is lovely, and my new neighbors are gracious and understanding. But you? You are not taking rejection well."

He gave a low chuckle. "And I don't plan to."

Now his hand touched hers, side by side on the balustrade. She moved hers away, and when he followed, she gave up with a sigh and allowed it.

"You are being childish," she said.

"I am courting you. If you let me kiss you, we'll return to the dancing for the next waltz."

"Then kiss me and be done with it, for your skill will not persuade me."

"Skill? I am flattered."

He drew her into his arms, her breasts to the hard planes of his chest, her skirts entwined with his legs. Her heartbeat quickened, and it was as if she couldn't get enough air—all in reaction to his simplest touch. Why?

And then his lips met hers, soft and coaxing one moment, firm and commanding the next, demanding entrance to her mouth and insisting that she meet him in passion. And to her regret, she did, with an enthusiasm that was embarrassing and exhilarating at the same time.

At last he lifted his head, and she managed to say in a breathless voice, "There, we have scandalized our hostess enough."

"Or made her sigh with the romance of it all."

He was probably more correct than she was.

"But what if no one knows what we're doing out here," he continued, his arms still holding her firm against him, "and we're discovered? You would have to marry me then."

"I am a widow, Robert, given far more freedom than any maiden to have an affair. I cannot be forced into marriage by this sort of scandal."

"Then we may have an affair?"

She groaned. "Not this again. You must let go of this fantasy of us together."

"No."

He wasn't teasing now, she could hear it in his voice. He was determined, and for the first time, she wondered if he could defeat all of her promises to herself.

No, she wouldn't let that happen. "Take me inside, please. I'm cold."

Chapter 19

~~~∞∞~~~

Robert escorted them home, then headed back to Hedgerley to take a room at the inn for the night. Audrey knew he wanted her to ask him to spend the night, and that he would have tried to persuade her, had Blythe not been in the carriage with them. Thank goodness for her sister, because Audrey remembered how easily she'd let Robert seduce her on her very own dining table, where her servants might have found them. She winced at the memory, and had to force away the images of the pleasure she hadn't known she was capable of.

To her surprise, Blythe followed her into her bedroom.

"Molly," Blythe said, "I'll help Audrey undress for the night. And then she can help me."

Audrey frowned at Molly. "You should be sleeping, not waiting up for us. You're still recovering."

"So I dozed upon your bed," Molly said. "I knew you wouldn't mind. Thank you, Miss

Blythe, I will accept your kind offer, and I'll tell Charlotte you don't need her. But before I go, did you both enjoy your dinner?"

"You should have seen her waltz with Lord Knightsbridge!" Blythe gushed, before Audrey had the chance to speak. "They made the most romantic couple there."

Audrey was surprised to feel her cheeks heat, knowing Molly still thought they were truly engaged. "Blythe—"

Molly gave an exaggerated sigh. "Oh, it must have been wonderful."

"He even led her out on the terrace," Blythe confided.

"Ooh!"

"You never did tell me what he . . . *said* out there." Blythe's voice hinted at laughter and happiness.

Audrey hesitated. Both her sister and Molly wanted to believe that even the most impractical of dreams could come true. And that wasn't going to happen. "Enough, ladies. We are all very tired. Good night, Molly. And next time, tell me when you're going to alter the bodice of my gowns."

Molly didn't sound apologetic as she said, "You looked stunning, didn't you?"

"Oh, she did," Blythe chimed in.

"And Lord Knightsbridge couldn't take his eyes from you."

"No, he couldn't," Blythe agreed. "And neither could several of the other men."

Would this blushing never cease? "Good night, Molly."

Molly departed and Blythe began to unhook the back of Audrey's gown.

"Men were not looking at me, Blythe, at least not in the way you meant," Audrey insisted. "Why did you mislead Molly?"

"Of course they were looking at you. And why should they not? You are beautiful, Audrey. People will stare at first because of your blindness, and yes, that happened tonight. When I was young—"

"And you are so very old now," Audrey teased.

"Shh, let me finish! I am trying to apologize or to explain or . . . I don't know."

Audrey heard the sorrow, and turned about, even though her gown was only just starting to part at the top. "Blythe, this isn't necessary. I know you're sorry. We all make stupid mistakes in our youth. And I made several of them, so I certainly understand."

"Just let me say this," Blythe whispered, then cleared her throat. "I don't know why I used to behave this way—it seems so ridiculous and childish now—but I used to be so sad and defensive when people stared at you."

"You *were* a child," Audrey said with kindness. "I don't hold that against you."

"Even Father told me to ignore everyone. And then . . . and then he made certain we'd never have to see how people looked at you. We denied you any friendships, Audrey, a social life."

"Oh, Blythe, don't cry," Audrey said, putting her arms around her sister. "That was Father's influence. I know that. And perhaps he thought he was trying to protect me."

"You mean rather than trying to avoid his own feelings of embarrassment?" Blythe said bitterly.

"I know he felt that way, too."

"I wish that things had been different," Blythe whispered raggedly, "that I'd been more mature. We lost so much time together."

Audrey's eyes stung and her smile wobbled. "But we have all the time in the world now. We'll be able to visit each other's homes, and spend lots of time together."

"That's good."

They hugged again, then with tired fingers, fumbled through unhooking each other's gowns.

"Good night, Audrey," Blythe said, then added, "I love you."

"I love you, too," Audrey said, and when she heard the door shut, she felt the drip of happy tears she could no longer suppress.

When Audrey came downstairs the next morning, Robert was waiting in the drawing room. He rose as he saw her descend the last stair, and called her name.

Her head angled toward the room and she approached, her expression one of disapproval that he didn't quite believe. Her cheeks were pink, and he knew his attentions reached her, though she didn't want them to.

"So you didn't go home," she said impassively.

"Did you think I would?"

"No." She gave a reluctant smile.

"What are we doing today? Your feast is approaching. Have the invitations gone out? I didn't receive one."

She shook her head, looking amused and exasperated all at the same time. "Molly isn't finished with them yet. I am still insisting she resume her duties at a slow pace."

"But will I be invited?"

She hesitated a long time, but he wasn't worried.

"You'd come anyway, wouldn't you?" she asked.

"I would."

"Then you'll receive an invitation."

"It would seem awkward to exclude your future husband, the local earl."

Before she could respond with her own jibe, Robert heard the wail of a child.

Audrey turned her head toward the back of the house, looking not at all surprised.

"What the hell is that?" Robert demanded.

"There is no need to curse," she admonished, entering the drawing room and closing the door behind her.

She stood facing him, hesitation in her every manner, as if she didn't know how to tell him—or if she'd even planned to. He crossed his arms over his chest and waited.

"That little boy is Mrs. Sanford's grandchild, son of her older daughter, Louisa."

"A widow, or so I heard."

Audrey seemed to grow a little taller, shoulders back like a foot soldier reporting unwelcome news.

"She is not a widow. I recently discovered that the child is my husband's bastard."

Robert's sudden fury with Martin Blake was only eclipsed by the thought of the pain this must have given her. Gently, he said, "So this is the secret your servants have been protecting all along."

She nodded. "Martin took advantage of a young woman in his employ, and I will not compound his terrible errors by making this girl or her family suffer. At least he provided for the child, which is how I discovered the truth."

"And what do you plan to do with this knowledge?"

She blinked at him. "Nothing. Louisa is welcome in this household."

He frowned. "Are you certain that's wise?"

As if she didn't want to hear any words of caution, she opened the door. "I will do what I think best," she answered. "And now I need to greet Louisa. Please wait here."

That wasn't going to happen. He followed several paces behind her, then leaned against the doorjamb as the domestic scene in the kitchen unfolded. Mrs. Sanford worked at her wooden table, a large cauldron bubbling over the fire. A young woman with the same blond hair as the maid, Evelyn, sat on another stool, holding a squirming little boy on her lap. He had Blake's black hair, and the same impudent expression that the man had worn heading into each battle, as if he knew something the enemy didn't. Robert was glad Audrey couldn't see the resemblance.

He watched as Mrs. Sanford and her daughter greeted Audrey's entrance with resignation, but there was fear in their eyes when they looked at him. He said nothing, for once glad of the reputation a title could provide.

"Louisa, is that you?" Audrey asked.

Louisa shot a frightened look at her mother, then answered, "Aye, ma'am, 'tis me—and Arthur, of course."

Audrey smiled. "Of course. I could hear his exuberance."

Robert wondered how Audrey could smile at this reminder of her husband's disregard of her. He knew it wasn't the child's fault, but how saintly could Audrey be?

Her expression grew sober. "Louisa, I know it is too late, but I would like to apologize for my husband's abominable behavior toward you."

Louisa burst into tears and hid her face against little Arthur's head. The boy kept trying to turn around as if he didn't know what was going on. Robert didn't blame him.

"It was me own fault, Mrs. Blake," Louisa said between sobs. "I was so foolish and I felt sorry for him married to an invalid—oh heavens!"

She looked at Audrey in horror and went off on a fresh wail. Mrs. Sanford left her mixing bowls and after lifting the boy onto one hip, slipped an arm around her daughter's back. Louisa covered her face with both hands.

"Louisa, I do not blame you," Audrey said.

She had far more generosity than Robert would have had.

"Mr. Blake was not a man to consider others," she continued, "and he used you for his own purposes, just as he did me. He obviously exaggerated my blindness."

Louisa nodded, dropping her hands to reveal her tear-ravaged, blotchy face.

"People have always wanted to consider me an invalid, and I have done my best to show otherwise. I won't forget the debts Mr. Blake owes to Arthur. I will continue to help provide his care, and if you'd like, you are welcome to move back here with your family."

Robert would have thought that Louisa would be overjoyed.

There was a hesitation in her manner as she said, "You—you would not mind, ma'am?"

"Not at all. I imagine you've been lonely."

New tears slid down the girl's cheeks as she nodded, but she didn't smile at the prospect of being reunited with her family.

"Audrey, I'd like to speak with you," Robert said at last.

Mrs. Sanford and her daughter flinched at the sound of his voice, and the little boy craned his neck around with curiosity. Only Audrey seemed unsurprised as she nodded and followed him back to the drawing room.

He shut the door after her entrance. "Audrey, I

understand your compassion for this young girl having been taken advantage of—"

"Taken advantage of by my own husband," she interrupted.

"True, but that was not your fault, nor do you owe her anything beyond support from Blake's estate. But offering a home? That is a terrible idea."

"Why? Her only family is here, and she's living alone somewhere, ostracized. I've been told that most villagers know she is not a widow, so her last attempt at respectability is gone. This is Martin's fault, Robert."

"But not yours. And you knew I'd disagree with how you're handling this—why else keep me in the dark about the child?"

"Perhaps because you have no say in my decisions," she said pointedly. "We are not engaged."

"Regardless, this decision is bad for *you*, Audrey. You'll be living with a constant reminder of your husband's infidelity."

"You act as if I need reminders of what he did?" she asked in disbelief. "He took my money and he left me trapped with my father—I'm not likely to forget that."

"And so you think you can never trust a man again," he said sadly.

She seemed to hesitate, which gave him hope.

"You have to accept my decisions, Robert. I won't marry you."

"I can't accept that," he said.

And as he looked at Audrey, unbowed by the terrible pain inflicted upon her, he realized that her pain was his. He didn't know what that meant, only that he wanted to make the worst of it go away, to see her truly happy. And he was starting to wonder if she was as against marriage to him as she claimed.

"Audrey!"

They both heard Blythe's excited voice from the entrance hall, and then she came rushing in, a squirming bundle of furry black and white puppy in her arms.

Blythe smiled at him, but went directly to her sister. "I have a gift for you. Hold out your arms."

Frowning, Audrey did so, and then her eyes went wide as the puppy snuggled against her.

"Isn't he adorable?" Blythe asked. "He's finally old enough to leave his mother back in the barn. I think you should have him."

The puppy started licking Audrey's face, and soon she was laughing. "Oh, I don't know if I'm capable of such a responsibility, Blythe."

"Of course you are. Play with him for a while. There's even a rope to use as a leash should you need to take him outside. Molly and I can share the responsibility with you. But right now I cannot. Mr. Yardley is waiting to take me for a carriage ride."

"He is Miss Yardley's brother," Audrey said. "You met him at the Flitcroft dinner?"

"I did. He is a kind man, too old and somber for me, but I could not refuse a simple ride. I'll be back soon!"

Smiling, Blythe tossed the rope to Robert, then caught up her shawl and hurried out the front door.

Audrey petted the puppy in bewilderment. "I . . . I'm not sure this is such a good idea. I won't be able to see what he's up to."

"You can hear him, and once he's older and trained, he'll be a good companion."

"Then I certainly won't need a husband." She bit her lip as if to contain a smile.

"I'm not laughing."

"You know what Blythe is trying to do," Audrey said tiredly. She stroked the puppy's little head as it kept trying to lick her chin.

"Give you a gift?"

"She's trying to distract me from—from everything. She means well."

"Are you distracted?"

"I'm worried this is just one more responsibility that I am not equipped to handle."

"You handle everything in your path, Audrey. You'll handle this."

The puppy was squirming so much, she had to put him down. He sniffed at her skirts, at Robert's boots, then started to search the corners.

"What is he doing?" she asked.

"Exploring. And looking for a certain spot. If you take him outside every few hours, he'll learn to piss out there. He's used to that already."

"Robert, your language."

He stooped to tie the rope around the puppy's neck. "Then find a better word. And a name. I'll walk him outside."

"Thank you."

The puppy was all big paws and floppy ears, and pulled as hard as he could to lead Robert around the back, toward his home in the barn.

Mr. Sanford was repairing a broken rail in the paddock fence, then glanced up as Robert approached. He frowned down at the puppy. "I told Miss Collins the puppy weren't a good idea. Mrs. Blake is sendin' it back?"

"Not at all, I'm simply taking it for a stroll."

Mr. Sanford's expression only darkened. "A puppy is just another thing a blind woman can't take care of. Comin' here, tryin' to prove herself independent—it isn't right to worry her father like this. And I know all about worry."

Robert eyed the man with speculation. Much as he wanted to rebuke him, he remained silent to see what else he might say.

"She should go home," Mr. Sanford continued, "not that it's me place to say such a thing, beggin' yer pardon, milord."

Why bring up Audrey's father as her guardian rather than him, the man who intended to marry her?

The servants had been a puzzle from the beginning, and Robert wasn't satisfied that all was well between them and Audrey. After the puppy had relieved himself, he led him back inside. It took some time to find Audrey, because he hadn't thought she'd have reason to be in the kitchen.

He found her holding Louisa's little boy, talking to him earnestly as he met her gaze. Louisa was stirring a pot over the fire, looking over her shoulder again and again at Audrey.

Robert felt a chill of unease. "Audrey?"

She lifted her head and her smile seemed all that was normal. "Do you still have the puppy, Robert?"

"I do."

"I was just telling Arthur about him." She set the little boy on his feet. "We still have to think of a name, Arthur."

The puppy sniffed the boy's toes, making him laugh.

Audrey smiled up at Robert, and it was probably a good thing she couldn't see that he didn't return her smile.

"Why are you here?" he asked quietly.

Her smile faded. "You sound concerned, when it's unnecessary. I am simply helping where I'm needed." She lowered her voice. "I have a duty to this baby, almost as if he were my ward."

Robert felt her words like a twist to his gut. "Blake's estate provides for him. You owe him nothing else."

"I understand your words, but I can't quite feel that way."

It was because of the babe she lost, he knew, the babe that would have been Arthur's age. He couldn't even imagine the heartache she had felt, the memories this little boy stirred up. But he couldn't talk to her about it without betraying Blythe's confidences, just as the sisters were becoming closer.

"Arthur," Louisa said, walking across the kitchen toward them, "come to me and leave his lordship be."

Audrey patted Arthur briefly on the head, and seemed to have no qualms about returning him to the care of his mother. But it couldn't be good for her to see the boy day in and day out, to dwell on all she had lost. Somehow, he had to make her see that with him, she could have her own babies, that they could have a good life together—that he could make her happy.

But how to show her she could trust him? All he could do was continue to spend as much time as possible with her.

Robert followed Audrey back into the entrance hall, listening as she laughed at the puppy, who jumped repeatedly at her skirts.

"A puppy!" Molly rushed down the stairs, Francis behind her. "Francis told me, but I couldn't quite believe that Miss Blythe—" She broke off, blushing.

Audrey smiled. "It's hard to believe how different my relationship with my sister has become, isn't it?"

"Perhaps it was for the best I took ill when I did," Molly said. "It gave you two the chance to be together."

"I will never think it good that you took ill," Audrey scolded. "But doesn't the puppy just feel wonderfully soft? We must come up with a name."

Molly dropped to her knees, then smiled up into Francis's indulgent, besotted expression. Robert saw where this infatuation was headed, and knew that in his father's household, such fraternization would never have been tolerated. But Audrey was unconventional—everything about her. That was one of the reasons he was drawn to her.

"I'll take charge of the puppy, miss," Molly said. "It will do me good to have a little exercise."

"If you're certain . . ." Audrey began.

"She's certain," Robert interrupted. "Audrey, might I speak with you in the drawing room?"

She seemed almost nervous preceding him in, and she started talking before he could.

"I'm not just hosting a tenant feast, Robert. Eventually I'm going to have my own dinner party. You'll be able to reacquaint yourself with the young ladies of the village."

"Are you matchmaking to rid yourself of me?"

She blinked a moment, and he hoped she was considering how lonely they'd be without each other.

"I simply want you to see all the young women who'll be awaiting a heroic former officer."

"Heroic?" he echoed, the word distasteful in his mouth. "I'm no hero, Audrey. I've told you this before."

"Why do you sound so strained, Robert?" she asked. "You speak so little of your military life—frankly, you've said almost nothing at all."

He could tell she focused every one of her senses on him, and he didn't like what he'd revealed.

"Because it is not fit conversation for a lady," he answered.

There was a long, meaningful silence between

them, and he realized her struggle not to question him more. For just this moment, he was relieved she was trying to keep her distance.

But he was about to give her ample opportunity to discover more about him.

"I came here for another reason," he said. "I received word that my friend, Viscount Sergeant Blackthorne, is bringing his wife to visit me at Knightsbridge Hall tomorrow."

"Blackthorne? He is one of the men who served with you?"

"He is. Apparently he mentioned my newly engaged status to his wife, and she'd like to meet us both. She is the daughter of our former commander, a man we all admired."

And whose death we caused.

He had hoped he had his guilt well under control by helping Audrey, but perhaps it would never go away, he thought bleakly. It was a shameful secret that sometimes haunted his dreams.

Audrey was still hesitating, perhaps dissecting his words too much.

"And you can bring Blythe, of course, and who knows what men she'll meet? And Audrey," he added in a more thoughtful tone. "I'd like you to meet them."

"Very well," she said reluctantly. "We will come to you tomorrow."

"Then I will head home to make the arrangements. Go enjoy your new puppy."

He knew he'd not been quite fair, luring her with things she could not refuse. She'd probably realized it. But all was fair in love—or at least in courtship.

Chapter 20

That evening as they sat in the drawing room doing their needlework, Audrey told Blythe about Robert's invitation.

"Invited to Knightsbridge Hall?" Blythe said, excitement laced through her voice. "My friends have described it, and it sounds practically royal in size and decor."

Audrey didn't like the uneasiness that rattled her. She had faced and overcome so many challenges in her life. She concentrated on the fact that Robert wanted her to meet one of his closest friends. She shouldn't feel such a softening in her heart over this. But she couldn't help thinking that he was a man who was never embarrassed about her, not since the beginning. And he'd continued to prove it over and over, escorting her to her new village, to a stranger's house for dinner, and now to his own ancestral home.

And each day they were separated, she yearned to be with him, and only felt truly happy when she could hear his voice, consult him about her estate—her very life.

Was she making a mistake by denying him?

Had she been so focused on her past, and on what one shallow man had done to her, that she couldn't be open-minded, openhearted, about Robert? Just the thought that she was willing to entertain these ideas showed her he meant more to her than she'd ever planned. She wouldn't have Blythe forever, nor even Molly, who seemed more and more in love with her footman as he helped her back to health.

But she could have Robert—and perhaps a family.

The thought seemed to paralyze her with fear, and something must have shown on her face.

"Audrey, is something wrong?" Blythe asked. "You look . . . I don't know how you look. Oh, dear, I've been so selfish once again. You don't want to visit Robert's home, do you?"

Audrey licked her suddenly dry lips. "I admit I have my concerns, but I wouldn't have mentioned it if I hadn't already decided to accept the invitation."

"You like being with him, don't you?"

"He is a nice man."

Blythe actually laughed, and Audrey tossed a skein of yarn at her.

GAYLE CALLEN

"Nice man?" Blythe repeated, still giggling. "Oh, Audrey, you are falling in love with him. Why is that so terrible? He is nothing like your first husband."

Falling in love with him? She wouldn't even consider such a weakness, such an open avenue to heartache.

"I know he's not Martin. But this is in my home, where he's a guest. Perhaps . . . perhaps I want to see what he's like in his own home, with his friends."

"Ah, because you're finally giving some real thought to becoming his wife."

And that was true. And frightening. And—she didn't know what. It was as if now that she'd come to terms with Martin and what he'd done to her, she was able to put it behind her, to see a future uncluttered by betrayal. Could she find love—real love—with Robert?

When Audrey and Blythe arrived at Knightsbridge Hall early the next afternoon, Audrey had already listened impassively to Blythe's glowing description of the castle exterior, the oldest wings to the newest, and her imagination wasn't able to produce an image in her head. It all felt . . . unreal. When they arrived in the entrance hall, she could hear their footsteps echo away into vastness. Blythe gave an awestruck gasp. It was all Audrey needed to know about the impressiveness of Robert's country seat.

"Good morning, Audrey."

Robert's voice rang with pleasure, and she wasn't certain it was because of her, or because at last she'd come to see what she'd give up if she didn't marry him.

Did he not realize his large household might be an impediment to a blind woman? Not that she planned to make any decisions because of a house, but she found herself uneasy. There were so many steps to the nearest drawing room, and she'd heard Robert tell his butler to use the Blue Drawing Room, as if there were so many rooms they had to separate them by color.

As they walked, Robert took her arm and said quietly, "I'm so glad you came."

"Did you think I wouldn't?"

"No, you're a woman of your word. I just wanted you to know that I'm simply glad to see you here."

She lowered her voice. "Here in this home you think I can be a part of."

"Think? You would have this place in tip-top shape in no time. My butler is badly overtaxed, as is my housekeeper, since they only have me to consult—and didn't even have me for so many years."

Audrey said nothing, trying to imagine herself

here, where the furnishings were probably so far apart she'd have trouble counting steps between. It was a little intimidating—and challenging. She'd begun to realize in the last few weeks that she liked a challenge.

"We've entered the drawing room," he said in her ear. "Blackthorne and his wife are seated on the sofa facing us as we approach. Blackthorne is a soldier, one of those dark, brooding types who never planned to be anything but a soldier. No ambition in life."

"I heard that," said the man himself, his tone dry and amused.

"Then I shall be forced to introduce him," Robert continued. "Viscount Blackthorne, may I present my fiancée, Mrs. Audrey Blake, and her sister, Miss Blythe Collins."

"It is a pleasure to meet the woman who has tamed such a headstrong rogue," Lord Blackthorne said.

"Tamed?" Audrey echoed. "I am not certain that is the correct term. I believe he has quite trampled all over my intentions."

"I am not so headstrong as all that," Robert said. "Audrey, Blythe, meet Lady Blackthorne, once Lady Cecilia Mallory, daughter of our late commander, the Earl of Appertan."

"Ah," Audrey said, "so you met each other through the military. It sounds very romantic."

She heard Lord Blackthorne chuckle quietly, while his wife laughed aloud.

"Mrs. Blake," Lady Blackthorne said, "there was nothing romantic about it. I quite believe I was desperate for a husband."

Blythe spoke up. "And Audrey was desperate for a fiancé. You all have much in common."

Audrey winced at her sister's indelicacy. Perhaps Robert had wanted nothing mentioned about how they'd come to be together.

But Robert only laughed and said, "Let us sit down and exchange stories. There's a tea tray we may share until luncheon is ready."

A servant took their cloaks, and Audrey asked if she could serve the tea. Perhaps Robert would wish to show that she was *almost* just like any other young lady.

When they were sipping tea, Blythe was the first one who returned to the topic of marriage. "Lady Blackthorne, do forgive my curiosity, but how can a military marriage not be romantic?"

The woman sighed, yet her voice was amused as she said, "Due to many reasons, I needed access to my inheritance, and the only way I could have that, was to marry. I had been corresponding with

Michael for months after my father's death, and thought he'd be able to help me."

"Corresponding?" Audrey said. "He was still in India?"

"I attended the wedding," Robert said. "In India. Without a bride."

"You married by proxy," Blythe breathed, sounding awed. "Surely you had met him before."

"No, I hadn't," Lady Blackthorne answered. "I thought he was a man my father's age."

"She thought I'd keel over rather quickly," Lord Blackthorne explained. "Imagine her surprise when I showed up at her door a month ago."

Lady Blackthorne chuckled. "And he thought I was desperate to marry because I was a plain spinster."

"They make a very handsome couple," Blythe told Audrey. "And they seem very much in love."

Audrey winced. "Blythe, perhaps they don't want their personal business discussed so openly."

"Oh, no," Lady Blackthorne said, "Miss Collins is correct."

"We make a handsome couple," Lord Blackthorne said somberly.

Everyone laughed.

"But in truth," he continued, "we were very lucky to fall in love."

"I do believe it was destiny," his wife responded

softly, "since I had had no intention of ever even meeting Michael, or having a proper marriage."

Audrey could hear the emotion in their voices, imagined them looking into each other's eyes, and felt her own heart constrict. She'd been telling herself all along she'd never marry, just like Lady Blackthorne, but since she'd met Robert, one by one her defenses were falling apart, until she was left vulnerable to him. She hated feeling needy, but did every woman feel that way when confronted with the enormity of her growing emotional attachment to a man?

"And she must be in love with me," Lord Blackthorne said, "because I'll be remaining with the army, and she'll be living at least half of each year in India with me."

"Didn't you spend much of your childhood there, Lady Blackthorne?" Robert asked. "I remember your father speaking of you often and fondly."

"Thank you for telling me, Lord Knightsbridge," she said. "Not all of my memories of India are good ones, yet I will have much to occupy myself when we live there."

"It seems she has a better head for estate management than I do," Lord Blackthorne said. "My brother used to oversee my estate, but Cecilia will be taking over."

Surprised, Audrey added another intriguing layer to the puzzle of Robert's friends.

"Brilliant," Robert said, clapping his hands together. "Lady Blackthorne and Audrey should have much to discuss. Audrey inherited Blake's estate and has been in charge for several weeks now. It's going very well."

"You've been of much help, Robert," Audrey insisted, feeling her cheeks heat.

"Won't you all call me Cecilia?" she said. "We have so many interesting conversations ahead of us."

They all went into luncheon together, and Audrey thought about these two military men, each involved with unconventional women, and not threatened by it. How many other men could be like them? Could she risk letting Robert go, all because she was afraid?

And did she want to be alone? When she'd sent him away, she'd been so sad and lonely at the prospect of a day without a visit from him.

But maybe she was being selfish. Robert professed to admire her and like her, but no words of love had ever been exchanged. And she didn't even know if she loved *him*! How was she supposed to decide what was best for them both, if she didn't even know her own mind?

Throughout luncheon, Robert found his gaze returning again and again to Audrey from his place at the head of the table. She sat on his left, Michael on his right, two very important people in his life.

He hadn't known how the day might go, if Audrey would allow her embarrassment over their false engagement to leave her stilted with Michael and his wife, but that hadn't happened. Audrey had been as taken with Cecilia as Robert was, and was already plying her with many questions about the Appertan estates, which she'd been managing during her brother's minority. Robert guessed that there was more going on behind the Blackthornes' words, that their relationship had perhaps a rockier start than they were letting on, but that was something to question Michael about later.

During a lull in the conversation, he asked Michael, "Have you heard from Rothford?"

"The Duke of Rothford?" Blythe interjected, wide-eyed. "Robert, how do you know so many peers when you've been in India for so long?"

He smiled. "Rothford returned from India with us. He, too, had been with the Eighth Dragoons."

"I haven't gone to London since our initial arrival," Michael said. "You stayed there longer than I."

"And he was quite absent from any event I attended," Robert admitted. "I will be very curious when he finally does return to Society."

He saw Audrey looking intrigued, and Cecilia, staring down as she ate, wearing a knowing smile. Had Michael told Cecilia everything—every reason they had come to England? And had she accepted that guilt motivated their actions? Michael had tried to deny it to himself, felt he'd made a battlefield decision and should not feel guilty. And how had *that* worked out for him with his wife?

Robert steered the conversation away from Rothford and any other guilty memories. After luncheon, Cecilia asked for a tour of the mansion, and he obliged them, listening as Blythe expounded in detail where she thought her sister should know more.

He watched Audrey more than anyone, wondered if the thought of this old mausoleum would set her even further against him, but she seemed interested, asking questions about the history of the hall and his family.

At last the ladies decided to rest before dinner, and Robert looked at Michael. "Shall we have a brandy?"

"Most definitely."

Michael followed him, still with the slight limp from wounds he'd sustained several months before.

"You are doing well?" Robert asked as they entered his study, and he closed the door behind his friend.

"Much better, thank you. I no longer need the cane, at least."

As Robert poured, offered a glass, then sat beside his friend, he felt Michael's regard.

"When you planned to return home to help Audrey," Michael mused, "none of us knew she was blind."

Robert nodded, sipping, then feeling the heat of the brandy coat his stomach.

"And now you're engaged. That seems . . . quick."

"As quick as a proxy marriage?" Robert grinned.

Michael smiled back. "You have me there." His smile faded. "Take it from a man who almost lost his wife because she was determined to annul our marriage—"

"She had such a strong negative reaction once she met you?" Robert quipped.

"Just listen. I wasn't honest with her at the beginning about our involvement in the death of her father—in the death of Audrey's husband. Have you explained it all to her?"

Robert shook his head. "Not yet. I've been too busy trying to keep her from breaking the engagement."

"That sounds familiar," Michael said dryly. "But you should know that confessing our secret was not as bad as I thought, not when the woman is rational and understanding. Audrey seems that sort of woman."

"I know. But we have other issues between us that are more important to me."

"I won't delve into your private affairs, but secrecy will just make everything worse."

"I'll take your advice under consideration. Now tell me, are you certain you want to take such a flower of England back to that hot hellhole where we've served?"

Michael laughed.

That evening, when neighbors arrived to join them for dinner, Audrey listened to the ease with which Robert moved between so many levels of Society, from the servants to his friendship with the absent duke. She heard the respect in the voices of the servants, and the relief of the neighbors as they got to know Robert. From everything she'd heard, his father was not a man people liked, even if they respected him. The neighbors seemed glad to know Robert was his own man in that regard.

Audrey knew how hard he'd been working to be a better man than his father, so that his neighbors could know to trust him, so that his servants could act on their own without fear.

She could not contain the depths of her admiration for him, and feeling scared and worried and excited, she knew she was coming closer and closer to accepting his marriage proposal.

To top everything off, he asked Blythe to perform for his guests after dinner, allowing her to shine, and making Audrey feel all choked with emotion at his very goodness.

To her surprise, Blythe asked her to join in, and the two sisters sang a duet while Audrey played. Audrey later wondered how she'd gotten through it without crying. With Robert's help, she had her sister back again, and she was living the life she always wanted.

That's when she knew she was happy, happier than she'd ever been in her life. And all because of Robert. She had fallen in love with him. How could she be afraid of that?

But . . . what if he didn't have the same strong feelings?

After Blythe had retired for the night, Audrey wandered about the bedroom feeling restless, her thoughts churning. She counted paces between furnishings, wondering if that would at last tire her mind.

There was a faint knock on the door, and feeling relieved, she opened it. "Blythe, you couldn't sleep either?"

"It's me."

Robert's voice was quiet and deep, and she found herself clutching the door to keep from throwing herself into his arms.

"I—" she began, then had to moisten her lips. "I didn't expect you."

"I came to see if you enjoyed the day. Might I come in?"

She'd been alone with him so many times— why did this feel so different? Perhaps it was because of the big four-poster bed looming behind her, or that she was only wearing her nightdress and dressing gown.

She stepped back, opening the door wider. "Please come in." She shut the door behind him, and knew she'd taken a step into the unknown, where she might at last be able to find the answers she sought. Turning about and leaning against the door, she smiled at him. "I had a lovely day, Robert. Lord Blackthorne and his wife are gracious, kind people."

"I agree."

She gave a little start, surprised that he was so close.

"But do you want to know the best part of the day?" he continued, his voice becoming husky. "It was having you at my side, as my hostess. This place suddenly felt like a home to me."

"Oh, Robert."

When he took her upper arms in his hands, she lifted her face for his kiss. Their mouths were greedy in their exploration, hot and wet. She found herself falling back against the door, trapped by his big body pressing into hers. They were wearing so little clothing that she could feel the hard indentations of his chest, and the way his heart pounded against hers.

She felt herself coming alive. Robert was kissing her as if she were the finest wine and he'd never been so thirsty. He burrowed his face into her neck, tasting her skin, nipping at her until she shuddered.

And then she felt his hand move along her side and up her torso, cupping her breast, making her gasp at the burst of heat and sensitivity and exquisite pleasure. He kneaded her through the thin silk garments, rubbing the hard point of her nipple between his fingers.

She was restless and trembling against him, feeling as if she'd fall to the floor if she couldn't hold onto him. She bunched his shirt at the back and pulled, until she could touch the hot skin of his lower back. It seemed wicked and daring, and made her only want more.

She felt her dressing gown part, her hair come loose under his fingers, and he kissed his way down her neck. Dropping to his knees, he spread her gown wide even as he kissed a line down her collarbone and between her breasts. She felt the touch of his whiskered cheek against her breast a moment before he took her nipple into his mouth right through her nightdress. She cried out and arched her back, as if she could press all of her inside him.

He caught one of her knees up against his side, moving his torso between her thighs even as he continued to suckle and lick at her breasts. He felt strong and hot against the intimate depths of her body, and she shamelessly rubbed herself against him.

Her nightdress brushed against her legs as he slowly drew it up her body, separating just long enough to drag it along her sensitive skin. She was the one who took it on its last journey, pulling it up and over her head, feeling her hair fall down all around her nakedness, the brush of it suddenly as erotic as his fingers.

And then she realized how pale a thought that was, because his fingers began to touch her everywhere, even as he still knelt at her feet. Out of the darkness, his caresses skimmed her ribs, her hips, behind her knees, sliding along between her thighs. When his hands palmed her hips, she felt the brush of his thumbs along her curls, sliding deeper into her wetness, parting her.

And then he kissed her there, and she cried out, trembling, her hands pressed to his shoulders to hold herself up. He licked her, teased her, suckled her, and just when she climbed toward that peak of pleasure for only the second time in her life, he suddenly rose and swept her off her feet, carrying her to the bed. Though he set her down gently, she could hear movement, and knew he was tugging off his own garments. Not caring if she impeded him, she explored the flat ripples of his stomach, tugged at the buttons of his trousers, then heard him groan as she palmed the hard length of him through his undergarments as his trousers sagged down his hips.

"Hurry," she whispered, falling back on the bed.

Without shame, she threw her arms wide against all the pillows, arching her back, displaying herself for him, feeling beautiful and desirable, all the things he'd brought to life in her. The mattress sagged with his weight as he crawled toward her. He spread her thighs with his big hands, then settled between them, over her, holding most of his weight with his hands on either side of her head.

She felt his erection hot and hard against her, sliding the length of her once, twice, until she moaned her need of him and clutched his body closer. And then he slid home, deep inside her, and there was no pain, just the fullness of knowing they were joined together at last.

Chapter 21

Robert didn't move—couldn't move—staring down into Audrey's flushed face, her eyes half closed, her lips moistly parted. He'd never felt so connected to a woman, had never come so close to pure bliss, pure sensation.

But the urges were strong inside him, and she was making the most erotic little gasps of pleasure. He bent to kiss her, to take in the sounds she made when he first began to move.

They shared a moan, and he kissed her deeply, mimicking with his tongue what he was doing to her body. Her knees lifted, her thighs clutched his hips, and he rolled against her in slow building movements. He reached to capture the fullness of her breast again, and watched in wonder as she found her pleasure, the depths of her body shuddering all around him, her face full of joy and contentment as the last waves of it moved through her.

He couldn't wait any longer, driving into her

over and over until the passion took him away, and he poured himself inside her.

Then stillness came over him as he enjoyed the press of her moist skin along every inch of his. He braced himself on his elbows and looked down into her face. He wasn't certain of her expression, and he found his thoughts returning to the first moments in her room, how he hadn't even asked her permission, had just swept her away with his kisses and passion.

Had he seduced her in an attempt to control? He'd come to her room with deliberate intention after all. He found himself questioning everything he'd been doing all along, making her think he was indispensable when he'd told himself he was only trying to help. Had he just been trying to have his way?

But they could have a good marriage, he knew that, and they both wanted children. He could make this work.

"Are you all right?" he murmured, kissing her cheek and her temple and the tip of her nose.

"Hmm."

Her response was a hum, and her satisfied smile a balm to his guilty conscience.

"I saw your freckles at last."

She giggled, and even that slight movement of her body was enough to make him fully erect again.

With a little gasp, she moved beneath him. "So soon?"

"Not if you're tender," he insisted.

"Oh, I'm not tender."

And before he knew it, they were rolling around on the bed, until at last he pulled her on top and watched her discover the pleasures of mastering him.

"Oh my!" she gasped, falling down onto his chest when it was over.

Both of them were breathing hard, moist with perspiration.

"If I'd have known it was this much fun," she said, "I'd have been a scandalous widow before now."

He pinched her backside. "You'd better watch it. I've now seen all those freckles you thought you'd keep hidden."

She laughed and rolled off him, not even bothering with a sheet, comfortable with her nudity. And that aroused him all over again, but he restrained himself with difficulty. He came up on his side, resting his head on his bent arm, letting the other hand trail along the curves of her body. Her eyes were half closed, and she moaned softly when he lingered on her nipples.

"You must stop," she whispered. "You can't stay here tonight."

He thought about being with her every night, wanted to remind her that all she had to say was "yes," and they'd never be separated again.

But he didn't want passion to be the reason she accepted his proposal. That seemed too . . . underhanded on his part.

As if he hadn't been underhanded in so many other ways, he thought with regret.

He leaned down to give her a soft kiss. "It's difficult to leave you."

"But you must." She yawned. "You have exhausted me, and how will I face your guests with circles under my eyes? They'll know—"

"They'll know that an engaged couple couldn't keep their hands from one another for one more moment."

She smiled, but didn't respond, and at last, he sat up and left her bed. As he dressed, he watched her. She drew the sheet up at last, but he knew the chill of the room had more to do with that than shyness. She could never be shy with him again.

When he was ready to leave, he leaned over her, making her sink slowly back into her pillows until he was above her. He kissed her long and deep, not touching her in any other way.

"Good night, sweet Audrey," he murmured against her lips.

"Good night."

He thought she was about to say something else, but all she did was give him a soft smile that he took with him into his dreams.

Audrey awoke feeling more relaxed and happy than she'd ever felt in her life. Her body was tender in spots, but not painful, only a reminder of Robert's passion, and that felt delicious.

She thought she might feel embarrassed at breakfast, but any of that was overwhelmed by the somber knowledge that she was leaving right after. She tried to enjoy each conversation with Robert, Blythe, and the Blackthornes, to make the meal last, but soon enough it was time to leave.

At the carriage, Robert held both her hands. "It'll be a day or two before I can come to you, no later than your tenants' feast, I promise."

"It will seem a long time," she murmured, squeezing his hands.

"You'll miss me?"

"I always do."

And then he kissed her cheek in front of everyone, and she didn't mind in the least, only found her smile growing tremulous as she waved good-bye out the window.

"He still has his arm upraised," Blythe said, her words trailing off in a sigh of happiness. "I think he truly loves you. Don't you?"

"I—" Audrey hesitated. "I don't know about his feelings, but I love him."

Blythe gave her a swift hug before settling back on the bench at her side. "I knew it," she said with satisfaction.

Audrey could only laugh. She would not allow her doubts to assail her, only thought of the next time she would meet with Robert, the next time she could show him with her body how she felt. And she trembled at the memories, and hugged them tight to herself all the way home. She wasn't afraid anymore.

Two days passed swiftly, and Robert enjoyed his own home more than he ever had in his life. Sharing it with Michael and Cecilia made all the difference in the world—as did the knowledge that soon he'd be sharing it with Audrey. Regardless of her "scandalous widow" comment, he knew she wasn't the type of woman to have an affair and then forget him.

He still saw her face in his dreams, the last time he'd kissed her good-bye, the hope and the tenderness she hadn't bothered to hide. And when he wasn't seeing her face, he was remembering her passionate lovemaking until he could barely fall asleep at night for wanting her.

When Michael and Cecilia heard about Audrey's tenants' feast, they asked if they could attend, and the three of them arrived together. There were pavilions thrown up across the grounds, tables and chairs being set up by the Sanfords as well as workers Audrey had hired from the village. People scurried about, but with a sense of happy anticipation.

Robert smiled at it all, until he saw Audrey in the garden, holding Louisa Sanford's little boy, Molly standing nearby, the puppy on a leash. His eagerness to see Audrey felt doused with cold water, and he couldn't quite understand his own uneasiness.

"Who is the little boy Audrey is holding?" Cecilia asked as they walked through the grass.

"The son of one of Rose Cottage's maids," he said.

But Michael's gaze sharpened on him, as if Robert's voice had revealed too much to his good friend.

Audrey heard the gravel crunch beneath their feet and lifted her head, her brilliant smile for the boy fading.

"Good morning, Lord Knightsbridge," Molly said.

Audrey's expression softened with pleasure, and Robert felt some of his concerns fade—not all.

"Robert," Audrey said. "I've missed you."

"And I've missed you. But before we become all sentimental, I've brought Michael and Cecilia, too."

"What a lovely home you have, Audrey," Cecilia said.

Audrey's smile widened to a grin. "How wonderful that you've come! All our plans are going well, and everything will be ready for the feast this afternoon. Molly can show you both inside where you can refresh yourselves."

"I'll remain and speak with you," Robert said.

Her expression was quizzical, but she turned to Molly. "Can you return Arthur to Louisa? She must be done helping her mother with the tarts by now. I'll keep the dog. Bye-bye, Arthur."

She gave a little wave, and the boy waved back. Everyone headed for Rose Cottage, and Robert squatted down to pet the puppy.

"Does he have a name yet?" he asked.

"Victor," she said. "Molly came up with it. For Queen Victoria."

"A good name." And then he rose to his feet, and they stood there, separated, but so recently joined together. For just a moment, he let the pleasure of looking at her, being with her, overtake his concern.

She smiled almost shyly. "What are you doing?"

"Remembering." He cleared his throat, then

lowered his voice. "Remembering how you look naked, by candlelight."

She blushed, her eyelids lowered, a sweet smile curving her lips. "Robert, you shouldn't speak so."

"I think I'll have to make love to you outdoors."

Her eyes flew wide. "Robert!"

He laughed and took both her hands to kiss them, wishing no gloves separated her skin from his lips. "Then I'll change the subject to something more serious. Perhaps this will discomfit you, but I'm concerned about your closeness to Louisa's son."

To his surprise, her smile softened, and she reached up to touch his face. "I cannot believe how well you see what's inside me, Robert."

"You don't seem to mind my concern."

"I understand it. There were moments when I first learned of Arthur's existence, that I felt too . . . connected to him. He is Martin's son."

She hesitated, as if she was about to tell him about her son who'd died, and then changed her mind. He was surprised to feel sorrow because she didn't want to share her private pain with him—but he hadn't shared his secrets either.

"I even considered making him my ward, giving him the education Martin should have given him. But then I realized that Louisa was actually afraid of my involvement—that the whole family feared

I could take him away. That was a power I'd never had before, and I felt sickened that I didn't initially see how wrong it was. I was shocked back into realizing I couldn't live my life through other people."

"You don't need to do that, Audrey. Live your life with me, and we can have our own children."

To his surprise, she gave him an enigmatic, even flirtatious smile. "We'll talk later. I have guests to prepare for just now."

As he escorted her back to the house, Robert felt a renewed sense of hope. She'd made love with him, and she hadn't denied his desire to marry her. He felt like everything he'd ever wanted—the family he'd never truly had—would finally be his.

Audrey had never imagined how wonderful it would be to be a hostess to the people who depended on her just as she depended on them. She owned the land, but they had the labor to make it fertile, and she was so grateful to be able to show her thanks, and her promise of a long partnership in the future.

Her puppy, Victor, spent much of the afternoon with her as she moved from pavilion to pavilion, table to table. Sometimes Blythe was with her, other times Robert, and she heard in the voices of her tenants the gratitude at having a new landlord who cared, the promise of future stability. And it wasn't just because of Robert and his title, but her own belief, her own desire to be a part of this community.

Even Mr. Sanford sounded proud, and she knew that at last she'd won the trust of her servants, and she returned that trust in kind.

Blythe was more grown-up and gracious than Audrey had ever dared to hope, mingling with people of a different station than her own, but still winning them over with her charm and genuine joy, something Audrey had never heard in all the long years they'd lived together—no, that wasn't true. Blythe's unhappiness had only evolved since their mother's death, and their father's conviction like a stain upon the family that Audrey was too embarrassing to ever be seen. It seemed like a dream to her now, an ugly dream soon forgotten, now that the world had opened up to her.

And then there was Robert, moving smoothly between the Blackthornes and the meekest shepherd with equal ease. She had never imagined she would find a man to bring her happiness—and it was because of Martin she'd even met him. But she glowed with an inner fire when she was near him, could not stop smiling up at him, and accepted his hand whenever he reached for her. Their engagement was becoming real, and she felt so blessed and happy.

All she'd have to do was say the magic words, "Yes, I'll marry you," and her new life would spread out before her, with a loving husband and perhaps the children she'd been afraid to hope for.

It all came down to trust, and at last, she was starting to believe he was trustworthy.

That evening, after the grounds had been restored to pristine gardens and parkland, her grateful tenants had gone home with full bellies, and she entered her own home with a full heart. She moved quietly through the kitchens, where only Mrs. Sanford checked on the banked fire and wished her a good night.

"Mrs. Blake, would you like a candle to guide your way?" the housekeeper called as Audrey moved toward the front of the house.

Audrey turned back and grinned. "Thanks, but no."

Where once Mrs. Sanford would have been mortified by her gaffe, now she simply chuckled through her apology.

The other servants and Blythe had already gone to bed, and Audrey couldn't help wondering if Robert and the Blackthornes had also retired. With Blythe and the married couple in attendance, it had seemed acceptable to allow Robert to remain as well.

She found herself wishing she could sneak into

his room, knowing that in her small manor, it would be too noticeable. But a girl could dream . . .

And then she heard male voices in the drawing room and slowed to a stop. She didn't want to interrupt if—

"I'm going to tell her the truth, Michael," Robert was saying.

Audrey froze, a knot of worry unfurling inside her. She almost went up the stairs, telling herself it was none of her business, but she was a stronger woman than that now.

She reached for the door, found it partially closed, and pushed inside. The silence was deafening, but for the tick-ticking of the coal settling in the grate.

"What truth do you wish to tell me, Robert?" she asked in a cool voice.

"You can leave us, Michael," Robert said impassively.

"Good night, Audrey," Michael murmured as he went by.

Although she nodded, she didn't spare another thought for him, simply walked slowly toward where she believed Robert was standing. "Well?"

"I have two things to tell you," he began at last.

His voice was more somber than she'd ever heard before, and it gave her a sick twist of fear. She'd been so happy—had it all been a lie?

"I was referring to my part in the death of your husband, of our commander, and another soldier in our regiment."

"Your part?" she repeated faintly.

"Blackthorne, Rothford, and I. I feel you need to hear the whole story."

"All right."

"We were escorting what we thought were thieves and their families, women and children, all so hungry. They were prisoners, but it just didn't seem right to us, especially their destination—a place where they'd be interrogated further, using measures only used in time of war or great need."

She felt a spasm of queasiness at what might be done to people to coerce the truth out of them—innocent or not. "Go on."

"So we disobeyed orders. We *allowed* them to escape."

He emphasized "allowed" so she'd understand that they must have looked the other way.

"Did you think you were doing right?" she asked in bewilderment.

"We did."

"Then how can you blame yourselves for the decision?"

"Don't you understand, Audrey?" he demanded. "We let them return to their lives and their villages, as if we knew better than our superiors. Soldiers are taught respect and obedience, loyalty to one's commander—and we lost sight of that, and even our commander died as a result."

"They weren't villagers?" she whispered, twisting her fingers together, feeling the scene unfold in her imagination, the one she kept primed and ready to show her what she assumed the world looked like. Just now, it seemed like a curse.

"Perhaps they were, but they brought others with them when they attacked our regiment. Three men died, including our commander, Cecilia's father."

"And my husband," she said stonily.

"And your husband. From the beginning, Michael tried to insist that we'd made the best decision we could at the time, under great stress, that it wasn't our fault. I don't believe that, and neither does Rothford. I felt guilt for what we'd done, and it only continued to grow. And when Michael was to be sent home to recover from his wounds and meet his bride, Rothford and I decided to resign our commissions and return as well. We had to do something to atone for the consequences of our decision."

He stopped speaking, and she stood still, hugging herself, trying to think logically, without the emotions that were so powerful and overwhelming two years before. But there was bitterness beneath her words as she said, "So you came to me, Martin's widow, to express your condolences."

"And I offered you my help," he reminded her. "It was the least I could do after all you'd suffered. That was all you wanted from me—you made it perfectly clear you didn't want a husband."

"But you would have offered yourself like some sort of sacrifice?" she asked in outrage.

"I might have considered it, but I knew you were too proud, too independent."

"I was not independent when you met me."

"But you wanted to be, and I wanted to be of assistance."

She remained quiet for a moment, trying to rethink the last few weeks. He was right about everything he said—where she was concerned. But . . .

"I cannot lie to you and say that I loved Martin," she said. "Regardless, I'm able to see an honest mistake for what it was. You didn't mean to cause his death." *And perhaps the death of my child*, she thought, with the resulting flare of grief.

He took her hand and squeezed it. "You have every right to blame me for not telling you up front. But . . . I thought it would hurt you all over again, and perhaps complicate what I could do for you."

"And perhaps shower you with my grief?"

He hesitated. "I don't know. I honestly thought the news might hurt worse. I didn't know if you loved Blake or—"

"But none of this conjecture matters," she interrupted tiredly. "You offered your help, and I took it, and now I have my own household, and the love of my sister again. I could have been trapped there forever without you."

"Those are kind words, Audrey, and I appreciate them. But there's one last thing you need to know."

She sighed and closed her eyes. "I'm so tired, Robert. Can this not wait?"

"I know about the child you lost."

She went still, and though the grief was still there, confusion bubbled inside her. "But how . . ."

"Blythe accidentally told me."

She felt suddenly cold, as if she were growing distant from her body. "When?" she whispered. "You two were barely speaking when she first came to visit me."

"Over a week ago," he answered.

"That's not what I mean—was it before you suddenly wanted to marry me in truth?"

He didn't answer, and she didn't need to see his face to understand the reality. "You only wanted to marry me out of guilt and pity."

"Audrey, I had already come to admire everything about you. I cannot deny that hearing about your child altered things, but my feelings have continued to grow—"

"I'm not marrying you," she said flatly. "My God, I even—gave myself to you! How you must have pitied me." And she'd been so stupid as to fall in love with him. God, she was a fool. Everyone had tried to warn her, and she'd been so convinced she'd never fall for a man's lies again.

"I didn't pity you! I wanted you, Audrey, and you wanted me."

"But I can't trust your reasons anymore, Robert. I can't trust *you*. We'll simply end this now. You gave your pathetic blind widow her scandalous affair."

"I want more than an affair, Audrey," he said, taking her by the shoulders. "We deal so well together."

No words of love, but she couldn't be surprised. "We both have too much guilt, Robert—you for the death of my husband, and me for whatever I did that caused my child's death."

"Whatever you did? My God, Audrey, you learned that your husband had died. The grief—"

"Grief? I felt little for him after the way he'd treated me. But perhaps I caused my little boy's death with my terrible fear that they'd take him away from me. My father was horrified that his flawed daughter might give birth to an equally flawed grandchild. My baby was just a thing to him, and when he was born dead—I think they were all relieved. Now you can be relieved, too, for you've done enough for me."

"Audrey, don't—"

"I was right all along—only as a single, independent widow will I find even a modicum of happiness. I can't even trust my own motives where you're concerned—maybe I was going to use *you* to have a baby. God, I can't take this." She wouldn't have been hurt again if she'd never let anyone close—how had Robert made her forget that?

She turned and hurried away, forcing herself not to run. When she reached her bedroom, she couldn't even have the release of crying. Everything inside her felt so very cold and remote and—dead.

Chapter 22

❦

Audrey was sitting on the edge of her bed when the door opened. She prayed it would only be Molly, come to help her undress for bed, but she heard Blythe's cheerful voice. To her ears, it was like raucous screech of a bird, making her wince.

"I told Molly to go to bed, since she's been dealing with the puppy. I'm here to help."

And then she must have looked at Audrey, who couldn't master the emotions necessary to hide her despair.

"Audrey, what's wrong?" she cried.

When Blythe sat down on the bed beside her, tried to put her arm around her, it was too much. Audrey shook her off and rose to pace.

"Robert knows about my baby," she said, feeling her despair replaced by anger as she said the words aloud.

Blythe burst into noisy tears. "Don't blame him—it's my fault!"

At least she'd admitted it. "Tell me the truth—tell me everything! I cannot take another lie."

"Oh, Audrey, I didn't mean to. Robert and I were discussing how the servants seemed to be hiding Louisa's baby from you, and the truth just . . . came out." She blew her nose in a handkerchief. "I had no idea he didn't know. I've been trying so hard to be worthy of your trust, to prove that I've grown up. I spent so much of my childhood resenting that you were different, that Father made us treat you that way. You were always so independent, like you never needed us—I wanted to be needed," she added on a whisper. "I came here thinking I could be of help, even though Father sent me."

"What are you saying?"

"He thought—he thought you would want to come home, and I was to tell him when you were ready. I was supposed to tell him everything that happened, but I didn't, I swear. He even sent a letter to the Sanfords with your coachman on that first day, telling them that you were only hurting yourself, and that you should be at home."

Audrey closed her eyes on a groan. "Another reason they had problems with me from the start."

"But I saw you, Audrey, I knew you were going to be successful, and I wanted to be a part of it, to help you. And now I've ruined everything."

"You didn't ruin everything, Robert did," Audrey said coldly.

"Robert? Why are you blaming him when this is my fault?"

"Because once he knew about the baby, he courted me out of pity, made me fall in love with him—I am such a fool!" She fisted her hands.

"Oh, no, you're not!" Blythe insisted, catching her hand and making her stop pacing. "You need to hear what I've seen. I've been watching Robert all this time, and he's fallen in love with you right before my very eyes. There is such tenderness—"

"You mean pity," Audrey interrupted with bitterness.

"Eyes can be powerful, and you don't understand that. I know the difference between pity and love. Do you not think I have seen others show their pity on their faces? He *loves* you Audrey! It shines from him. Can you not feel it?"

"No," she whispered. "And he never said it. I don't trust a single thing I'm feeling, and I won't make another terrible marriage. I'd rather be alone."

"How can a marriage be terrible if you love him?" Blythe asked plaintively.

"During my first marriage, there was no love at all, and I still felt betrayed when Martin left me behind. But if I love Robert—imagine how he could hurt me? I won't do it, I won't marry him," she insisted, even as she knew she sounded almost hysterical.

Blythe only blew her nose again. "I . . . I feel responsible for this."

"You aren't. He should have told me he knew, and instead, he seduced me."

Blythe gave a little gasp. "Oh, Audrey . . ."

"Now don't you pity me, too, I couldn't take it!" She covered her face with both hands. "Just—just leave me be, Blythe. I forgive you, because it was just a slip of the tongue."

"I don't know if I deserve your forgiveness," she whispered.

"Then that makes me *certain* I forgive you. Go to bed, Blythe. I'll be all right."

Blythe put her arms around her, and Audrey accepted the hug, and even tightened it for a fierce moment. She would get through this, and she would have her sister, even if she never rid herself of this terrible ache deep inside where her bright love used to be.

Robert stood in one of the guest bedrooms at Rose Cottage, staring at the wall that separated Audrey and him, feeling tired and frustrated and angry with himself.

The guilt he bore for helping cause the death of her husband—*that* she'd understood and thought an honest mistake, though it changed everything about her life.

But withholding that he knew the truth about the death of her child? How had he not seen how important that would be to her?

Because, of course, he always thought he knew best. He'd spent his entire life trying to be a different man, a better man, and still hadn't managed it.

But it wasn't too late. He and Audrey were meant to be together, however their relationship had come about. The more he knew her, the more amazed he was by her strength, courage, and compassion. He no longer felt pity or duty-bound—he'd fallen in love with her. Every time he was separated from her, the days stretched out as if with no reason, if he couldn't share them with her.

But would she ever believe this? He had to find some way to convince her of the truth.

Audrey delayed coming down to breakfast, but it didn't matter. Robert was still there in the morning, waiting for her, his "Good morning" full of a resolution that didn't bode well for her peace of mind.

Peace of mind? She'd barely gotten a few hours' sleep, and her mind felt sluggish and sad. Any peace was cowering in a corner as her dark thoughts chased each other around.

When she heard no other voices or movement, she asked, "Where are my other guests?" keeping her voice impassive.

"They breakfasted and went walking with Blythe. Your sister said you usually walk with her, but she didn't want to disturb you."

Audrey only nodded.

"Michael and Cecilia will be leaving soon after." He paused, then asked softly, "How are you?"

She felt the barest brush along her arm and pulled away. "I can't force you to leave, Robert, but I need you to do so, to stop visiting me."

"I won't give up, Audrey. I've fallen in love with you, and somehow I'll find a way to prove it to you, to make you believe."

"You're just hurting me!" she whispered, backing away. "And for all I know, you're only concerned because there might be a child."

"And I would love our child, even as I love you."

She whirled and departed for her study, feeling the sting of tears she'd become so good at suppressing. She slammed the door hard, and barely resisted sliding down to the floor. She didn't want to think of their child, or how it would force her to marry, make her give up her independence. She wouldn't want her child to suffer Arthur's fate, that of a nameless bastard.

And she wanted to cry because she'd spent the last three days missing Robert terribly, had felt everything brighten the moment he'd arrived to share the tenant feast with her. And he'd destroyed all that. All along she'd been softening toward him, imagining him lonely but for the memories of a brother he'd never been permitted to love, parents who hadn't loved him. If he knew, he'd think she was pitying *him*, she thought bitterly. Everything was so complicated.

When Michael and Cecilia were preparing to leave later that morning, Audrey felt composed, although she imagined she could not hide that something was wrong. She was simply grateful that Robert would be leaving as well.

But he didn't plan to leave, had even brought his own horse, to her frustration.

As the men were saying their good-byes, she felt a touch on her arm.

"Audrey, may I speak privately with you?" Cecilia asked.

"Of course." Curious in spite of herself, Audrey led the way across the hall to her study, then turned to await what the other woman had planned.

"Robert has said nothing to either Michael or me, but I can see that problems have appeared overnight. You both seemed so happy yesterday."

Audrey hesitated, but she didn't want to lie—lies were what had put her in this position. "I discovered . . . some unsettling truths."

"Was it about their military service and the terrible tragedy that took my father's life, along with your husband's?"

Audrey nodded without elaborating, unable to bear the thought of one more person's pity. "Did Michael withhold the truth from you?"

Cecilia sighed aloud. "He did, and probably for the same reasons Robert did—guilt and shame. I don't think we could punish them any more than they've already punished themselves."

"This isn't about punishment," Audrey said tightly, "but trust."

"I withheld things from Michael, painful things about my family and our past. I told myself it wasn't his business, or even that I didn't want to relive everything."

"But this *was* my business—this concerned my dead husband." *And me, when Robert hid his reasons for courting me. How many times can I believe what a man tells me?*

She'd withheld the truth about her baby—but that didn't affect Robert at all. It was her private sorrow, something she was trying to leave in the past as she began her new life.

Or did it concern him? Did it give him a complete picture of her, one he deserved? She was so confused.

"Audrey," Cecilia said, "it is not my place to try to change your mind. I only ask that you give it much thought before making any final decisions. I cannot tell you how wonderfully happy the two of you looked together. Michael told me he'd always hoped Robert would at last find the family he deserved."

Those words were as sharp and painful as a knife, but she forced herself to nod. "Thank you for the advice, Cecilia. I will keep it in mind."

"Write to me, please? I would truly like to consider you a friend."

"I will. I have to warn you—my handwriting is atrocious."

Cecilia chuckled, and they hugged in parting.

After Michael and Cecilia had gone, Robert and Audrey stood in the entrance hall for a frozen moment. She heard the tap of Blythe's slippers as she walked away.

"Audrey, we should talk," Robert asked.

"No." She turned and closed the study door behind her.

But all day long, he remained at Rose Cottage,

and she was forced to encounter him whatever she did. He didn't try to force her to listen to explanations, he was always just . . . there.

For Robert, the day was interminable. He wasn't going to be like Audrey's puppy, trying to follow her around, but he ate meals with her, and in between walked the grounds he'd come to enjoy. The management of Rose Cottage and the larger estate had helped him come to grips with the management of his earldom, and he would always have fond thoughts of it. He'd hoped it might even become Audrey's dower property again when they married.

As the evening approached, and his presence in a feminine household risked scandalizing her neighbors, he realized she was just waiting him out, as if to see if he'd leave—or show himself as a man who'd risk a woman's reputation to have what he wanted. But he wouldn't do that, for those would only be the tactics of his father, and Robert didn't have to be him. Loving her had taught him that.

But maybe Audrey didn't know that.

After dinner, he found her alone in the drawing room, crocheting slowly, her expression one of concentration as she used her nimble fingers to count the stitches she'd already made. He imagined Blythe had retired early to bed after a day warily watching the two of them.

Audrey tilted her head toward the door.

"It's me," Robert said. "I'm leaving, but I'd like to talk to you before I do."

"I can't stop you."

He deserved that. He stepped inside, closed the door, then crossed to sit beside her on the sofa. At least she didn't stiffen, only continued to crochet.

"Ever since I became the earl, I've spent years trying to be different from my father."

"I know this."

"You don't know why. Just as you didn't want to talk about your baby, I didn't want to talk about another death, one that happened before I even bought my commission."

"You've told me about your brother, and I had already heard about your business partner who took his own life."

Robert stared at her. "So you knew something about my past, and didn't ask me about it, didn't speak up."

She lowered her crocheting. "It's not the same thing. Your actions after you learned about my baby's death are what I am most disappointed in."

"Then you can be disappointed even more when I tell you that I was so determined to get in early on the initial railway investments, that I manipulated Stephen Kepple. I wanted his participation, even though others told me he wasn't strong enough for the risky investment I'd proposed. So I befriended him, got him to invest, and the deal went bad. Everyone lost money. And Kepple killed himself. I'll never know if he realized he'd been manipulated into joining, or if he regretted how much money he'd invested. And then I knew that I was a bully, just like my father."

"A bully," she echoed.

He could hear the bitterness in her voice, but he put aside the pain of that. "I bought a commission the next day, determined to be the kind of man I'd once idolized, the retired army officer who lived near Knightsbridge Hall. He was the only man who'd ever stood up to my father, regardless of the difference in their stations. Following orders, being in command, all these things helped change me into a man who understood being part of a regiment, and not just out to do whatever I thought best."

"Then what happened when you met me?" she demanded.

"You wanted my help, and I was grateful to offer it. And once I knew you, I fell in love, yet I still hurt you. A man wants to be depended upon, to protect and cherish his wife—surely that can't be all bad. Or that's what I told myself. It was far easier to think that than to admit that it was all about me and how I couldn't live without you."

Audrey drew in a sharp breath, but said nothing.

"I started out trying to rescue you, to appease my guilt, but I think your love rescued me."

She held up a hand. "Robert—"

"Let me finish. I never could have done the things you have, left my family to begin anew, when Society doesn't encourage women to form households. I never thought of a woman being courageous until I met you. I've seen men in combat, but you're the bravest person I've ever known."

She bit her lip, her eyes downcast, and didn't respond.

"That's all I wanted to say." He stood up. "Think about our future, Audrey. Don't give up on me, on us. I love you."

And he walked out the door into a misty rain. He'd said all he could—now it was up to Audrey and the powerful love he hoped she bore him.

Audrey sat still, at war with herself. Part of her wanted to call him back, and the other part was relieved he was gone, so she wouldn't have to listen to his painful words, to risk being drawn back in against her will.

He'd tried to change himself, as had she. Neither of them had been perfect at it. But could she honestly trust him enough to put herself in his hands, to be vulnerable?

"I need to speak with you," Blythe said from the doorway.

Audrey sighed. "Doesn't everyone? Were you eavesdropping?"

"Only a bit, and only because you're making it absolutely necessary. And now it's my turn to speak my mind."

Audrey groaned and tossed her crocheting on the table in front of her. "Then do it quickly."

"You aren't going to want to hear it."

"Blythe!"

"I think you're afraid to marry Robert. You think that because you're blind, it gives you even more reason. But every woman who marries has to take an incredible risk, and you're no different just because you're blind."

"Well, thank you for that," Audrey said dryly.

"You know what I mean! Women put themselves in the hands of men every day, and sometimes it isn't a success, as you already know from bitter experience. Did you love Mr. Blake?"

"You know I didn't."

"He married you for your dowry. Why did you marry him?"

"I—" Audrey broke off and had to swallow. "To start my own family."

"And?"

"To get away from Father," she finished on a whisper. "I . . . I used Martin just as much as he used me."

"Then I guess you're just as flawed as the rest of us—as Robert."

Audrey bowed her head, and was shocked when tears dripped onto her clasped hands. "I'm so afraid to be hurt again, Blythe. It almost broke me when I understood how little regard Martin had for me. And then my sweet baby died, and I thought my life was over."

"But it wasn't. Your grief eased and you have begun a whole new life. Robert wants to be a part of it, however badly it all began between you. Do you want to be alone here but for the servants? You could have your own family, Audrey."

Could she give up the camaraderie she'd shared with Robert, and the sweetest pleasure she'd ever known? His kisses made her feel like the most desirable woman in the world. She *loved* him, loved the honor that brought him to her, and the way he treated her as any other woman. Was she going to deny her heart?

She stood up quickly. "I sent him away."

"I told him to stay, that I had some things you needed to hear. I'm interfering in your life. Get used to it."

While Audrey gaped, she heard Blythe walk to the door and throw it open.

"Robert, she's not done talking to you."

She heard his heavy steps, smelled the cool dampness of the outdoors all around him. And she was suddenly shaking.

"I'll leave you two alone," Blythe said, closing the door behind her.

"Are you cold?" Robert asked, coming closer.

She shook her head, letting herself be surrounded in his warmth, the sweetness of love.

"I didn't eavesdrop, if that's what you're wondering," he assured her.

She shook her head again. Oh, God, was she really going to do this?

The room seemed alive with him in it, and the chance to touch him was all she wanted, all she needed.

"Oh Robert," she whispered, reaching forward with her bare hand.

He took it, and she felt the dampness of his gloves. With a gasp, she ran her hands up his arms.

"You're all wet."

"I was out the door when Blythe called me back. She can be just as insistent as you."

She covered her mouth against a bubble of laughter. "Oh, Robert," she said again, closing her eyes as tears leaked between her lashes.

"Don't cry," he said hoarsely, gathering her against him.

She didn't care that she was getting wet. She flung her arms about his neck and pulled his head down toward her. "Don't leave me again. I love you."

With a groan, he kissed her, sweeping her up until her feet dangled, and all she had for support was his solid body.

"Audrey, I love you."

And then he was kissing her face over and over, and she was memorizing the feel of his, even though she knew she'd have a lifetime to do it.

"I trust you," she whispered. "I want to marry you. I'm ready to find our happiness."

"I think we've already found it," he murmured against her lips. "And we'll never take it for granted. I'll go purchase a Special License, because I can't wait through weeks of church banns to make you mine."

"I'm already yours." She cupped his beloved face in her hands. "I think I knew that all along. I promise never to fight my instincts again."

"As if I believe that."

They shared more kisses in the midst of laughter.